SLAY TWO
RUIN

LAURELIN PAIGE

Hot Alphas. Smart Women. Sexy Stories.

Editing: Erica Russikoff at Erica Edits

Proofing: Michele Ficht

Cover: Laurelin Paige

Formatting: Alyssa Garcia

Also by Laurelin Paige

Visit www.laurelinpaige.com for a more detailed reading order.

The Dirty Universe

Dirty Filthy Rich Boys - READ FREE
Dirty Duet: Dirty Filthy Rich Men | Dirty Filthy Rich Love
Dirty Sexy Bastard - READ FREE
Dirty Games Duet: Dirty Sexy Player | Dirty Sexy Games
Dirty Sweet Duet: Sweet Liar | Sweet Fate
Dirty Filthy Fix
Dirty Wild Trilogy: Coming 2020

The Fixed Universe

Fixed Series: Fixed on You | Found in You | Forever with You
Hudson | Fixed Forever
Found Duet: Free Me | Find Me
Chandler
Falling Under You
Dirty Filthy Fix
Slay Saga Slay One: Rivalry | Slay Two: Ruin
Slay Three: Revenge | Slay Four: Rising
The Open Door

First and Last Duet: First Touch | Last Kiss

Hollywood Standalones

One More Time
Close
Sex Symbol
Star Struck

Written with Sierra Simone

Porn Star | Hot Cop

Written with Kayti McGee under the name Laurelin McGee

Miss Match | Love Struck | MisTaken | Holiday for Hire

*For Liz who gives and gives
without ever getting.*

INTRO
Edward

I'd never believed in idle threats. When I told someone I intended to harm them in some way, I was always prepared to back it up.

I was prepared to kill Celia.

I just hadn't decided yet that I would.

Rather, I *had* decided, and now I was having second thoughts.

I wasn't a man who had second thoughts. I was a man who honored my commitments, both to myself and to others. Always. That was how I'd climbed out of the depths of poverty, how I'd risen out of nowhere, against all odds. I decided, and I did. Case closed.

There were always obstacles to overcome. Every goal worth achieving had some unaccounted for hindrance along the way, usually showing up at the most inopportune time. That was how progress worked. Steps forward, a step back. The trick was to not get caught up in the stumble.

Take a breath, find balance, then proceed.

But Celia Werner wasn't just a rock on the pathway. She hadn't just tripped me up. She hadn't made me simply stumble. She was a ledge, crumbling under my hold, and no matter how I dug my fingernails into the ground at her feet, I was beginning to fear I might fall.

It was possible I already had.

My mistake had been in fucking her. There, in the grip of her orgasm, when she was vulnerable and real, it was impossible not to see what could be between us. I hadn't even topped her that first time, not really. I hadn't probed into her psyche beforehand the way I normally liked, hadn't brought her walls down, hadn't taken her to ruin, and still I'd slipped in somehow. Slipped in behind her facade where she was unguarded and defenseless, and the authenticity of what I found there was overwhelming.

It wasn't supposed to have been like that.

There'd been a plan. A scheme years in the making, an improbable scheme at that, and yet everything had fallen into place, as though even the stars believed in my operation of revenge. She'd accepted my ridiculous proposal. She'd been satisfied with a prenup. She hadn't made a single bit of effort to redraft her will and trust.

It had been too easy. Every obstacle on the way had been met and breached without incident. When she'd shifted, I'd shifted with her. Without effort. It had been a cakewalk. Logistically, anyway. I'd known she'd be sharp and wily and fierce. I'd prepared for that.

What I hadn't known was that I'd like it.

Like *her*.

Did I like her? It was hard to accept if I did, but I couldn't deny there was something there. Something raw and out of control, yet identifiable as its own, unlike so much of what I'd grown accustomed to feeling in the near three decades that had passed since my parents' deaths.

I hesitated to say it was a nice change, only because of what that would mean for the future of my scheme, but it was a change. And, if I were honest, I liked the change.

Before her, there'd only been blackness inside. Not because I had felt nothing, but because I felt too much. Too much anger, too much regret, too much heartache, too much love. Too much responsibility.

Too much *everything*.

And it all mixed together, all the individual *too much* of emotion until it was impossible to distinguish one from another, the same way a child's overzealous watercolor project turned into mud with the application of too many colors.

That was how my feelings existed inside me—as mud. Darker than that, though. An inky blob. A black hole. The perception of black holes very often is that they are large areas of nothing, but they're just the opposite. They are the densest objects in the universe. They suck at the life around them. They tear apart any matter that comes close to them because of their massive gravity.

That was what I was inside before her.

My emotions had mass.

My emotions had gravity.

My emotions were capable of tearing a person apart to ruin.

ONE
Celia

I t was bullshit.

I called him on it too. "Bullshit."

As terrifying as the words were coming from Edward's mouth, *"My little bird, I intend to kill you,"* that's all they were—words. He didn't mean to kill me. Of course he didn't. He wanted me off balance, that was all.

He stared at me for a beat, the anger he'd exhibited a moment before easing into something else. Something calmer, more controlled, yet just as vehement.

Without taking his eyes off me, he settled into the chair behind his desk. "I can understand why you'd choose not to believe me."

"Because you're dramatic and full of nonsense threats? Yeah. Pretty unbelievable." Almost as unbelievable as the fact that I was standing before him half-naked, covered in his cum since only a handful of minutes before his ominous declaration, he'd fucked me, wildly, claiming my body as his as he did.

I'd loved it. I'd even loved the painful and intense spanking I'd received that had precipitated the fucking.

He'd loved it too. I had no doubt of that. He might hate himself for loving it, for whatever reason I couldn't know, but there was no faking that he'd been into it.

Which made his stupid threat more hurtful than frightening. "You have regrets about fucking me, fine. But be a grown-up about it. Childish taunts are not your style."

I snagged a fistful of tissues from the box on his desk and reached around my torso to wipe the sticky mess he'd made on my backside as best I could before pulling on my bottoms. Wadding the tissue up in a ball, I threw it into his lap.

So maybe childish taunts were *my* style. Quid pro quo and all that.

With my jaw set, I crossed my arms over my breasts and met his steady gaze.

Edward let the ball of tissue fall from his lap to the floor, barely giving it a glance as he leaned back in his chair. His lips curled slowly. "You continue to fascinate me, little bird. I'll give you that. And you are correct. Childish taunts are not my style. Which is why you should be most assured that I mean what I've said."

So he was going to cling to that then. How immature.

Unless he actually meant it.

A shiver crawled up my spine. I shook it away. He was trying to get under my skin. He'd only win if I let him.

The best move was to ignore his scare tactics and focus on what he'd given me—an admission.

"Why did you call me that?" I knew the answer, but

there was a chance I could be wrong. That the nickname was a coincidence.

"I've just told you I plan to kill you, and you're more concerned with the name I've given you. Fascinating indeed." He was good, I had to give him that. I'd often held onto a ruse way past the time it should be surrendered, but never with such commitment.

Never so convincing.

"Just stop. You don't mean it."

Edward cocked his head slightly. "Don't I?"

"You don't. You're trying to scare me." But my mouth felt dry and my hands were sweaty despite the fact that I was only wearing a bikini in an air-conditioned room.

"Is it working?"

Yes.

But what I said was, "No. Now I'm just pissed off."

His grin widened. "That makes two of us."

He didn't need to tell me. He'd been mad before I'd even entered the room, deservedly so, after I'd pushed him all day, openly flirting with his staff. It had gotten me what I'd wanted—him. Inside me. Unleashed and unbridled.

I'd told myself I wanted him so I could win The Game, but it had been a lie. I'd just wanted him, and having had him, I wanted more of him, and for the first time in years— in a decade—I could see a future for myself that didn't center around the games that Hudson had taught me so well to play, that didn't involve lies and manipulation. A future filled *with* instead of the nothing that had lived so long inside of me.

I wanted Edward, but it was painfully clear that, no matter how much he might want me back, he wouldn't allow it.

I was scared, yes, and pissed. But mostly hurt.

I remembered this emotion. I remembered rejection. I remembered this kind of pain.

I'd rather play The Game.

"Why did you call me that?" I asked again, more sternly, as though I had power to make any demands. So he'd made me feel things. I didn't have to acknowledge that. I knew how to be empty. I could be empty again.

Edward rested his ankle on his opposite thigh, a more casual posture than I'd seen him take before, the nonchalant behavior adding to my unease. "Why did I call you that just now or why did I call you that before?"

Before. It was so vague. He'd called me "little bird" twice now in this conversation. His reference to before could simply mean the first time tonight, and not the time he'd said it to me outside The Open Door. It was a clever tactic, refusing to give anything away. Requiring me to be the one to admit that I'd been there that night or let the mention slide.

I considered it for only a handful of seconds. While I hated being backed into a corner as I had been, I wanted answers more. "How did you know it was me?"

My disguise hadn't been perfect the night I'd attended the sex party and seen him there as well, but it was a stretch to think that anyone would have realized who I was. My hair had been dyed. My outfit had been specifically one I'd never wear. I'd worn a mask that fully covered my face. A feathered mask of a dragon that Edward had mistaken for a bird.

More likely it hadn't been a mistake but a deliberate choice meant to knock me back a peg or two.

Still, as he'd demeaned me with the nickname, I'd believed he'd done so as a stranger. To discover that he'd known all along was the real blow to my esteem.

He studied me, his hand rubbing over the scruff of beard on his chin—the Van Dyke that I'd suggested he grow—and for a tense instant, I thought he might deny knowing what I was talking about. That would be just like him, wouldn't it? Get me to confess and then refuse to acknowledge it.

But if the thought had crossed his mind, he didn't go with it. "I think the better question," he said, "is how did we end up at the same party together."

The rhythm of my heart stuttered, two beats coming so fast that I could actually feel them against the inside wall of my chest. He hadn't just known it was me. He'd known I'd be there.

Now that was terrifying.

And exciting.

And impossible. How the hell had he known? I ventured a guess. "You had me followed."

"Did I?" His brows arched inward as though he were trying to recall the details of the event. So fucking performative. "I believe I was there first."

"Then you figured out I was going to be there. Somehow." I threw up my hands, already tired of the tug of war.

Perhaps in response to my impatience, he threw me a bone. A clue. "How did *you* end up at that party?"

"I was invited."

"By whom?"

"By..." Oh, fuck.

I quickly went over the circumstances that had led me there that night. Having learned from Blanche that Edward liked kinky parties, I'd gone searching for one he might attend, putting a call out on kink-related forums under an anonymous username for such events.

One person had reached out in response, inviting me to join The Open Door, an underground organization that hosted weekly sex parties. I'd been wary about accepting, worried that the membership fee would be traced to my bank account, but I hadn't for a minute been concerned about the stranger who'd invited me.

Had FeelslikePAIN been Edward?

I needed to sit down.

As soon as I sank into the chair facing his desk, I regretted it. My ass had cooled down, but sitting reignited the sting of his severe spanking.

Not a chance I was letting him know that.

"That's impossible," I said through gritted teeth, bearing down through the pain. "That couldn't have been you. You couldn't have known that username was me."

"Are you sure?"

With my elbow propped on the arm of the chair, I ran my fingers across my forehead. "This is tedious, Edward. Would you just tell me?"

His lips twitched in a way that suggested my impatience amused him, which only made me more irritable. Of course. As he surely knew it would.

Abruptly he sat forward, setting his elbows on the desk and clasping his hands together, tucking all of his fingers in except the two pointers, which he steepled together and aimed in my direction. "How about *you* tell *me* something?" he asked, his expression wicked with curiosity. "How did it feel to watch me that night?"

"What do you mean?" *Sneaky, exhilarating, conniving.* Was that what he was after?

"How did it feel to watch me touching another woman? Making another woman come in front of you."

My stomach dropped as simultaneously the space between my thighs began to buzz. Against my will the memories crashed into the forefront of my mind. He'd sat across from me, his eyes locked with mine as he'd assisted the woman on his lap in masturbating to orgasm.

"Sasha," I said mindlessly. "Her name was Sasha." Because concentrating on that point was safer than answering him. Even the question had heated my face, not because it was humiliating to be asked—though it definitely was— but because both the memory and the forwardness of his inquiry aroused me, much to my annoyance.

"Her name doesn't matter. It only matters that she wasn't you. Tell me how you felt."

She wasn't you. It came off as a deliberate slap in the face.

The pointed comment also brought my emotions from that night into vivid focus. I'd been vulnerable then. I'd felt exposed, and that was with a disguise. A pointless disguise, it turned out, but I hadn't known that at the time.

Just thinking about what he must have seen in me in that moment made my skin crawl.

There was no way I could share those feelings with him. They were too personal. Too real, and here, under the intensity of his gaze, there was nothing I could hide behind.

"I'm not doing this," I said, as I stood up and turned to leave.

"Sit down, Celia."

The command was sharp and sinister, a verbal lasso wrapping around my torso, holding me in place. I was only a handful of strides away from the doorway. So close to escape.

And yet I couldn't go.

I didn't generally have a problem defying him. I could now. Easily.

Only, as blasé as I'd been throughout our conversation, I actually was scared. More than I wanted to admit, even to myself. I didn't believe that he would kill me, necessarily.

Just.

What if I was wrong?

With my chin held high, I returned to my chair, wincing as my ass touched the surface. "There. I sat down. But only because you're going to give me answers. How did you figure out that was me on that forum? And why did you want me to go to that party?"

Edward sat up to his full height, his eyes narrowing as he stared at me. Into me. "Let me be clear," he said with cool authority. "You are not in a position to ask to see my cards. It's your turn to show yours, and, if I'm satisfied after I see them, I may choose to show you some of mine."

I swallowed hard.

Though his face remained perfectly composed, his hands were in fists resting on the desk, and I couldn't help but suspect that he was trying very hard to control his rage. "Now, answer my question."

"And if I do you'll give me answers?" My voice sounded weak, and for good reason, since I'd basically just been told he was in charge and stop defying him or else.

I seemed to have a real problem with authority.

Edward appeared to find that problem amusing. His lip twitched as though trying not to smile. "Perhaps. But I'm not answering anything you ask until I'm happy with what I hear from you."

"Nothing," I said stubbornly. "I felt nothing."

"If you're not going to be honest, then you might as well leave, which will not only end the discussion now but any possibility of discussion in the future."

Whether he meant that this was the only time *he'd* be *willing* to talk or that, later, *I* would be *unable* to talk, I didn't know.

Either way, he'd trapped me once again into answering.

"It was hot," I said, with obvious annoyance. "Okay? The way you touched her was hot."

"And?"

Jesus Christ, he was impossible.

"And dirty."

"And?"

"I don't know..." I shook my head, trying to guess what he might want me to say. "Unsettling."

"And...?"

"And mean. And manipulative. And exciting. And if you want something different from me, then I don't know what it is because I haven't read the Guide to Pleasing Edward Fasbender, and I'm going to need the CliffsNotes."

"I want you to be honest." His tone said his patience

was wearing thin.

Well, mine was too. And honesty? That wasn't something I'd been good with in a long time, let alone emotions.

At my hesitation, he prodded. "Close your eyes, Celia, and stop trying. Just imagine I'm touching her now. I'm kissing her. My mouth is on her breasts. My hands are on her cunt. Inside her cunt. Now, tell me what you're thinking."

My eyes were closed, and I could see it all like it was happening right then. I could feel the twist in my stomach, the rush of blood in my ears, the pang of envy.

I opened my mouth and let the words fall out. "I wished it were me you were touching."

And with that admission, I knew in my gut that whatever answers he gave me, if any, or whatever move he made next in this stupid fucked-up game, it didn't matter.

I'd already lost.

TWO

I heard his chair move before I opened my eyes, and when I did, he wasn't sitting behind the desk anymore. He was easy to find. He'd moved a few feet away to the mini bar. I already knew that the amber-colored liquor that poured out of the carafe into the tumbler was brandy.

When the glass held two fingers of liquor, he brought it over to me. "That was good," he said as he held his offering toward me. "Was that so hard?"

Was it hard to admit that I'd wanted him?

I'd been openly trying to seduce him for weeks. But I'd been able to convince myself that my only reasons for doing so were to win. Now, with my plans exposed and The Game out of my mind, it was different. It *was* hard. It made me weak.

I hated it.

"I hate you," I said, snatching the glass from his hand, pretty sure I meant it, vehemently, even, despite not having felt anything passionate for years. I brought the tumbler to my lips and took a long swallow. My stomach was empty, and I didn't really want the drink, but he'd made a point to pour it and bring it over, which meant he thought I needed it, and I didn't have the energy to argue about it.

And maybe I did need it.

Edward hadn't moved from my side. He lifted his hand and ran his knuckles across my cheek, a gesture so unexpected, I almost flinched.

"Would it make you feel better to know that I wished it had been you I was touching too, my little bird?"

My skin felt hot, and not from the liquor. I hated that too—how my body reacted to him. How it lit up at his touch, how his words sent my stomach fluttering and my heart racing, my organs not caring that he was a controlling asshole or that he (supposedly) wanted me dead.

Well, I wasn't my body.

I leaned away from his hand, wrapping one arm around myself while the other kept the glass near my mouth, a pathetic shield of sorts. "Stop calling me that. I'm not your anything."

"*Au contraire*. You are my wife." He circled back around toward his chair, and I immediately missed the warmth of his skin against mine.

Or my body did.

I wanted him as far from me as possible. Him on the other side of his desk was good. It was the farthest I'd likely get him until this was over. Until he decided he was bored with the conversation and let me leave.

If I was being forced to stay, I damn well meant to take advantage of the situation. "How did you know that was me on the forum?" I repeated my earlier question. "Even if you knew my IP address, it's supposed to be blocked to others on that site."

A loud clap of thunder boomed overhead. I glanced toward the window in time to see the flash of lightning that followed it, showing a thick layer of clouds covering the sky and sheets of pouring rain.

I was so surprised to realize it was storming that I almost missed Edward's response.

"...is blocked. But I had software installed directly on your laptop that captured all your activity."

What?

He had my full attention now. "How the fuck…?" Quickly my mind searched for the answer to my own question. How would he have gotten to my laptop? Who would have…

"Blanche," I said, her name coming out like a curse word. "You used Blanche Martin. She sent that email to me with those pictures that I, stupidly, downloaded. I should have known! It was awfully convenient that she'd shown up at the same time you did." *Stupid, stupid, stupid!*

"That's not a bad guess, but no. Not Blanche. She was a strange coincidence. When I saw you with her at Orsay, I actually thought you'd had the upper hand on me."

It was a relief to know Blanche hadn't been my mistake. And I still needed to know how he'd gotten into my laptop, but now I also had to know what I should have learned from Blanche that I didn't. "What did I miss? She couldn't tell me anything about you, except that she'd heard rumors that you liked kinky parties."

"I was wondering what gave you the idea to go looking for me on those forums."

"A lot of good that did." I realized I'd admitted more

than I'd meant to. "And I wasn't looking for you. Who said I was looking for you?"

His expression said he wasn't fooled. "It seems you formulated a whole plan to bring me down based on that little snippet of information. From your internet searches on consensual versus non-consensual sexual practices within marriage and the law surrounding those practices, I surmise you had intended to use what you assumed about my sexual proclivities to your advantage."

I was fucked, and I knew it.

But I'd never been good about letting things go when I should, and I clung to my innocence like he was clinging to his I'm-going-to-kill-you stance. "That's an awfully big assumption. Narcissist much? Not everything is about you."

"What else were you using the information for?"

"Maybe I was researching for a friend. Or writing a dark romance book."

"I'm sure that's what it was." His mouth twitched as though he were trying not to smile. "You weren't at all hoping to get me to, let's see, what exactly did your digital notebook say? 'Wives assaulted through non-consensual sexual practices have a strong case for nullifying prenuptial agreements.'"

Yep. Totally fucked.

My cheeks heated. I took another swallow of my drink, hoping the burn could wash down some of the humiliation of defeat.

"I'm intrigued about just what it is you imagine that I do in the bedroom, Celia. And offended that you think I don't require consent in my relationships."

"Yeah, well." I'd never presumed anything about consent. The truth wasn't what mattered in my games. "Your word against mine."

"Ah. So that's how you intended to play it. I was right on that then."

I mentally kicked myself. I was giving more than I was getting, and that needed to change.

In an attempt to reassert myself, I turned the conversation back to the information I really wanted. "If it wasn't Blanche who got you to my laptop, then who?"

He shook his head. "It's my turn to hear from you."

Cue eye roll. "You already seem to know everything about me. What do you need me for?"

"Which was what started this conversation in the first place, wasn't it?"

A chill ran down my spine. *I intend to kill you.* His words echoed in my brain. He sure knew how to retaliate against a bratty statement. I had to give him that.

And, as ridiculous as it was, his tactic was working. I was afraid of him. More afraid than made me comfortable.

Why was that also a turn-on?

And how the fuck did he get to me?

"Renee." The answer hit me like a ton of bricks, spilling out of my mouth on impact. "Oh my God. You got to Renee."

"You make it sound like I took a hit out on her. It wasn't like that at all." The squint of his eye said he was pleased—either with himself or that I'd guessed right, I wasn't sure.

Whichever it was, it encouraged me to follow down

the rabbit hole. "Somehow you got her to upload something on my computer for you."

"No. She simply gave me access to it. I did what I needed to from there."

Dammit. Really? Renee? She'd worked for me for years. We'd never been close, but I'd thought we had a decent boss/employee relationship. "She just handed it over to you? Without any questions? Did she know what you did to it?"

I wasn't so naive as to be surprised by betrayal, but still. This discovery came as a shock.

Edward waved a hand in the air, dismissing my questions. "It's not important."

"Not to you, maybe, but to me, you better believe it is." When he shrugged, I pressed on. "Did you pay her off? Is that why she quit?"

He studied me again as he considered his answer, or whether he would answer at all. "Nothing so nefarious," he said finally. "I offered her a better opportunity, and she took it."

"Did you sleep with her?" It was another thought that left my mouth as soon as it entered my head, and I was surprised by the gnawing in my chest that accompanied it.

He leaned forward abruptly. "Do you care?"

I asked, so of course I cared, and no matter what I tried to say, he knew it. It was a victory for him, but it felt like an even bigger loss for me.

Especially because I still didn't have the answer, and not knowing bothered me. Almost as much as the idea of Edward sharing his hands, his mouth, his cock with Renee.

I pushed down the sudden urge to cry. I wasn't used to

losing, and I was pretty sure I had. I didn't even know *how* to lose. How to act, what to say.

And I didn't *want* to lose.

I turned my head toward the windows where the storm pressed on with torrents of rain. "What was even the point of all of it? Why did you want to see what was on my computer? Why did you care? To convince me to accept your proposal?"

I switched my attention back to him for his answer.

"Whatever it took to nudge you in that direction, yes." His eyes hooded. "You should know I'd been prepared to do a lot more."

My breath tripped in my chest. He hadn't meant it to be seductive, he couldn't possibly. And yet I felt the sharp pang of desire low in my belly.

My reaction said more about me than his statement said about him. Said things I didn't want to know.

I forced myself to focus. "All to get to Werner Media? You have your own company. Why does my father's matter so much to you?"

"It just does."

It was my turn to study him. His blue eyes were as set as his jaw. He gave nothing away but determination, no matter how I searched for more.

No matter how I wished he'd give more.

It was beyond stupid that I cared. Stupid and downright irritating.

I crossed one leg over the other and lifted my chin in defiance of him and my feelings. "Well, it was all for nothing because you're crazy if you think I'm suggesting my father let you helm his company now."

"As if you'd ever planned to do that in the first place."

No matter what I had to say, he had to one-up me. No matter what my hand, his was better.

And, frankly, none of his motivations made any sense. "If you didn't think that I would ever convince my father to select you—the whole point of our marriage, according to your proposal—then why did you put so much effort into getting me to marry you?"

"I believe I've already given you that answer." He sat back in his chair again, cool and smooth.

I considered the answer, his threat. I was sure he wasn't serious, because, mainly, who did that? Who schemed to marry a prominent woman and then killed her?

But if he really never believed I could further his chances with my father, and yet he'd gone to all those lengths to make sure I did indeed marry him, then what had he hoped to gain? What had been his plan?

There was only one answer that made logical sense, as impossible as it was to believe.

"You can't kill me," I said, my voice more steady than I felt. "People would notice."

"I expect people to notice." Edward picked up a fountain pen off his desk and twirled it absentmindedly. "I have a first-rate funeral planned. I expect many will attend, even though it will be held in London. I don't have time right now to go to the U.S., which I'm sure your parents would prefer, but that isn't theirs to decide. It will be a nice event, I assure you. I've even saved you the coveted spot in the family plot next to my parents."

No. He didn't mean it. He didn't mean any of it.

But my stomach twisted all the same, and bile rose to

the back of my throat, because even if he didn't mean it, it was an awfully deranged scenario he'd painted.

A scenario that I didn't intend entertaining a minute longer.

I stood up and glared down at him. "You're a sick asshole, you know that? A perverted lunatic, and I don't have to listen to this."

I set the brandy tumbler on his desk and spun toward the doors, determined to make it out this time.

"Did I say you could leave?" His voice boomed through the room with as much fury as the thunder outside, and something in his tone, something that he'd only hinted at before, suggested very strongly that he wasn't to be disobeyed.

Frustrated, I whirled back around to face him. "What is it you want from me?"

He was standing now. At his full height, I was very much aware that he was bigger than me. That he was stronger than me. That we were alone in a storm, and I was helpless, if he wanted me to be.

And he very much wanted me to be.

"Sit down," he ordered, the narrow focus of his eyes daring me to defy him.

I took two reluctant steps toward the chair, but stopped when I remembered the tender state of my ass. "I'd rather stand, if you don't mind."

"I do mind." His flash of teeth told me he knew exactly why standing was my preference. And that, for the same reason, he was determined I sit.

I paused, deciding.

"Sit," he said again, his voice so controlled that it sent

dread coursing through my veins.

I sat down, wincing openly this time as I did.

Edward remained standing, peering down at me with a smug smile.

He liked that. Having me uncomfortable. Having me hurt. The glint in his eye paired with his evil smirk gave him away. That's how much he liked it.

From the hint of color in his face, I would even go so far as saying that it turned him on.

I'd maybe have feelings about that if I weren't so rattled. If I weren't so scared.

"You want my father's shares," I said, thinly, stating the obvious so I could have time to think. "That's what this is about. How will killing me get you that? They're his shares. They aren't in my name."

"They weren't. But as of nine days ago, on the date of your marriage, they now belong to you."

My stomach dropped, and I could feel the color drain from my face. I'd forgotten that. How had I forgotten?

"No one knows that." My voice was nearly a whisper.

His knuckles pressed into the desk as he leaned into them. "I've done my research, too, sweetheart."

It was a change my father made to my trust years ago, when he'd thought I'd marry Hudson Pierce. Some stupid loophole he'd found to avoid paying taxes. His shares would be transferred to my name at the time of my marriage. He'd never expected to actually give up control of Werner Media, though, until he retired. That was supposed to be protected by my prenup, and it was.

A prenup didn't do anything, though, in a case of death.

Oh, God.

He wasn't bluffing. He meant what he'd said. He really did mean to kill me.

There was something Edward didn't know, however. If he did, this whole scheme of his would be null and void. He didn't know that Hudson Pierce secretly owned more shares than my father. My father didn't even know it. If Edward was after control of Werner Media, killing me would get him close, but it wouldn't get him where he wanted to be.

If I told him now, would he realize the futility of his plan and let me go?

Possibly.

It would also make me worth nothing. And now that he'd threatened my life, he couldn't let me walk away and not expect repercussions. I was fucked if he didn't know the truth. I was doubly fucked if he did.

I folded my hands in my lap, aware that they were shaking, hoping he didn't see how much. "So...what? You just come back from this honeymoon a single man?"

He paused only for the space of a breath. "It had been the plan."

"And now?"

"Now, I'm willing to renegotiate."

Hope rushed through me before reality set in. "There isn't anything you can offer that will get me to sign those shares over to you. Threaten me all you want. I'm not handing over my father's company to his arch nemesis." My father would kill me if Edward didn't.

"Forget the shares for the moment." He tossed the subject away casually, as though we were talking about bed linens instead of the state of my life. "Let's talk about what you'd planned to do to me. You wanted to convict me of some sexual crime, but to do so, you would have had to endure whatever it is that I prefer in the bedroom. I'm guessing that you still don't know what that is exactly."

"Uh." It was difficult to focus on anything but my predicament, so I focused on the effort. *Bedroom. What he likes there.* In truth I didn't know exactly what he did with his lovers, but wasn't the gist obvious? "I have some thoughts."

"I'm sure you do," he said, patronizingly. "But let me tell you so you know for sure—I like to see a woman broken down."

I shook my head. "Whatever that means, I have no doubt I could have handled it just fine."

He lifted his hands off the table and thrust them in his pockets, once again towering over me at his full height. "Let's find out," he said.

"I don't know what you're saying." I was starting to get a headache and the lack of food was getting to me. I needed things spelled out.

So Edward started spelling. "I'm saying, that's my deal. You want to live? Then let me break you down."

THREE

Lightning flashed, and with a loud crack of thunder, the lights went out, underscoring Edward's offer, because even nature was under his command. Why was I not surprised?

The blanket of darkness was a welcome relief. This time, Edward couldn't see the latest shiver that his words precipitated. He couldn't see the new stippling of goose-flesh along my arms. Couldn't see whatever I was sure my expression hadn't managed to conceal.

Break you down.

What the hell was that supposed to mean?

But now wasn't the time to ask, in the dark, with the wind and rain hitting so forcefully against the windows that I wasn't entirely sure they wouldn't break.

I could hear Edward across from me, a drawer of his desk opening and closing before a light shone brightly in my eyes.

I put my hand up to block my vision, my eyes squinting. The light remained there for several seconds then dropped down slightly, settling on my mouth.

"There are emergency lights in the kitchen," Edward said, and I could see now that what he was holding was only his cell phone.

I'd stopped carrying mine since I'd been on the island. The cellular service was too spotty and unreliable. Now the once relied-on gadget was only good for an alarm clock. Flashlight was another notable use, apparently.

The beam dropped from my face to the floor, moving around the desk along with the man holding it.

"Come," he said, and I was on my feet before I even thought of following his order. Once I was standing, his fingertips gripped tightly at my elbow, as though he didn't believe I'd accompany him otherwise.

Honestly, he might not have been wrong. Power out or not, I wasn't keen on letting him be my hero. With his hand tugging me along, I didn't have much choice in the matter.

He led me swiftly through the library doors into the hall. My nipples immediately stiffened as the temperature out here varied significantly from the warmer cocoon of his office space. Again, I was glad that the lights had gone out so that Edward wouldn't see the noticeable peaks through my bikini top. I'd be damned if he thought they were for him.

Funny how less than an hour ago, they had been for him.

His hand had crushed the flesh of my breast while he'd fucked me from behind, and I'd not only welcomed it all but urged him for more.

The memory brought a fresh wave of warmth between my legs. My stupid libido still responded to him. I didn't know who I hated more for that—him or my body.

Besides the effect it had on my nipples, the cool air brought on another shiver, one that Edward wouldn't miss with his hand on my elbow the way it was.

He stopped abruptly, surprising me. I tripped forward, only managing to stay upright because he was already holding me. His other hand, still holding his cell phone, moved to my other arm, as though automatically, steadying me. His touch was hot, and I despised how comforting it felt against my skin.

As soon as I'd found my balance, I jerked away.

He let me, dropping even his hand from my elbow. "Stay," he ordered, and as I watched the light of his cell bounce down the hall in the opposite direction toward his bedroom, as I stayed in the place he'd left me, I wondered if that was how he'd speak to me from now on, with one word commands like I was a dog.

It wouldn't be quite so disgusting if I wasn't compelled to obey.

Curiosity. That was the only reason I was still there. And I needed a light. And even if I found my way to the kitchen on my own, I didn't know where to find supplies and the search would be difficult without him.

Without his cell phone, I corrected mentally. Because like hell was I relying on him for anything.

He returned a short minute later, and, as soon as he did, I felt the warmth of a plush robe being wrapped around me. Despite myself, I thrust my arms through one hole then the other before allowing him to tie a knot securely at my waist. Impressive considering he was still holding his phone.

When he'd bundled me up, he lingered, and, with the light pointing at me, I had the impression he was studying me, as he had earlier, as he did so often. Not for the first time, I wondered what he saw. What brought him back to look time and time again?

And why did I hope he never stopped?

I pulled away first, tugging the collar of the robe up to my nose to sniff. It smelled ordinary, like laundry detergent. Not like him. Not unlike him.

"Is this yours?" I asked, unable to help myself, when what I really should have said was thank you.

"No." His answer came quickly, and he stirred into action, once again taking me at my elbow and leading me with him.

My lips puckered into a pout that he couldn't see. *Not his robe.* Whose robe, then? Why had it been in his room? Why did my chest burn at the thought that it was some other woman's? A woman who he'd allowed into his bedroom, into his bed. Into his life.

A woman he didn't want to murder.

It wasn't jealousy. I refused to be jealous for the attention of someone who openly despised me. Just more curiosity.

I would tell myself that as long as I had to. Maybe, eventually, I'd mean it.

Once he'd pushed through the swinging door into the kitchen, he let me go and proceeded to the pantry, the light disappearing as he withdrew into the storeroom. There was one window in the room, but the blinds had been drawn leaving the space in near total darkness.

As though reacting to the location, my stomach growled, reminding me of its empty state. There'd be something to snack on in the refrigerator, which wouldn't have had enough time to warm up at this early point in the power outage. It was on the other side of the room, and would be easiest to get to if I waited until Edward returned with the light.

But I was irritated at being abandoned and even more irritated at having to depend on anyone—that man in particular—so fuck waiting. Holding my hands out in front of me, I shuffled in the direction I thought made sense, only to stub my toe on the leg of the kitchen table.

"Goddammit." Even whispered, the curse was audible in the quiet.

The pantry door swung swiftly open and the light found me bent over, rubbing the pain from my injury.

Edward chuckled. "I suppose that's my fault for not telling you to stay."

"Fuck you. I'm not your pet." I let my foot fall with a thump.

"No, a pet would have more sense than to bumble around in the dark." Instead of returning to the pantry, he crossed over to the sink, the light spraying against the stainless steel. There the sound of tin met the counter as he set something down and then opened a drawer. Seconds later, a match was lit and then another, brighter flame, filled the room, the scent of kerosene in the air.

He turned toward me, and now the hurricane lamp he'd found was in my view. "I have one in my bedroom. I can send this one with you when you go to bed. If you'd rather, I can find you a working flashlight. The batteries on the first couple I tried seem to have died. It's been a while since we've needed to use them here. Usually the backup generator kicks in. I'll have Louvens look at it in the morning."

"The lamp is fine," I said, wrapping my arms around myself. The lamp illuminated the room quite well, and having grown accustomed to the safety of the dark, I felt suddenly exposed.

"Fine. Then on to other business, which is..." He didn't finish his sentence, crossing instead toward the refrigerator where he opened the door and pulled out a tray that he set on the counter by the lamp. He turned once more in my direction, gesturing to me with two fingers.

I took an involuntary step toward him before stopping myself. He already thought I was at his beck and call. I most certainly wouldn't respond to a hand gesture.

He laughed again, a sound so quiet it was definitely for himself. "Come here, you obstinate creature," he said, less of an order than anything else he'd said since the power had gone out. "I'm trying to feed you."

Too hungry to resist, I shuffled toward him, nodding at the tray he'd set out. "What is it?"

"A charcuterie. Joette prepared it for our dinner."

Leaning my hip into the counter next to him, I studied the plate of food, my arms still crossed. "I thought you already ate what Joette left."

"I ate the sandwiches. I didn't say that was all she'd left." When I hesitated, he reached for a piece of roquefort. "It's not poisonous. Shall I prove it?"

He brought it to his mouth, and I had to bite back a smile. It was meant to be a joke, but I didn't want to find him humorous. Especially not with a joke about killing me. It was too real.

But I was starving. And the charcuterie looked amazing. And I was pretty sure he wasn't going to kill me right now.

I picked up a bunch of grapes and popped four in my mouth, one after another. Edward reached next for a slice of capicola, using the bamboo spreader to dab mustard on it. After he'd eaten it, he moved over to a cabinet and pulled out two wine glasses. It was my turn to study him as he easily found a corkscrew and a bottle of something burgundy. He had the sleeves of his linen shirt pushed up to his biceps, showing off the muscular landscape of his arms. He was stunning, really, every part of him. The furrow of his brow as he worked open the wine. The determined set of his jaw as he poured. The smooth glide as he returned with the glasses, handing one out to me.

I took it, careful not to touch him as I did, ignoring the way my fingers ached to stretch out toward his. With my glass delivered, he lifted his own, nodding it first in my direction in a subtle toast before bringing it to his lips.

My skin tingled underneath the safety of the robe as I watched the alluring tilt of his head followed by the bob of his throat as he swallowed.

I looked away, taking my own quick sip and then setting the glass down to concentrate on what item I wanted to eat next.

Or to pretend to concentrate.

Absentmindedly, my fingers closed around a slice of manchego while my head swam in confusion. The robe, the lamp, the food, the wine—my husband had actively been caring for me in a way that made my knees weak. It was unlike the man I knew him to be on an ordinary day.

That he was behaving this way so soon after threatening my life was nearly impossible to process.

It felt wrong and surreal. Like the child being fattened up by the witch before she was thrown in the oven, except this time the child knew exactly what was happening from the onset.

And the child was stupid enough to stay.

I shook my head at myself and threw a butter cracker in my mouth. At least he was fattening me up with the good stuff.

"Feeling better?" he asked, and though I'd been determined not to look at him for the last several minutes, I could tell he was watching me.

"No," I answered honestly. My hunger was abating, but my stomach still felt twisted.

"What would make you feel better?"

I couldn't help it—my gaze flew back to his, wanting to see his expression to help read the subtext of his question.

Of course his face gave nothing away.

"Oh, I don't know," I said with dripping sarcasm. "Perhaps knowing my husband really wasn't planning my funeral might be a nice start."

"The only one who can determine that is you." He took another swallow of his wine, his eyes never leaving mine.

"Right, right." My body suddenly felt heavy. I hadn't realized until that moment that I'd hoped the whole caretaking routine was evidence that his murder plan was a ruse. "You said you want to break me down. What the hell does that even mean? You want me to be your submissive? You want to inflict pain on me? What?"

I popped another grape in my mouth and then pushed the tray away, having lost my appetite.

Edward set his glass down but kept his hand on it, his thumb stroking the stem. "It's not really a process that can be explained. There's submission involved, yes. It's often painful. It can be extremely satisfying as well."

"For you, you mean."

"Yes. For me."

I'd expected him to protest and try to convince me that there was pleasure in being dominated, blah blah blah. His answer instead, honest as it was, caused my breath to catch and the hair to lift at my neck. Was that what he wanted from me? Fear?

He had it. Fuck him for that, but there was no use denying he had me scared.

He must have read the apprehension in my face, and clever as he was, knew exactly how to counter it. With a challenge. "You thought you could endure it. Don't you want to see if it's true?"

I did when there was a reward at the end. "What do I get out of it?"

"You get to live." His tone suggested it was stupid to ask. That I wasn't in the place to be bartering. That he'd called this a negotiation, but it was really only an offer and both choices he was giving were shitty.

The insanity of it all suddenly hit me. "This is ridiculous. I'm not playing games with you. As soon as the sun is up, I'm out of here."

"You are?" He mimicked my pose, casually leaning his hip against the counter. "How do you plan to manage that? Can you man a boat? I'm pretty sure you don't know how to fly a plane. Uber doesn't come out here. You'd better think twice if you think any of my staff is going to help you. With this storm and our location, it will be impossible to get cell service."

My insides felt hard and cold, the blood in my veins was ice. I was stuck here. I'd already been trapped into submission. I was helpless. A slave to his whims.

This was real fear.

I scanned the room, looking for a weapon, for something I could use against him.

It was a subtle move of my eyes, but he read me like a book. "Do you know where the knives are kept?" His voice was low and ominous. "I do."

If I went for a drawer it would only be a guess. He'd get a hold of a knife before I did, and even if I managed to find the right drawer on the first try, he'd beat me there. He'd overpower me.

I had no choice.

But maybe I did. If I told Tom and Joette what Edward was doing to me, they'd surely help me.

I wouldn't be able to get to them until tomorrow though. "Can I have time to think?" I asked.

"Think about if you want to live? Sure. I'm in no rush to snap that neck. It really is pretty." He took a step toward me, and now he was close enough to trail his thumb down my neck, making me shudder. "But I doubt you're really looking for reasons to accept my offer and are instead looking for an escape. There isn't any way off my island."

Anger bloomed hot and new inside of me. He thought he knew everything? Thought he could guess every one of my moves? So he'd been right a few times...okay, a bunch of times, but that made me even more pissed off.

Pissed off enough to poke the bear.

"But maybe I'll kill you first," I said, trying to ignore the pad of his thumb at the hollow of my neck. "Did you think about that?"

He laughed, the amusement extending to his eyes. "You really are a pistol, aren't you?"

I swallowed, and he caressed his thumb against the movement, his gaze caught there at my throat for long seconds before moving up to my lips.

Then his hand moved to cup behind my neck, bringing my head up as he stepped into me. His mouth came down toward mine, and my pulse sped up with want.

At the last second, I got my wits together and turned my head away.

His lips landed on my jaw. He kept them there, sighing against my skin. "You were begging for me an hour ago."

"And then you told me you wanted me dead."

"Details."

He kissed along my jawline and up toward my ear, awakening every nerve in my body. My thighs felt slick and hot, and I could feel the steel press of his erection at my belly, and, even with all the bullshit and the scare tactics, there was a part of me that wanted him. A part of me that reveled in him wanting me. A part of me that felt validated by the evidence that the chemistry between us wasn't one-sided.

But that part of me was stupid and wrong.

The smart part of me recognized him for the predator he was. A predator who planned to eat me alive.

"You're not touching me again," I said, resolutely, despite the fact that he currently was touching me.

His mouth was at my ear, his breath warm. "You do realize fucking is part of this bargain."

"I haven't accepted this bargain yet."

His grip tightened at my neck, an obvious threat. "You mean you haven't yet accepted this bargain is your only option."

There was nothing to say to that.

Scratch that, there was one thing to say to that which was that I accepted his unfair bargain and would play whatever cruel game he wanted me to play.

I opened my mouth, but the words refused to come out.

And then I didn't need to say them, because Edward kissed the side of my head before dropping his hand and stepping away. "Take a bit of time to think. We have a few days before I need to leave. I can't stay past Sunday, though. I'll need your answer by then."

He pulled his cell from his pocket and turned the light on. He'd made it to the door before he turned back and nodded toward the stove. "By the way, the knives are there. Top drawer to the right."

Then, by the light of his cell phone, he left me, with the lamp, in the kitchen, with a drawer of knives he knew I'd never be brave enough to use.

FOUR

The power was back in the morning. In the daylight, with the storm over, I could think more clearly. Yes, I was trapped on the island, but only while we were on the island. All I had to do was agree to Edward's fucked-up game, and, as soon as we were back in London, there would be plenty of opportunities to get away. Not everyone worked for Edward. Not everyone was on his side.

When I woke up, I considered telling him right away, just to get it over with, but as I opened my door to go look for him, I thought better of it. It was Wednesday morning. If I agreed now, that gave him four days to begin "breaking me down" before we left Amelie. If I waited until the last minute, he couldn't do anything until we were back in the UK, and even if he got ambitious and attempted something on the plane, it would be far less abuse for me to suffer than if he got a head start.

So I shut the door and undertook a very different mission than my previous one—avoid my husband.

It shouldn't have come as a surprise, but this mission was much harder than the last. While he'd been nearly impossible to find in the first week of our honeymoon, now he was there at every turn. In the pool, on the beach, reading on the lanai—all the places I'd adopted as my hangouts when he'd locked himself away in his library. Whatever time I arrived at the kitchen for breakfast, he'd show up soon after. The same thing happened at lunch. By Friday, I was taking most of my meals by myself. I was barely leaving my room at all.

Dinner was the one occasion I had to spend in his presence. He'd never said so, exactly, but the staff still gathered for the meal, and my absence would be something he'd have to explain.

Not that I cared much about inconveniencing the man. Just, it didn't feel like I was in a position to piss him off.

Besides, being around the staff felt safe, even if they all were under Edward's employ. And they were nice, too. Fun. The women had lived very different lives than I had and were not the type of friends I'd pick if I were to choose, but, in reality, I'd never picked friends well, which was maybe what made their differences refreshing. Tom, Dreya, and Eliana especially fascinated me. They were always in a humorous mood in stark contrast to my constant seriousness. Their jokes were often crude and they teased incessantly, but their intentions were kind, and I enjoyed their company more than I liked to admit.

Joette, whose cooking had attracted Edward in the first place, was a particular favorite. She was about a decade older than my mother, and nothing like the woman who'd raised me, or, rather, the woman who'd paid a full-time nanny to do the work for her. Madge Werner was the quintessential socialite, an elitist, always at the ready with a snide remark and a fake smile. I loved her, of course I did, and we were close in many aspects, but it was never easy spending time with her. My stomach was always knotted in her presence, my back always straight, my mind constantly aware and waiting for her next attack.

Joette was everything Madge wasn't. She was expressive and warm, her smile always wide and genuine. When I retreated to my room, she checked in on me without making me feel like my privacy had been invaded. She was attentive without smothering. Curious but not nosy. And her cooking was absolutely divine. She'd be the thing I missed most when I was free of Edward.

Not the only thing, but I didn't like to think about that enough to name what those other things might be.

After dinner was where things became tricky. Previously, when I'd been desperate for Edward's attention, he'd disappear with the men into the library as soon as the meal was over. Now, everyone remained together. The sliding glass wall would be opened up to the patio, alcohol would be poured, cigars would be brought out, and the socializing would continue well into the night.

Edward was still himself in these instances, still composed and well-bred, but it was a more relaxed version of the man I'd been exposed to. His smile came naturally, meeting his eyes more often than not. He wasn't particularly chatty or entertaining, but he was engaged, and if a stranger had walked into the group, it would be obvious to him that Edward was the most important figure of the bunch. It was in the way the others angled their bodies, the way they looked to him for approval, the way they attended to his drink.

It made sense, of course. He was the one with the money. He was the one who paid the bills and owned the island and everything—everyone?—on it. But I had the feeling that the reaction to him would have been the same even if his name wasn't on the land title. He had a certain air about him, a magnetism, an authority that exuded from his very being, daring anyone to challenge him as king. As the devil.

Sometimes, seeing him like this, recognizing this about him, I was surprised that I'd ever dared to provoke him. That I'd dare to again if given the right opportunity, at the right time.

That time wasn't now. This was his show, and I let it be.

While the rest of the couples intermingled, Edward would invariably find a spot near me. He'd hand me a brandy then rest his arm next to me, his hand casually placed on my knee, and behind the laughs and the camaraderie, no one had any idea that I was a captive. That my husband had issued the gravest of threats. That his hold on me, a sure sign of ownership, had my heart pounding against my chest with trepidation.

Maybe not just trepidation. Maybe his touch did more to me than that. Still. Even now.

I didn't know what to expect after our guests left for their own residences. If his hand would rise higher up my thigh, between my legs, if his mouth would seek again to find mine. The minute someone yawned or initiated cleaning up, I excused myself to my bedroom so I wouldn't be left alone with the man I'd married. I didn't want to know what would happen if I stayed, and, thank God, he never followed me to my room.

Until Saturday night, the night before he'd told me he needed to leave.

I'd packed my bags earlier, quietly, careful not to draw his attention. I wanted to be ready to go in the morning, as soon as I gave him my answer about his offer. The luggage was stowed away in my closet, out of sight. The evening had proceeded as usual with the dinner and mingling. As soon as Marge had looked at Erris with that look that said, *Is it time to go?,* I made my own farewells and slipped away to my room. There, I'd showered in my ensuite, then, with a towel on my head and another wrapped around me, I wandered to my bedroom in search of body lotion.

I found Edward instead.

The entire time we'd been on the island, he'd never once entered my rooms, and seeing him there now, sitting in my armchair, his leg nonchalantly crossed at the ankle over the other knee made me startle. Made my stomach flip. Made my knees go weak.

"I wasn't expecting you." Somehow my voice sounded unaffected.

"We have a matter to settle."

"Do we?" I pulled the towel from my head and began patting dry the still-wet ends. There was nothing to gain from acting flippant, but I couldn't help myself. I wanted to be as casual as he was, even if it was all an act.

His blink was heavy and filled with annoyance. "I'd like to get an early start in the morning, but that depends on my agenda for the morning. Have you made a decision?"

He meant it depended on if he had to fit killing his wife into his schedule or not. The pomposity of it made me want to kick something.

I managed to hold my temper. Somewhat. "You haven't really left me much choice."

"No, I haven't."

"Then, there's my answer," I said, tossing the towel I'd used on my hair to the bed.

"Good. I'm pleased." He stood and nodded as if to seal the arrangement. "We'll get started when I get back."

He was almost out of the room when his words sunk in. "You mean when *we* get back. To London." Right?

He paused at the door, turning only his head toward me, one hand bracing the frame. "No, I mean when *I* get back. *From* London." His clarification delivered, he continued out of the room.

The floor felt like it was dropping from beneath me. "No, no, no, hold on." Gripping the towel around me, I scampered after him. "You can't possibly be suggesting that you're going to leave me here."

"No, I'm not *suggesting* that. I'm saying that exactly." He kept walking. Didn't even look back at me as he spoke.

Though he was still moving, I stopped, shocked. "No way. You can't leave me here. How can you leave me here?"

"Very easily. I simply get on my plane and don't allow you to board with me."

He was all the way through the family room and rounding the kitchen by the time I got my feet to move again. "But I agreed to your stupid plan! I gave you what you want! You can take me with you. You won. I lost. It's over."

"It's not over. It's just beginning." Halting, he twisted his body toward me. "And you know why I can't take you with me."

The way his eyes looked into me—looked *through* me, holding me in place—I knew he was a step ahead of me.

As always.

"No, actually, I don't," I said, refusing to accept it. As always.

With a sigh, he took two steps toward me. "Celia, we need to be beyond these little lies. If you're really going to submit to letting me break you down, there needs to be honesty between us."

God, he was so patronizing.

He was right about me and my motives, but that he was so sure he was right was infuriating.

It made me more determined than ever to stick to my story.

"Fine," I said, readjusting the towel since it had slipped in my pursuit. "If we're being honest, tell me honestly why I can't go to London with you."

His head cocked slightly, his gaze piercing deeper into my skin, into my bones. His expression was a challenge, as if to say, *Really? You really want me to spell out why you can't be trusted?*

"Whatever you're thinking I'll do, I won't do it. I promise." I'd gotten good at being able to lie while making direct eye contact.

"You won't run away? You won't try to escape the first opportunity you find? Forgive me for not believing you." He didn't give me a chance to refute, turning and walking away once again.

I scurried after him. "What's the point of honesty if you aren't going to believe anything I say?"

"Trust is earned. Once you've been honest for a significant amount of time, once you've proven your honesty over and over, then I will trust you. Until then, you'll remain here." He paused inside his room to toe off his shoes, then threw me a brow-raised glance, as if to reprimand me for entering his private quarters without his permission.

I hesitated, waiting to see if his reprimand would go further, but it didn't. Seeming to decide I wasn't worth the trouble, he pivoted away from me and crossed to his bed where he removed his watch and set it on the nightstand.

Quickly running through my options, I decided to change my tactic. "How long? How long before you come back?" Maybe he'd be back soon. An extra week on the island wasn't worth arguing about.

His forehead creased as he considered. "I need to catch up on work for a bit. Then it's the holidays, which always put things behind. I'll need some time to catch up from that as well. I should be able to get away again by the end of February."

"THE END OF FEBRUARY?" I was officially shouting. "You can't just abandon me here for three months!"

"Can't I?" The twinkle in his eye, that smirk—this clearly entertained him.

But he hadn't thought it all through. There was no way he had. "What will people say? My family? How are you going to explain this to my mother and father? If they haven't heard from me for a while, they'll at least expect a phone call for Christmas."

He wasn't at all fazed.

"I'm sure no one would question why my wife would want to spend the winter in the Caribbean rather than England." He unbuttoned his shirt as he spoke, his attention only half reserved for me. "As for your parents, I won't have to explain anything. You'll explain things just fine."

"I'll explain things?" I tried to guess what he meant.

"If you think you're going to get me to lie to them—"

He cut me off sharply. "You seem to have forgotten the information I've accessed on your laptop."

Meaning he had the passwords to my email accounts. He could easily email them as me. He could even look at past correspondence to copy my voice. I could picture what he'd say—*I loved Amelie so much I'm staying until spring. The internet doesn't work so I can't be reached. I'm only able to send this because I took a day trip to Nassau.*

He really did have me trapped. Had me captive in every way possible. And all my scheming, all my calculating was for naught.

Adrenaline coursed through my body as rage took over. All week I'd been a dormant volcano on the brink of turning active, the fire inside me heating up and now I'd reached a boiling point. He wanted me to break? Well, I wanted *him* to break. I wanted him to hurt.

Quickly, I scanned my surroundings and found a ceramic vase on his dresser top, a piece that was probably some antique worth some ungodly amount.

I didn't care.

I picked it up and flung it at him as hard as I could.

Of course he saw it coming and ducked out of the way. The vase exploded against the wall behind him, shattering into several pieces.

The gaze Edward pinned on me then was cool and narrow. "Temper, temper, little bird."

That's all I was to him. Something insignificant. A bird. A broken bird, at that, because he'd clipped my wings.

"Is this part of it? You've already started, haven't you?" If he meant to break me down, he was on his way to succeeding.

He didn't answer, shrugging his shirt off his shoulders as he crossed the room to toss it on the chair against the opposite wall. When he turned back to me, he nodded toward the pottery pieces. "I hope you don't plan on leaving your mess for Sanyjah to clean up."

My hands were balled into fists at my sides, my breath coming fast and shallow in my chest. I already wanted to punch him. Suggesting I get on my knees and straighten up was the last straw.

Bending down, I picked up a shard that had landed nearby. Then, when I found the piece had a sufficiently jagged edge, I didn't hesitate. I didn't think. I just did.

Holding the fragment up in the air, I charged toward him. I lost my towel on the way. I was naked, and I didn't care. The desire to hurt him was too real, too sharp, as sharp as the ceramic in my hand.

He caught me at my forearm, because he was faster and stronger than I was. He gripped the other as well, jerking it behind my back, drawing me near so that the tips of my breasts brushed against his chest. It didn't escape me that this was the closest I'd been to having my bare skin against his. Less than a week ago, I would have considered the position a win, would have fallen willingly into him. Would have given him all of me.

Now he wanted all of me, and I wanted him dead.

And he knew it.

But instead of wrenching the weapon away from me, he moved the tip to his throat. Lifting his chin, exposing his neck, he offered himself. "Do it. Right there. The carotid artery is your best shot at a clean kill. Swipe all the way across to get both branches. It takes more strength than you think it will, so be sure to push deep."

I held my hand still, keeping the point at his skin, and I thought about it. For a second, I really thought about it.

Then, with a sigh that sounded more like a growl, I dropped the shard, letting it fall to the tile floor with a clunk.

"There now, that's more honest. We both know you don't have the stomach for murder." Though it loosened, Edward's grip on my forearms remained. His thumb traced along the inside of my wrist. Up, down, sending goosebumps across my arm, causing my thighs to vibrate.

"I hate you," I seethed.

"That doesn't bother me."

I wrestled out of his hold and took a step back from him. His eyes perused me, scanning up from my toes to my lips, lingering on the parts of my body that interested him most. He was so fucking arrogant. As if he had a right to look at me that way.

Snatching his discarded shirt, I wrapped it around me. "I wouldn't get so cocky if I were you. I might not be a murderer right now, but three months on this island is a long time. A lot could change."

With that, I left him along with the mess I'd made. If he really wanted it cleaned, he could take care of it himself. He wanted me to submit to him, then fine. But if we weren't beginning until he returned, I had three months to do whatever the hell I wanted, and I planned to do just that.

I hardly slept. Variations of the dream I'd had during my nap days ago played out throughout the night. Sometimes I was being chased, sometimes I was the one chasing, but it was always me and a man. The anonymous man, who wasn't quite so anonymous anymore. While I could never see his face, I knew in my gut who it was. Who else would I run after?

Who else would make me run?

I gave up hope for sleep around dawn. Then I just lay there waiting, listening for sounds of Edward stirring in the main part of the house.

I finally heard him around eight. After throwing on a sundress and slipping on a pair of flip-flops, I came out to talk to him. A quick look in the hall mirror showed that I looked as bad as I felt—dark circles under my eyes, my face blotchy. I cringed, but the poor appearance would help.

With my arms wrapped around myself and my head bowed, I found him in the living room giving instructions to Mateo regarding his luggage.

"How sweet," he said when he saw me. "You came to say goodbye." With a nod, he ushered Mateo out to the jeep.

"Can I see you to the plane?" I asked, demurely.

"No, but you can see me to the door."

We walked the distance in silence. I could feel the heat of him at my side, but I wouldn't let it warm me. I stayed cold. I stayed focused.

"I need something," I said, turning toward him when we reached the door. "I need some reassurance. When this is all done, you'll let me go? We'll get a divorce and part with no other baggage between us?"

"Yes." His voice was gentle. Soothing almost.

"You mean that?"

"I do."

I searched his eyes while he searched mine, looking for a speck of compassion I could prey on. I was nearly sure I saw it—a flash of something kind behind his cool blue eyes.

I stepped closer to him. "And when you come back, in February, and you begin...your thing," I couldn't force myself to use his words for what he planned to do to me, "how long will I be here after that?"

"As long as it takes."

"I need an expiration. Otherwise I could be here forever."

"Or you could be dead."

That word again. It could have been devastating to hear so many times. If I weren't so fucking pissed.

Knowing this was my last chance, I pulled out all the stops. I laid it on thick. "Please, Edward." I reached out to curl my fingers in his shirt, linen again. Black this time. Fitting for the demon that he was. "I know I was awful to you, that I'm an awful person. I know I deserve whatever you have planned for me, but you're better than that. You're better than me. Please take me with you. I won't survive three months here. I'll do what you want. I'll be the perfect wife, whatever you want, just take me with you."

The words were staged, but I hadn't planned the tears. The tears, I was pretty sure, were real.

His hand came up to settle over mine. "Stop, bird," he said softly. "Stop with the lies."

He had no heart. He was nothing inside.

How well I knew what that was like.

The tears fell harder, and my grip tightened on his shirt as I grew spiteful. "What's going to stop me from going after you when you let me go? I'll tell everyone what you've done, that you've abducted me and forced me into your sick games. You'll be ruined."

"You aren't really helping your case here, Celia."

"There's no way what I'm saying is a revelation. I'm trying to insure that I get out of here alive." I brought my other fist to meet the one already on his chest, and I wasn't sure anymore if I wanted to beat him with them or hold him so tightly that he couldn't possibly leave without dragging me with him.

"You'll get out of here alive. As soon as you're broken down. And when that truly happens, there's no way you'd turn me in to anyone."

"Oh really." I tried to drop my hands, but he clasped them both under his, holding them in place. I could feel his heartbeat under my palm. Steady and strong. Calm.

"You seem to not understand what you'll become when you're broken down," he said, stroking his fingers over my skin. It was a lover's caress.

He was as good at pretending as I was.

It distracted me, but not enough to not ask the question he was leading me to ask. "What's that?"

He leaned forward, his lips ghosting along my forehead. "Mine."

FIVE

As soon as Edward was gone, I began looking for a way to escape.

He'd warned me that his staff was loyal to him, but with eleven adults on the island, there had to be someone who had a conscience. Someone who knew keeping a grown woman captive was wrong. These were good people, too. I'd spent time with them now, and couldn't believe that there wasn't one of them that would try to help me.

I chose who I'd approach carefully. Joette was the matriarch, the woman that Edward had initially befriended. Winning her favor would likely be the hardest, no matter how friendly and doting she'd been. It followed that her children would stand by her in most things, which was why I decided to approach one of the spouses.

Sanyjah, Mateo's wife, was the obvious choice.

Quieter than most of the women, Sanyjah was one of the primary housekeepers and spent a good deal of time around the main house. That meant I saw her more than almost anyone else except Joette and Tom, who did the daily cooking.

I found her later in the morning in Edward's room, cleaning up the ceramic from the vase I'd broken the night before.

"I'll be done in a few minutes," she said when I came in, obviously thinking I wanted use of the room.

"Actually, I came to talk to you."

She stood up straight, leaning on the broom, her expression mildly surprised. "Do you need something? Did Tom forget to stock your cupboards with toilet paper?"

The staff had never acted like servants around Edward. There could only be a handful of reasons why they'd behave differently with me. Either he'd told them to, which seemed unnecessary, and Edward never did anything unnecessarily. Or I hadn't given them any reason to act any other way.

The latter was more likely. I'd been nice enough with all of them but not particularly friendly. Obviously, I'd been a shitty guest.

I hoped that didn't bite me in the ass now. Hopefully, an explanation of my plight would forgive my previous conduct.

"No, nothing like that. Here, let me help." I bent down to pick up the shards I should have cleaned up the night before. When she protested, I dismissed her. "This was my fault, anyway. Only right that I'm the one to clean it up."

"You knocked it over?" The suspicion in her voice was reasonable. The vase had been placed across the room.

"I threw it. I was angry." I tossed the pieces into the garbage bag at Sanyjah's side then stood again. "I was angry because Edward is keeping me captive here. He won't let me leave. But now he's gone, and so I'm begging you to help me. Please, help me?"

Sanyjah peered at me curiously, as though she thought I might be testing her. Then she laughed and went back to sweeping the particles that had been left behind. "Sure I'll help you. I'll help by cleaning up after you."

"I know this sounds ridiculous, but I'm telling the truth. He tricked me into coming here, and now he's left me here."

"Tricked you? You married him, didn't you?"

"Yes, but." Of course anything I said about that would make my credibility worse. "I did willingly marry him," I said, thinking fast. "I didn't know what kind of a man he was when I did. He hid his true colors, and now I'm his prisoner."

She laughed again, shaking her head. Maybe I'd picked the wrong spouse after all.

I tried again. "I know there's a phone somewhere on the island with satellite reception. If you could just get me to it, I can call my father and…"

"I'm sorry, I can't do that," she said, serious now. "Now, if you'll excuse me, I need to finish my work."

She turned her back toward me, ending the discussion.

My attempts with Marge and Peter went similarly. In desperation, I moved onto Joette's children, but trying to plea to Mateo and Dreya was just as fruitless. Either I wasn't taken seriously or I was flatly dismissed. Clearly, they'd been given orders and those orders wouldn't be ignored.

I considered appealing to everyone all at once at dinner. Maybe with all of them together they'd see reason.

But, while we'd had dinner together nightly when Edward was on the island, that evening I was left only with a premade meal in the fridge from Joette.

The next day I tried something more demure with Tom, asking for use of the phone to call Edward. "We're newlyweds and all, and I already miss him."

She winked. "Exactly why he needs some time away from you. Pretty, young wives are distracting. Who's gonna pay the bills if you don't let the man work?"

Escaping was going to be harder than I'd thought.

I waited out the week. Though Joette and Tom and Sanyjah came almost daily, the house was quieter than it had been my entire honeymoon. Thanksgiving came and went, uncelebrated by Bahamian natives.

Whatever. It had never been my favorite holiday anyway. All those calories that had to be sweat off with extra workouts. Not that I didn't have time to exercise. Being stuck on Amelie was the perfect excuse to get in better shape. What else was there to do? It was paradise, but even paradise got boring after a while.

When Edward had been gone a week, I tried another approach, asking Eliana if I could tag along on her trip to Nassau for groceries.

She tilted her head up as if she was considering, and my chest fluttered with hope.

"I don't think that's a good idea," she said after a minute. "It's not safe."

"Not safe?"

"For a woman in your condition."

"A woman in my condition?" I was repeating everything she said in horror. What had Edward said about me?

"Did he tell you I was pregnant?"

"No!" she said, her eyes wide. "Congratulations!"

"I'm not pregnant," I said with a frustrated scowl. "I meant, what do you mean about my condition?"

"It's best we not talk about serious things like that," she said mysteriously. "And leave grocery shopping to me. You stay here where you're looked after. Everything will be all right."

No, everything would not be all right. I was trapped, and no one would give me a straight reason for not wanting to help me.

So I tried to hide on the boat. Actually, I first tried to steal the boat. Sure, I'd never driven one before, but it couldn't be that hard.

Except it completely was. I found the steering wheel and where to put a key, but the rest of the buttons were meaningless. And, even if I wanted to brave it, I soon learned the keys were locked up in a safe. There was a sailboat as well, but it was chained to the dock and secured with a padlock. That key, I presumed, was also in the safe.

And thus I was forced to try to hide instead. I buried myself under some blankets at the stern of the boat and waited.

Mateo caught me right away.

I tried again the following week. Monday was always grocery day, which meant I didn't have to cause suspicion by asking when the next boat would go out. I hoped that not mentioning wanting to go with Eliana this time would make it seem like it had left my mind. I got to the dock way before the time she usually left and found a better hiding spot on the cruiser.

Again, Mateo discovered me.

The next week it was Louvens who found me. Which meant I still might have a shot. He was the single man of the bunch and his sneaky stares at me in my bikini and on my daily runs had not gone unnoticed.

"We should take a ride to the mainland together," I said, sidling up to him. "Just you and me."

He wasn't unaffected. The quickness in his breathing gave him away.

"Think how much fun we could have," I pressed. My voice was sticky sweet, and the way I smoothed my palm down his chest was borderline inappropriate.

He grabbed my wrist before I could get anywhere interesting. "If you keep this up, I'm going to have to limit your access to just the house."

The island already felt small and claustrophobic. I couldn't survive confined to the house.

Interpreting my frown, he added, "It's for your safety."

For your safety. There was that phrase again.

"What exactly did my husband say to you about me?" I asked, my tone close to pleading.

Lou frowned and looked out over the horizon. "I'm afraid I'm not the one to ask."

There was no question who *was* the one to ask. When I got back to the house, I stormed into the kitchen where I could hear Tom and Joette singing together while they peeled potatoes.

"What did he tell you?" I demanded. "What did Edward tell you that convinced you that keeping me a prisoner was a matter of my safety?"

Tom looked to her mother. Joette sighed and wiped her hands on her apron. "Why don't you sit down?"

I didn't want to sit down.

But it was mid-December. Including the time with Edward, I'd been on the island five weeks, and if I had any hope of leaving, I realized I had to change my tactics.

I sat down.

Joette took my hand in hers, and as much as I wanted to find it patronizing, I didn't. It felt warm and comforting, even as the terrible words crossed her lips.

"Edward confided in us the truth," she said, tenderly. "About your mental health. About your delusions. Of course he isn't keeping you captive here, darling. He's trying to protect you. We all are. What a wonderful husband you have that he devotes such attention to his sick wife, even from afar."

I snatched my hand away from hers and tried to swallow past the lump in my throat. *My word against yours.* That's what I'd said to him. That's what my plan had been in trapping him with my game. He'd beat me to it. Whatever credibility I might have had with his staff was taken away by him simply telling them that I was crazy.

I'd said it before, but I hadn't believed it until right then. Hadn't truly believed it. I was Edward's prisoner. The only way I'd leave the island was if he chose to let me go.

SIX

The gifts began arriving as soon as I stopped trying to leave.

The first was the clothes. I'd already been quite vocal to everyone who would hear it about my limited wardrobe. I'd come to the island expecting to be there for two weeks. Two weeks that I'd planned to do nothing but seduce my husband, which meant I'd brought lots of short dresses and skimpy swimsuits. Though December in the Caribbean was still fairly temperate, the rainy season was in full swing and more than once I'd wished for a pair of yoga pants. And a sweater. And some jeans. A pantsuit.

More than once I'd thought about the monthly stipend Edward had promised me as his wife. More than once I fantasized spending it. One hundred thousand pounds could go a long way on Fifth Avenue.

In the end, I hadn't had to spend my money on clothing at all—if I actually had any money. Because when Eliana returned the following week from her grocery run, she'd come back with boxes and boxes of clothes.

"Thank you for finally listening," I exclaimed as I tore

into the first box, noting the designer label on the outside of the package.

"You're welcome, but it wasn't me," she said with a shrug. "This is all thanks to your husband."

I considered taking a pair of scissors to whatever I found inside, but it was too perfect—a red jersey wrap dress that was just my style. They were all perfect, every item. Every outfit was tailored to me, as though I'd been measured, as though I'd personally selected them.

And there was clothing for a range of occasions, from fancy to casual, all of them designer made. With designer shoes to match.

So he'd found a personal shopper and given her a big check. That wasn't hard. I was grateful for the clothes, but I wasn't grateful to *him*.

Except, then I found the notes, handwritten and tucked inside each item. Simple, brief notes that said things such as *Reminds me of the dress you wore to that first dinner at my house* on a floral sundress, and *A casual Sunday look* on a printed jumpsuit, and *White, the color that wedding dresses should be* on a white pair of linen pants.

He'd had a hand in the selection. Even if he hadn't done the shopping himself, he'd chosen with thought and then made sure I knew it.

But he was still my captor.

I crumpled all the notes and threw them into my bathroom wastebasket.

Then, after putting away all my clothes, one hundred pieces in all, I pulled the notes back out of the wastebasket and shoved them into the drawer of my nightstand. I wouldn't read them again; I didn't care about what they said or what they meant, but neither could I bear to let them go.

The next day Dreya invited me to morning yoga.

"I used to lead classes at the resorts in Nassau. Now I teach it to the kids." Dreya, I'd learned, was primarily responsible for homeschooling and caring for the fourteen children that lived on the island. She didn't shoulder the burden completely on her own; the other men and women rotated their duties to assist her, and though the youngest, Marge and Erris's baby, was only four months old, Mateo and Sanyjah's eldest two girls, at fourteen and fifteen years of age, were tasked with a fair amount of childcare as well as grandma watching.

And all of them, including Azariah, Joette's eighty-five-year-old mother, apparently met on the beach near the staff quarters every morning for yoga.

I'd always hated yoga. I hated group exercise in general, but particularly one that had me twisting in silly positions with weird names.

But island life had left me lonely. I had no internet. I had no phone. And most of my interactions with the staff had remained transactional. I ate my meals alone. I took my daily run alone. I spent my time alone.

So I accepted the invitation to yoga. I bent and stretched and laughed when five-year-old Jaden toppled over out of Vrksasana and smiled impressively when Azariah did a full back bend that I was smart enough not to even attempt.

And when the whole sequence was almost done and I lay in Balasana, child's pose, my forehead on the mat that Dreya had provided, the sound of gentle sighs around me mixing with the crash of ocean waves behind us, I realized I could breathe easier and deeper than I had in a very long time.

"Will you join us tomorrow?" Dreya asked when the mats were all cleared up, and I had nothing to do but leave to go back to the main house.

"I'll be here any day you let me," I answered honestly.

"Every weekday then."

I gave her an answering smile. "I'd like that."

"Your husband will be pleased to hear."

I didn't let that final remark ruin it, letting it fall off me as I turned to go on my way, but I knew without being explicitly told that the invitation hadn't really come from Dreya at all.

The following day was Christmas Eve. I remarked on it, casually, to Tom.

"Perhaps you want to write a letter to your family?"

The suggestion was startling. And exhilarating.

"Can I?" I clarified. "I mean, am I allowed?"

"Why wouldn't you be allowed?"

I could think of several reasons, the most obvious being that I'd tell them I was being held captive and to get the

FBI involved in finding me ASAFP.

But Tom was digging out stationery and a pen, and I wasn't about to clue her in on her mistake.

I kept it simple, sticking to facts and details needed to initiate a rescue mission. I addressed it to my father, knowing he was the one who had the power to do things, the man who would make things happen. I didn't tell him he'd been right, that Edward Fasbender was no good, that he was a devil, that I should have avoided him at all costs.

He'd already know that without me saying it.

I sealed the note in the envelope Tom had provided and handed her the letter, feeling more hopeful than I had in weeks.

The next gift came Christmas morning, along with another invitation.

I'd expected to be alone for the day, and that idea had brought on the worst bout of melancholy yet. Though I wasn't emotionally close to my parents, we were close in other ways. We did things together. We went to the ballet, the opera, charity fundraisers. We spent holidays together. We exchanged cliché, meaningless gifts, but we were together.

Except for the year I was in the hospital, I'd always spent Christmas in their condo, snuggled up in my pajamas, watching *It's a Wonderful Life* and *Miracle on 34th Street*. There'd be an early dinner first, with the Pierces, either at our house or at theirs, but classic movies was the evening routine. My father would leave less than half-way through the first one and my mother would drink too much sherry, but it was tradition. It was what I knew, and I missed it more than I thought I could.

I missed them. More than I should. More than they likely missed me.

But I had dealt with those feelings laying in bed on Christmas Eve. And after acknowledging them, I'd made a plan for distraction. I'd spend the day reading something from the library—one of the countless business commu-nication books or one of the worn paperback romances that I assumed belonged to Edward's sister, Camilla, or his ex-wife, Marion. The pickings were slim, but I'd always enjoyed reading. There would be something to occupy my mind, even if I had to reread something I'd already read.

Instead, I awoke to the smell of something delicious baking and the sounds of commotion.

"What's going on?" I asked Tom when I found her in the kitchen pulling cinnamon rolls out of the oven.

"These should do you for breakfast," she said, as if that was an answer. "Sorry this is all I have time for before get-ting back to my own. We'll have dinner at our quarters at three. Dress casual."

"Okay." I hadn't thought for a moment I'd be welcome at their family Christmas celebrations, and I wasn't about to question the invitation. "I heard noise in the library too. What's going on in there?"

"Oh, that's your Christmas present from Edward. I think you'll be quite delighted with his choices."

Without hesitation, I left to see what she was talking about. There were a few people in the library—Louvens and Peter as well as the two eldest of Peter and Tom's kids. While Lou was breaking down boxes, the rest were loading empty shelves with books. I surveyed the titles. There were a lot of classics but more contemporary reads, titles that I recognized but hadn't yet picked up. Titles that were definitely on my TBR.

Edward had guessed my taste in books as well as he'd guessed my taste in clothes.

Except, guess wasn't the right word for it. He'd studied me. He'd learned me.

My throat felt suddenly tight.

Unwittingly, a memory popped in my mind, one of the last games I'd played with Hudson. Or I'd thought it was a game. He'd decided it was something different. The subject was Alayna Withers, the woman who would one day become his wife. He'd called me from the Hamptons with a list of books he needed me to purchase and have delivered to his penthouse immediately.

He hadn't told me, but I'd known they were for her. Even then, I'd suspected where things were headed. That he was done with me.

The books he'd chosen had been personal, it was obvious. He'd put care and thought into the selections, and a strange throb had begun in my chest. Like a knocking against my ribcage from deep inside. I wouldn't let the emotion out, wouldn't let it show itself, but I'd recognized it.

It was envy.

What would that feel like, to have a man care about me so much, to have him be that attentive and adoring that he'd fill shelves and shelves with exactly the books I wanted to read?

When Louvens and Peter and Tom left a short while later, I knelt on the library floor, stared at the shelves of new books, and took long, deep breaths until the dizziness went away. Until the tightness loosened in my chest. Until I could make my mind separate the gift from the man who'd given it.

The gifts continued the next week and into the new year, if gifts were what they were. The allowances. The evidences that I remained on Edward's mind.

First, on the next grocery day, came a beautiful hand-crafted wooden chess set and a book on how to play. Which was fine and all, but I knew how to play already, though it had been ages since I had, and who was supposed to oppose me?

I found myself reading the book anyway, learning new moves, brushing up on techniques. I set the board up and played against myself as best I could.

The next week, Eliana began joining me for afternoon games. She beat me most of the time, but I was a quick study, and the company was good.

One day when she came to play, she noticed the copy of *One Hundred Years of Solitude* that I had on the table near the sofa, face down to keep my place.

"If you have specific books you'd like, let me know," she said. "I'll see what I can do to get them."

I wasn't sure if that meant she'd go through Edward or

she'd simply pick them up on grocery day. There wasn't much I wanted, at the moment. He'd stocked me up fairly well.

Except, there was a subject I was interested in, a topic I wanted to know more about before my husband returned. "Could you maybe see if you could get me some books about BDSM?"

"Romance books?" she asked, her expression strange.

"No. Nonfiction. About being a submissive. A how-to guide or whatever you can find."

The following week, she brought me three—*Exploring Kink, A Dominant's Guide for Submissives*, and *Sadistic Desires*. I felt powerful with them in my possession. It gave me a guide for my future.

And if Edward knew about them, fine. Perhaps it was good he knew that I was prepared.

The same week, I learned that Marge had been a massage therapist before she'd moved to the island. I discovered it when, after yoga one morning, she announced that I was to follow her to the pool house. It was right outside the main house, but I'd never bothered to go in. Now I discovered I'd been missing out. It was well-equipped with a steam room and boxing ring and, surprise, surprise, a massage room. For two hours, I lay on that table and Marge worked every muscle until I was a noodle.

"See if you can stay that loose until next week," she said when she was done.

"What's next week?"

"Your next massage. Mister Fasbender has decided they'll be weekly."

I knew by now that everything happened at *Mister*

Fasbender's request, and still, each declaration to that effect made my stomach drop and flutter all at once.

That night I wrote another letter to my parents. The first one had gone unanswered, and I suspected it had never been sent at all. This one wouldn't reach them either, but it felt good to talk to them. Felt good to open up and say things, honest things. Things I wished I could say to someone. Anyone.

It's beautiful here.

I miss my home. I miss my freedom. But I'm not any more alone here than I was in New York.

Something's changing in me, and I don't know who I am anymore. Tell me who I am.

I sealed the envelope and gave it to Tom, futile as I knew it was.

The next week a Hispanic beautician came back with Eliana from Nassau. She couldn't speak a lick of English, and I could only speak a handful of words in Spanish, which I was sure was intentional. Language barrier or not, she understood what I wanted with my hair and after three hours of fussing with it, my highlights and length were back to what I preferred.

The following week beauty supplies were sent. High-quality skin care products and makeup, more than one person could ever use with ingredients that almost made me stop jonesing for my Botox.

The next week it was a Korean woman who arrived from Nassau, with perfect eyebrows and full pink lips. She spoke more English than the hairdresser, but it still took me quite a while to understand her. At first, I thought she'd come to do my nails. When she pulled out a wax warmer and applicator sticks, I figured she was there to shape my brows into perfect arches like her own. And she did do that.

But when she was finished, she gestured lower, toward my shorts.

I did usually keep things neat down there. I'd attempted a trim or two while on the island, but I'd pretty much surrendered to letting it turn into a jungle. I could say it didn't matter without having a man around who'd see it, but the truth was I'd always waxed for myself. I liked the feeling of being mostly bare. I liked the way my underwear rubbed against my skin, the way my bikinis smoothed without a tuft of hair underneath.

I should have been appreciative that Edward had thought of this. Of even this.

But this wasn't a gift. This was going too far.

Leaving the beautician in confusion, I stormed out of the pool house where all my beauty procedures had been performed, and into the house to find someone—anyone—who would listen to my complaint.

Unfortunately for her, I found Tom.

"This has gone too far," I said, my tone harsh and louder than necessary. "He's trying to butter me up. Trying to make me forget I'm in captivity by playing nice with all these favors. But I haven't forgotten. And these aren't favors—not really. They're for him. The clothes? The hair? The makeup? A bikini wax? This is for him. This is what he wants from a wife—a perfect, pretty Barbie doll. He has no right demanding this from me. He has no right!"

Tom looked up from the dough she'd been kneading and wiped a bead of sweat from her forehead with her knuckle. "What about the chess? And the massages? What about the books? Are those all for him too?"

The question threw me off guard, but I was too worked up to let it go. I paced the kitchen as I talked. "Yes. Yes! Because he's dictating my life. It doesn't matter that I like it or want it. He's deciding. He's not even here. He's however many hundreds of miles away, and he's still controlling everything. He's choosing what I fill my days with and shaping me in whatever way he likes as though he expects me to follow his commands. As though I'm his fucking submissive. As though I'm—" *His.*

I cut off before the word passed my lips, but it stopped me in my tracks.

Tom rose one expectant brow, waiting for the end of a sentence I would never finish. I couldn't say it out loud, but this was my fate, I realized. This was what I'd agreed to. To break down. To submit. To become his.

Scowling, I spun around and headed back to the pool house where I let the Korean woman wax my pussy. She took everything off, leaving me bare. Usually I left a strip, but it didn't matter what my preference was. This was what Edward wanted, and that's what he'd get.

Later, I sat out on the lanai, my knees cradled to my chest as I stared numbly out at the ocean. Joette stuck her head out, most likely to tell me she was leaving for the day, but, seeing me, she came outside completely. She didn't say anything, just stood there, patiently, making herself available.

Without looking at her, I spoke. "I know what you said. I know what he told you about why I'm here and that you believed him. How can you not see what this really is?"

"How can *you* not?"

My head swung sharply in her direction. A frown tugged at my lips, confusion knitted my brow.

She perched on the edge of the deck chair next to me. "I've known Edward for quite some time. He's a man who holds much inside him. Rage, mostly. Destruction. He can be compassionate and thoughtful, but his darkness has always remained at his core, an infection that has no cure.

"Until now. Until you."

I opened my mouth to speak, but no sound came out. I didn't understand what she was saying well enough to protest, and I certainly didn't agree.

"He's different with you," she went on. "It's not something you can see because you've only ever known him as the man who's met you. But he *is* different. He's more the man I think he wants to be. The man he needs to be, even if he doesn't see it yet. It scares him, I'm sure, and perhaps he isn't behaving the way he should with you, and for that I'm sorry. But I can see something coming—for both of you—and that's what I'm holding on for. I hope you can find a way to hold on for the same."

She was loyal, there was no doubt about that. And optimistic. And I wanted to say her rose-colored view was a bold-faced lie.

But she stood up to leave, and I said nothing at all.

The following Friday, the second week of February, I decided to do something new—I invited everyone to dinner.

Well, not everyone. The main house was big, but not quite big enough to handle twelve adults and fourteen children.

But when Edward had been here, he'd had most of the grown-ups over every night so I did the same. I approached Tom about the idea first thing in the morning, and by noon she'd confirmed that most of them would be there.

"We're looking forward to it," she said with such sincerity that I chose to believe her.

That evening, we gathered. Joette, Mateo and Sanyjah, Tom and Peter, Dreya and Eliana. I'd been told earlier that Erris and Marge had volunteered to stay with the kids, so I hadn't expected them.

"Where's Louvens?" I asked when I looked around the table and noticed him missing.

Dreya and Eliana exchanged a glance that made me regret asking. As easy as they made it seem, they were a broken family of sorts. Louvens and Eliana had been married and had four children together before Eliana had fallen in love with Lou's little sister. They all seemed to get along whenever I saw them, but perhaps there were disagreements that I wasn't party to.

"He'll be here," Joette said dismissively. "How's the plantain?"

The plantain was delicious. The whole meal was delicious, Joette's cooking made better by eating it in the company of others. It was noisy and chaotic and that was wonderful. The conversation engaged me. The private stories of their families held my interest in a way I'd never thought domestic tales would interest me. I laughed—really laughed—for the first time in months. Maybe even longer.

I felt, shockingly, at home.

We were midway through the meal when I heard the front door open, and less than a minute later, I discovered why Louvens had missed dinner, where he had been.

He'd been at the airstrip.

He'd been picking up Edward.

SEVEN

"Edward." It felt like I talked about him all the time, like he was always present in my mind, but seeing him in the flesh felt like seeing a stranger. And as much as I hated him, my breath caught in my chest, my heart tripping with elation.

His eyes held mine as he approached me, one hand held behind his back.

I stood automatically. "I didn't know you were... What are you doing here?" I hadn't expected him for another couple of weeks.

"Could I really stay away from my wife this weekend? It's our first Valentine's Day together. I wouldn't miss it for the world."

Valentine's Day. Time lost all meaning on Amelie. I barely knew it was Friday let alone that there was a holiday tomorrow.

Especially when the holiday wasn't important.

Valentine's Day wasn't why Edward was here.

This was for show, as was the bouquet of calla lilies

and roses that he presented from behind his back, but the flowers and the tender kiss on the lips did something to me. Dazed me. Made it hard to think.

I swallowed, running my sweaty palms along the front of my dress in a pretense of smoothing my skirt. Tom was already up and taking care of the flowers, finding them a vase, and Mateo had another chair and place set before I could get my wits together.

Edward sat, taking my hand in his so I sat as well. His attention, though, was on those around him, listening and smiling as his staff brought him up to speed on island life.

I picked at my food after that, sipped anxiously at my wine. My stomach was in knots and the press of Edward's fingers laced through mine was distracting. The tug of an unanswered question swirled through my mind, wanting resolution.

When the group was preoccupied with an unimportant family debate, I couldn't take it anymore. I leaned toward him, keeping my voice quiet. "What happens now?"

"We finish dinner." Letting go of my hand and stretching his arm around my chair—a natural move for a husband who'd missed his bride—he bent into me, the warm air of his breath tickling my ear. "Then, tonight, we begin."

When Edward had been on the island before, the socializing had gone on long after the meal was over. This night, as though everyone had been given orders I wasn't aware of, the group departed as soon as the table was cleared.

Edward must have slipped away during the goodbyes because, immediately after our guests had left, he instructed me. "I've laid out clothes for you on your bed. Wear them and nothing else. Meet me in the library when you're finished."

With tingling fingers and toes, I nodded and left for my room. I hadn't decided if I meant to make this easy for him or not. I was still angry with him—outrageously angry—but two and a half months had made me more comfortable with that anger. It no longer spewed from me. I was able now to hold it, to wait.

Wait for what, I wasn't sure. I'd know when the time was right to draw it out.

Curiosity now dominated my emotions. And nervousness. What would Edward do to me? Would it hurt too much? Would it not hurt enough?

I was beyond ready to know.

On my bed, I found the items he'd set out. They hadn't been with the clothes he'd sent me, so he must have brought it. I would have tossed them out otherwise. The underwear were plain white cotton briefs. The matching bra had no wire and did nothing in the way of support. The white dress—smock was a better term for it—had no shape. It hung past my knees, accentuating absolutely nothing about my body. White ballet flats accompanied the outfit. The best thing I could say about them was that they fit.

I lingered in front of my bathroom mirror for almost a full minute. I'd given up doing my makeup since I'd been on the island, and, while my body had developed a nice tan, sunscreen had kept my face blotchy and uneven. Edward hadn't specified anything about cosmetics, but he seemed to be going for plain, a look that I didn't wear comfortably.

Some foundation and a bit of rouge would make me feel better. I had a feeling that was the reason he wouldn't want me applying them.

I settled for freshening my lipgloss, leaving my lips a natural pink, then headed to the library to find my husband.

"This isn't sexy," I said when I arrived.

He glanced up at me from behind his computer. "I know."

Ouch.

But now I had to wonder—was this plain Jane appearance meant to throw me off balance or keep him from losing his?

The possibility that it was the latter felt warm in my belly.

A few taps of keys and the printer behind Edward woke up, shooting out several pages. "These are for you," he said, gathering the items and handing them to me.

I could feel the crease in my brow as I looked them over. Right away I noticed something very startling—the pages were emails.

"You just printed these. How are you on the internet? The Wi-Fi has never worked." I'd tried an unbelievable amount of times to connect with no success. There was only one server option. No password required. It wasn't like that was the reason I'd been locked out.

"Because I've had the server disconnected. I had it turned back on when I arrived."

"There's been a working server here the whole time?" I didn't know how he continued to surprise me.

He looked at me like I was ridiculous. "How else would I be able to work while I'm here? And don't get any ideas.

It's password protected."

Password protected and disconnected server—the man really didn't trust me.

I considered lashing out about it and quickly decided not to. I'd already been confined to the island with no contact with the outside world. It wasn't like this was a new horror, even if it was new to discover the details around it.

With a sigh, I turned my focus back to the papers in my hand. They'd been printed from my email account. I scanned the top, my eyes rushing lower when I realized the top section was in reply to something below. I recognized the words there. They were my words. For the most part. They'd been edited to exclude the main point, which was that my husband had taken me captive, but the little that was left were the words I'd written to my parents in my first letter.

I shot daggers at him, again contemplating giving him my wrath, but really. What had I expected? I'd never really believed that those letters would get through, that he'd let me talk freely to my parents.

It was a pointless argument.

Taking another deep breath, I read through my mother's replies. Each were cordial and succinct. My mother preferred conversing on the phone, and she said as much in one of the emails, *It's too bad you don't have service there so you can call.*

Beyond that, there was nothing overtly warm. Nothing that expressed concern for me or my new marriage beyond the stock *We miss you* at the bottom of each message.

I tossed them down on Edward's desk, dismissively. "Can we start now?"

"They did send you a Christmas gift," he said gesturing to a Tiffany box on the corner of his desk that I'd over-looked. A bracelet, judging from the size. Probably diamonds. Not the most expensive item in the inventory but not the least either.

I didn't need to see it to know almost exactly what it was.

It was devastating that the gift that Edward sent, the books that currently surrounded me, were of more value to me than what my parents had sent.

Not wanting to give any of that away, I simply shrugged. "I'll look at it later, if you don't mind. When I'm alone."

"We gave them tickets to the symphony, by the way. Box seats."

I half chuckled because the gift was so exactly what I would have selected that they wouldn't have thought for a moment that I hadn't. "You're good," I said, flatly. "I have to give you that."

He nodded once as though he already knew. "Then let's go, shall we?"

My curiosity was killing me, but I managed to remain silent while Edward led me out the front doors and across the driveway to the path that ran the circumference of the island. Since I'd only ever walked it at night, I hadn't realized that the way was lit. They were possibly even lights that didn't come on with a timer and that Edward had turned them on tonight so I may have never noticed them. But the lights weren't the interesting thing about our journey.

The interesting thing was that I'd been this way enough in the daylight to know that there was nothing along the path for us to go to. The staff quarters were in the opposite direction, and, unless Edward enjoyed a romp out in the jungle, the only reason I could imagine he would take me this way was to lead me to the cliffs that bordered the west side of the island.

Nervousness turned into fear.

"Where are you taking me?" I couldn't manage to keep the apprehension out of my voice.

Edward, who'd been a step ahead the whole time, turned back so he could walk alongside me, his hand pressed at my lower back.

It wasn't more comforting, if that's what he'd intended.

"We have a destination," he said, not sounding at all like a man who was about to kill his wife, but what did a man in that position sound like? "Not too much farther."

"It's not the journey there that concerns me. I'm concerned that I might not be making the journey back."

The walkway was lit only at our feet, but I could still see the hint of a smirk on his lips. "While it would be awfully fun to let that doubt remain, that isn't what tonight is about. Yes, you will be making the journey back."

I was only somewhat mollified. "What is tonight about, exactly?"

"Trust."

Any tension he'd relieved from his answer before returned with bravado. There were a hundred ways he could test my trust, ways I was certain not to like, and I wasn't entirely sure the cliffs weren't part of that, but I kept my mouth clamped shut and focused on holding onto my courage rather than what my courage might be used for.

Five minutes later, Edward directed me off the path toward the fence that bordered the island's edge. Beyond, the rock dropped off to the ocean one hundred feet below. I hadn't wandered over to this particular spot, but I'd pressed my body against the wood barrier at a place farther along the path and smiled over the dramatic expanse of sea beneath me.

My heart sped up to double its speed as we approached.

Once at the fence, he flipped a latch I hadn't known was there, and a portion of it swung out, opening to let us onto a stairway that I'd never known was there, pressed into the side of the mountain, kept hidden from other viewpoints. One flight down, and I could finally see where we were headed—a small, one-story bungalow with its own private beach.

"Is this your dungeon?" I asked at the door as Edward unlocked the front door with a key from his pocket.

He chuckled, a sound that I'd forgotten made my thighs draw up and tighten. "Nothing that nefarious."

"Your playroom?"

"Something like that." The door open, he reached in to flick on a light switch, then stepped aside to let me in.

I walked in and paused to survey my surroundings— the stone tile floor, the bamboo ceiling, the oriental-style windows, the wrap-around white couch with alternating black and gray and brown pillows, the matching love seat across from it, the square mocha coffee table that anchored the room.

Edward stood beside me, the heat of him radiating toward me. "I've brought women to the island before. I prefer to keep them out of the space I share with my children."

I finished where that thought led. "So you bring them here."

"So I've brought them here. Yes."

That felt heavy inside me and light at the same time. I didn't like the idea that I was in a space that he'd shared with others, but, in bringing me here, he'd inadvertently told me that he didn't bring women to the main house. And he'd taken me there first.

It was clever, really. A cozy place he could fill with all sorts of sex toys without being afraid of his children stumbling upon them. Not that there were any obvious toys in sight, but there appeared to be at least one bedroom where he could hide away his whips and chains and fetish equipment.

I walked in farther to draw attention away from the shudder that ran through me at the thought. Even after all the time I'd spent preparing myself for whatever tortures he had in store for me, physical pain was still more a turn-off than a turn-on.

Well, *severe* physical pain, anyway. I'd really liked the hard spanking he'd given me, as much as I hated admitting it.

Hopefully he'd start off slow.

"Should we get to this?" I clapped my palms together, ignoring how damp they were.

Looking both amused and smug, he gestured for me to sit on the sofa. "I can make you a drink if you think that will help." He'd already crossed to the bar to make his own.

Liquor was tempting. It would ease the tension in my shoulders, calm my nerves. Lessen my inhibitions.

The last one was exactly the reason I decided to decline. Whatever was about to happen, whatever Edward was going to do to me, I needed my faculties present.

"Very well then." He took his tumbler of cognac and

crossed to the love seat across from me, unbuttoning his jacket before he sat. He was wearing a suit, leading me to suspect he'd gone directly from work to the airport. He must be exhausted, but he didn't seem the least bit tired. In fact, he seemed acutely alert. Like the predator he was.

I waited.

He waited.

"This is an interesting setup," I said, beyond the time when it felt something should be said by someone. "Me here. You over there. Do you break me down simply with the power of your mind?"

He crossed one leg over the other and perched his hand holding the glass on his thigh. "This is how this will work," he said, and I had to force myself not to lean forward. "We will sit here, and, when you're ready, you will tell me about something in your life, something that affected you deeply. Something not pleasant. Something that required you to rebuild yourself in the aftermath."

That had not been at all what I'd been expecting.

I repeated his words in my head before clarifying. "You want me to tell you a story?"

He shook his head impatiently. "Definitely not a story, at least not in the fictional sense. It will be from your life, and it will be true. You will describe the event and all the relevant circumstances surrounding it in exact detail. I may ask questions as you proceed. I'll expect answers. All of it, every single word that comes from your mouth, must be authentic."

Now I knew why he'd offered the drink.

I crossed my legs, mirroring his position. Already my head was whirring with the tales I could spin, petty, plausible fables from a rich girl's pretty life.

This was the stuff I was good at. This was going to be cake.

"I'll know it's not true, Celia," he warned, reading my mind like he lived inside it.

"How?" I challenged.

"I just will."

"But how?"

"Celia…" He gave me a stern stare that reminded me of the one my grandpa Werner used to terrify me with as a child whenever I was found doing something I wasn't supposed to do. "I'll know."

"What happens if you don't believe me?"

"If you're telling the truth, I *will* believe you."

I debated pushing the issue further because, really. How would he know? Even if I was honest and drudged up some hurt from the past and shared it with him in excruciating detail, he could accuse me of lying.

But just before I opened my mouth to say that, I looked at him again, really looked at him, and the sharp intensity of his gaze reminded me—he'd always seen me.

He'd see me now too.

There was something I was missing, though. None of the books about BDSM had covered anything like this. And I was pretty sure he was a sadist. Where did the pain come in?

"And then what happens?" I asked, no longer caring that I looked desperate in my need to know.

He looked at me plainly, as though the answer was obvious. "Then, depending on how you do, I'll respond."

There it was. What I'd been looking for. Where the

pain would come in. "You'll take me to the bedroom, tie me up, and flog me until I'm screaming, you mean."

He tilted his head, his eyes narrowing as he studied me.

I'd gotten something wrong. I tried to guess what. Perhaps the flogger wasn't his instrument of choice. A cane then. Or maybe he was more inventive with his play. Or more hands-on. Choking, perhaps. Or he'd use his fists.

My stomach lurched at the thought of fists.

After what felt like an eternity, he spoke. "You seem to be under the impression that I beat women up."

"Don't you?" He was probably one of those guys who preferred to use words that didn't make his violent side sound so violent.

"Not typically."

I rolled my eyes, tired of this chasing around the bush. "Look, I know you do. Sasha said you did."

He lifted his chin inquisitively. "She did?"

"Yes. She said…" I tried to remember exactly what the woman at The Open Door party had said about Edward. *He's really good…if you can take a beating.* Which obviously meant that…

Oh, God.

It was a figure of speech.

This was the type of beating he meant to give me, not with physical pain, not with implements that weighed down my nipples or made my ass vibrate, but with words. My own words. My own pain used against me.

I swallowed, carefully. "So you just want me to pick some terrible thing that happened in my lifetime and tell you all about it like we're best girlfriends who've had too much wine?"

That smirk again. "I expect you to be vulnerable, yes."

If I hadn't understood the point of the game before, I did now. And, in every way I couldn't have imagined, this was worse than I'd prepared for.

I really wished I'd taken that drink.

Eight

"Take all the time you need," Edward said, stretching his arm across the sofa, settling in. His self-satisfied look told me what my own expression must have given away, and I remembered again why I hated him.

"I have one already," I said flippantly. "I met with this businessman on the pretense that he wanted to hire me. Oh, by the way, sorry I wasn't around to finish your office. Something came up." He'd never really intended for me to redesign his space, but I'd undertaken the task with sincerity. It pissed me off as much as anything else he'd done that I hadn't been able to see it to completion.

"The pieces you ordered came in. It got finished without you." His tone was flat and uninterested.

"And?"

He took a swallow of his cognac before answering. "Everything looks nice."

It looked fan-fucking-tastic, I was sure of it. He knew it too, but there was no way he'd give me anything, even that.

"Anyway." I let my focus drift, as though I was telling something romantic or whimsical. "I gave up my business, moved across an ocean, and married him. Then he told me he wanted to kill me. Now he's keeping me captive on his pleasure island." I brought my gaze back to him, narrowed and piercing.

If he wanted me to talk about something that affected me, then this definitely should count. There were very few moments in my life that had changed the course of my life the way that meeting him had.

His breaths were usually measured, but this one was deep. I saw it in the slight rise of his torso, the one tell he had that I wasn't as easy for him to manage as he liked me to believe.

He took another swallow of his drink then set it down on the side table. With laser focus, he regarded me. "Is this really what you want to talk about?"

Yes. Yes, it really was.

Except...

He'd said he might ask questions. He'd said he wanted me vulnerable. There were so many ways he could poke and prod at me in this arena, and it was an arena that truly did belong to him. I might be a bull, determined and horned, but he was a skilled matador, and no matter how tempting he was with that cape, he'd be sure to sidestep when I charged.

There were other things to tell. Things that were harder to say but impossible for him to subvert.

Needing an escape from his unrelenting stare, I closed my eyes. Without meaning to go there, I found myself at the beginning, in a time when I was still only innocent, in a country garden, on a rope swing with a wooden seat.

Bile burned at the back of my throat. These weren't memories I ever allowed, and I felt their foreignness like an illness. My body fought to remove them. My head ached with their presence.

But the actual beginning came before, in the reason I'd been in that garden in the first place. "I was close to my grandpa Werner," I said, feeling the tremble in my voice. "I spent a month with him every summer, four glorious weeks without my mother and father. It was just me and him, and I was spoiled and loved. When he died—"

"You were six," Edward said cutting me off. "This isn't what I'm looking for, and you know it."

My muscles tensed as though preparing to fight. He thought I was giving him something basic. Too basic. He assumed I was going to tell him how my granddaddy died when I was a kid and how it broke my heart and how I'd never been the same after, and while all of those things were true, it had only been the prologue to the real story.

But it was good he'd stopped me.

This wasn't something I wanted to tell either. Not now. Not ever.

With a soft laugh, I shook my head, surprised with myself for starting down that path. Irritated that he'd been the one to draw me back when it should have been me.

I propped my elbows on my lap and leaned my forehead into my palms. My fingers rubbed into my skin, massaging my brow. I knew what story to tell. It was the one that I told myself meant the most, which was a bold-faced lie, but it was easier to clutch to it as the cause of all my pain than giving acknowledgment to the others.

For one last moment, I let myself contemplate telling

a lie instead. I believed I could get away with it, but I also believed that, if I couldn't, the consequences would be significant.

And what would happen if I told the truth? I sort of wanted to find out.

With my mind made, I dropped my hands to my lap and sat back. Composed. "There was a boy I grew up with. A boy who changed everything. And don't stop me this time because this is real."

He nodded for me to continue.

"Our mothers were friends. Our families got together a lot. Holidays, summers, vacations. We probably should have thought of each other as brother and sister, and maybe he did..." I trailed off for a moment, wondering if that had been the case for Hudson. "Anyway, I never did. My mom believed we'd get married one day, and maybe that's why I did too. It had been bred into me to be his bride, and so it was natural to fall in love with him.

"All through high school, I crushed on him, putting myself out there, waiting for him to make a move. Watching as he went through girls like they were tissues."

"Girlfriends?" Edward asked. "Or just lovers?"

The difference was relevant.

"Lovers," I said quickly. "Never a girlfriend. Which was why I held out hope. I mean, I wasn't the only girl fawning over him. He was super attractive, lean and gray-eyed. He came from mega money and everyone knew he was the guy who'd take his inheritance and quadruple it before he was thirty—which he did. He had the serious thing going for him. He was scary smart and controlled and calculating and strategic. Always a step ahead of everyone else."

"So you have a type." His smug smile made me light-headed while at the same time want to kick him in the balls.

I gritted my teeth. "The type that likes to fuck with my emotions, yeah. I guess I do."

"What's his name?"

I paused, about to give it. But his wanting to know, even if I couldn't guess why, made it valuable information. "It doesn't matter," I said.

"I'll decide if it matters."

"No, actually, you won't. This is my story—" I corrected myself at his brow raise. "A true story, but totally mine, and that means I'm the one who knows what details are significant and which ones aren't. His name is not."

His jaw flexed, and for the first time ever, I felt him warring for control.

"We'll leave it then," he said, handing me this one win. "For now."

It was impossible not to be pleased with myself, and I didn't bother to hide my grin. "As I was saying, he wasn't popular in the way popular kids usually are, but people knew him. Girls knew him. And if they weren't scared of him, they were into him."

"I imagine some were both." *Like you with me,* his tone said clearly.

I ignored the pointed remark and went on. "I didn't care about the other girls, though. Because he was mine. I was the one he grew up with. I was the one who knew him—well, as much as he let anyone know him. I was the one he had a nickname for when he never had one for anyone, including his siblings. By all rights, he was mine."

"What did he call you?"

"Ceeley." That wasn't technically true—Ceeley hadn't been a nickname that Hudson started, my mother had. He'd simply adopted it, probably because he'd heard me called that more than Celia for much of our younger years. It was a relevant detail to omit, but I was who I was and that meant I reveled in slipping in something that Edward would never know to counter.

"Original," he huffed. "I thought you said he was sharp."

"We were *kids,*" I reminded him. *Asshole.*

I took a breath, hearing my own words echo in the room, letting them sink in for both of us. "We were kids," I said again, "and it was a kid crush, and by the time I graduated high school I realized that it wasn't going anywhere, and I needed to move on."

I got up, wary that I hadn't been given permission, careful to portray that I didn't believe I needed it, and wandered around the back of the couch to the bar. When Edward made no protest, I crouched down to examine the contents of the wine fridge.

"I wasn't what you'd call studious. I had good grades, and I was smart, but I didn't get into it the way a lot of the preppy kids did, and, having spent all my teen years believing I didn't have to grow up and *do* anything except marry my friend, I had no real plan for college." I pulled out a Malbec and stood. "I liked art and literature. I could study those anywhere. So my only real requirement for choosing a school was that it be far from wherever he was going to be. He was staying east, so I went west. UC Berkeley."

I had to rummage through three drawers before finding the corkscrew, which was only annoying because Edward had chosen to watch me search rather than stand up and help me.

"No, no, don't get up," I said sarcastically when I began the awkward job of removing the cork. "I've got it."

I *did* have it, and I didn't actually want him helping me. I especially didn't want him close to me. I preferred him over *there,* with a distance between us. It wasn't something I was willing to give up just so he could open up my wine.

When the struggle was over and the cork had eased from the bottle with a satisfying pop, I plucked a wine glass from the rack and poured. Then I turned back toward Edward, resting my ass on the bar as I took a swallow.

I let the taste register as I decided what to say next. It had a black-cherry flavor, full-bodied with a hint of chili. "Nice," I said, because I wanted to prove I could give a compliment even if he couldn't.

He didn't react except to prompt me. "Berkeley?"

"I met a guy there. Dirk."

"His name was Dirk?" He didn't hide the mockery in his inflection. That had been Hudson's reaction, too, if I remembered correctly.

I really did have a type.

"Dirk Pennington," I said, unfazed. "He was…" I searched for how to describe a man I'd barely thought about in a decade. "I don't know, he was a good guy. He was nice. Genuine. Sweet." I played up the adjectives with my vocalization, throwing them in the face of a man who wouldn't see himself in any of them.

"In other words, boring."

"A lot of women find the good guys more attractive than the bad."

"But not you."

My stomach flipped at his accurate pronouncement. I despised that he saw that about me even more than I despised that it was true, so, of course, I became overly defensive. "I really liked him! We were good together."

"Did you fuck him?"

"Are you jealous?" There'd been no hint of it in his remark, but I couldn't help myself.

Edward said nothing, expressionless and impervious to my charm.

I sighed. "Not that it's relevant, but yes. He wasn't my first either, so don't try to make that into anything it's not."

"So you fucked him, he wasn't your first, and he was nice," he said in summarization.

I took a swallow of my wine. "Right."

"And he made you forget all about the nameless guy."

"That's right," I said cautiously, feeling there was a challenge in his last statement that I couldn't quite pinpoint.

"I see," he said in a way that made me sure he didn't see at all. At least, he didn't see what I wanted him to see. "And then what happened?"

"Then I came home for the summer. Dirk stayed in California because that was where he was from. He invited me to move in with him, which I considered, but I was young, and I missed home."

"You wanted to go back and flaunt Dirk in the nameless guy's face."

"No." It *had* been the first thing I'd told Hudson when I saw him again. My mother had plans for us to go to a garden show that afternoon, and I didn't have much time to visit, but I'd snuck off to his summer house just to tell him. "No, not to flaunt. I wanted him to know I was over him, though, yes."

"Uh-huh," he said, unconvinced.

"Because I didn't want my old crush to be an obstacle in our friendship."

"I don't believe you."

His skepticism was maddening.

"I wasn't trying to make him jealous," I insisted. If that's what he was suggesting. "What I had with Dirk was real. I thought he could have been it for me."

He let that sit for a moment, letting me absorb the truth of what I'd just said, or the untruth, as he believed.

But it *was* true. Wasn't it?

"So then you wanted to see the old crush to test yourself," he said when I didn't say anything else. "To be sure."

My cheeks flamed with guilt. "Okay, maybe a bit of that too." I pushed myself off the bar with my hip and walked back around the couch and sat down. "But I truly didn't have some glorified plan to make him fall for me. I had fond feelings for him, and I wanted to find a new way to be in his life. So I told him all about Dirk, and it worked. I had a boyfriend and wasn't after him anymore so suddenly I wasn't someone he needed to avoid. We were together so much that summer, going to the movies and the beach and parties of people we knew in high school. Except for my parents and my best friend, Christina, I saw him more than anyone else.

"It was all fine until the end of August. We'd gotten close, really close, and, sure, I still felt things for him. Those aren't the kinds of feelings that go away easily, but I was okay with what we were and what we weren't, and

I had Dirk, who I talked to every day." I checked myself. "Maybe not *every* day. Not at the end."

"Because the boy was seeming interested."

I scowled because I hated how Edward thought he knew everything. But he was right this time. Which I hated even more. "Yeah. He did seem interested."

I took another swallow of the Malbec and ignored the way Edward made me feel with his presence in order to better remember how Hudson had made me feel in the past. Literally manipulated me into feeling, to be truthful, but I wouldn't know that for sure for another several months. "He would brush up against me, accidentally. Or he'd sweep the hair from my face. Touching, he was always touching me, and that had never been like him before. He'd never been a real physical guy. And he was thoughtful about me. I'd lamented to him about not knowing what to major in, and he'd researched my school and gotten all these brochures on interior design and gave me a gorgeous coffee-table book about it."

The memory made me smile. It had seemed utterly romantic to me—a guy going out of his way to help decide what I should do with my life. What I should *be*. It was the best proof of mattering. A guy wouldn't go out of his way like that, wouldn't notice, if I didn't matter. That kind of gesture got me fluttery every time.

Though there hadn't been that many. The last time a man paid that much attention to me…

I glanced quickly at Edward, as if he could read my thoughts, as if he could know I'd almost compared his gifts over the last three months to the gift Hudson had given that had swept me away.

They weren't the same. I refused to think of them as

the same.

"Is there something else?" he asked, trying to interpret my train of thought.

"I didn't sleep with him." I couldn't tell from his expression if that had been truly what he'd assumed. "I did kiss him. Or I let him kiss me. I'm not sure which it was anymore. And I wanted him to kiss me."

I'd wanted him to do more than kiss me. I would have let him, if things had gone the way I'd wanted. I'd thought it was inevitable after that kiss. That we'd be together. That we'd be a couple.

I could still feel that wanting, under layers of years and walls and nothing. Like a bruise that never healed but only hurt when I pressed on it. Of all the made-up things there had been between Hudson and me, before and after, that moment was real. That wanting was real.

Wanting that was magnified by believing he felt it too.

I'd thought all that had stood between us was Dirk, a guy who, as Edward had pointed out, was good but bland.

"I wasn't a terrible person." How long had it been since I'd been able to say those words? "Not yet, anyway. So I did the honorable thing, and tried to call Dirk to break up. But he was at work so I had to leave a message and when he called back I was already at this big party Christina was having, which wasn't the place to break up with a guy, and I knew it, but..." My only excuse had been eagerness, and that sounded petty, so I left it there. "He was hurt. I could tell. Even over the phone." *Let's wait and talk this over when we get back for the new semester,* he'd begged. "It hurt more than I'd imagined it would, hurting him like that. I had to leave for a bit to take a drive and get my head together afterward because it hurt so bad. But when

I came back, I was better and ready, and I saw...I saw the boy's car, so I knew he was inside, and I looked for him everywhere. Asked everyone. Searched every room, and when someone said he thought he was hanging in Christina's room, I ran up there."

I could still see it like it was happening. Me flinging open the door, and *them*. The image permanently seared into my mind.

"He was fucking her. Fucking my best friend. As if we hadn't kissed the night before. As if we hadn't agreed to talk more about our relationship at the party. As if I hadn't told him I loved him." It sounded so insignificant in the telling compared to how it had felt to witness.

The worst part, though, hadn't even been that moment but after, when I'd confronted Hudson, and he'd pretended there'd been nothing, that all the signs I'd read were mistaken. He'd told me to grow up.

What did you think was going to happen between us? You thought I was going to love you? You thought we were going to ride off into the sunset together?

"And all I could think was how duped I'd been. Because I hadn't thought he was going to love me until he made me believe he would." It was strange how mad I could still be about it, even after everything that followed. How hurt and abused. How raw. "He'd insinuated the only thing holding him back from me was my relationship with Dirk. And so I'd ended that! To be with him! I'd had real feelings for him, and me? I'd been nothing more than something to do. Nothing more than a game."

It was over. I'd said it all. I'd told it the way it happened, in a way I'd never told anyone, and, yeah, I felt vulnerable. It was cathartic too. Cleansing.

Edward remained silent for long beats after, as he'd been through much of my wandering through the past, and while I'd never forgotten he was there, he had made it easier to feel like the telling was natural. My parents had always poo-pooed therapy, and I wondered if it was like this—sitting on a couch, uncomfortable, trapped. Waiting for the therapist to speak and declare you sane.

"That must have made you feel very betrayed," he said eventually. Which would have been comforting if he hadn't added more on. "Being someone else's game." His subtext was clear.

Shame pricked at my insides. Maybe this had been the wrong story to tell him after all.

No, it still could be the right story. If I told it to the very end.

I leaned forward. "So you know what I did? I left him at that stupid party and went back to his place. Then I fucked his father in the pool house for two hours. Did I feel betrayed? Yes. And then I got even."

Edward held my stare for a long time. I could tell his thoughts were brewing, but his expression gave nothing away. My heart hammered in my chest as I waited for his response. I'd bared myself. Then I'd reminded him that I was vengeful, but I'd bared myself first.

Finally, after an eternity, he spoke. "This boy betrayed you, so you ruined both his parents' marriage and your mother's friendship by fucking his father. That's what you're saying, isn't it?"

I could feel the color drain from my face. That was what I was saying, but put like that, it sounded...well, it sounded reprehensible.

And it *was* reprehensible.

Even though I'd left out the fact that Jack already cheated on his wife all the time, and that it had been another decade before anyone found out about it, so my mother's friendship had remained intact. Even with those details, what I'd done was fucked up.

Which was the most horrible part of the story, if I was honest with myself.

The pain that still lingered all this time later wasn't from what Hudson had done to me, but what I'd done to Hudson. What kind of messed-up person did that shit? What kind of fucked-up human was I?

I turned my head, afraid that Edward would see that I understood what I was, what I'd done. Because if he saw that, I'd really be exposed.

I couldn't bear being that vulnerable.

He rose then, and I could feel his anger rise with him like fanned flames. "This evening has been a waste of my time," he said, his voice eerily controlled. "This isn't breaking down. This is bragging."

Without giving me another look, he pivoted and headed to the door. Before he disappeared beyond it, he said, "I'll give you my response tomorrow. You're free to do as you please until then."

He shut the door behind him with an uncharacteristic slam.

I sat stunned. And mad. And hurt. And embarrassed. But mostly mad.

I'd done what he'd wanted. I'd given him his stupid-ass story. And now I was free to do as I pleased? Fuck him because that was a lie. I wasn't free to leave the island.

And fuck him for thinking he knew anything about me,

about what was and wasn't breaking down. I'd opened up to him. What I'd said was horrible, but it was hard. Sharing what I'd shared had been hard.

I reached for my wine and chugged the rest down in an attempt to push down the emotions building up inside of me. When it was empty, and the feelings remained, I threw the glass against the wall.

Shattering items was becoming a habit.

If only it were just Edward's antique vases and glassware being shattered and not also me.

NINE

As bitter as the night before had ended, I woke up with a tickle of excitement. He was here, on the island, and that meant that no matter what happened, the day would be different than they had been when he was away.

Plus, there was the added expectation of his response. I lay awake in bed for nearly half an hour wondering what it would be, imagining the ways his reaction to my tale could play out. Now that he'd made clear his sadism centered around the psychological rather than the physical, the boundaries of what might happen felt exponentially larger. The possibilities of what would happen next were titillating and unfathomable and frightening, and the dread I'd felt about what he'd do to me when I'd thought pain would be involved had been replaced by intrigue. I wanted to find out. I wanted to know.

Once out of bed, though, the thrill simmered down.

The house was quiet, Edward wasn't around. It was exactly like every other Saturday on Amelie, when Joette and Tom and the staff had the day off and the meals were prepared beforehand and the day belonged to myself. There wasn't even yoga on the weekends. Ideally, the privacy was a good setup for newlyweds who hadn't seen each other in months.

Edward and I had never fit the notion of "ideally."

With no interest in being the one to seek him out, I went about my routine in the ways I normally did, lounging by the pool, reading *An American Marriage* until the story of a black man's twelve-year incarceration for a crime he didn't commit began to diminish the terribleness of my own imprisonment, and I had to set it down. It was hard to complain about my situation in comparison. My jail was a paradise, sure. And it could be argued that I deserved it, since I was far from innocent. It could definitely be worse, *was* worse for other real people.

I saw that, but I didn't want to. I wanted to believe I had it bad. I wanted to be angry. I wanted to be pissed. I wanted to be self-righteous and indignant and full of contempt.

The fact that those emotions weren't as readily accessible as they'd once been was both surprising and surreal, and it was definitely discomforting.

Edward arrived back from wherever he'd been in the early afternoon. I didn't see him come in, but I felt the atmosphere change, felt *him*, and, when I looked up, he was at his library window watching me. He saw me notice him and didn't flinch, as though he had every right to be staring at me.

My pulse sped up and my cheeks flushed, and, especially perceptible because of all the weeks he'd been away, I realized how much I liked having someone around to look at me. How much I liked him looking at me.

Before I could help it, I smiled.

Immediately, I thought better and scowled, hating myself for getting caught up in his stupid gaze. Hating him for having a gaze worthy of being caught up in.

I'd turned away too quickly to find out his reaction to my mistake, but, imagined or not, I felt his smirk on my profile and hated him for that too.

When I finally came in an hour later, the house was buzzing with the makings of a big dinner, the kind we'd had regularly on our honeymoon, and that sent me fuming again, for no reason I could discern. Then, later, as I cleaned up and applied makeup in my bathroom, I realized the reason was because company for dinner very likely meant company *after* dinner. Which meant waiting another day for Edward's response.

It also meant sharing him with others, and I wanted him all to myself. With that awareness, another wave of anger rolled through me.

My mascara applied to one eye only, I leaned back to study the woman in the mirror. My blonde hair was coiffed in a low chignon, sun-kissed highlights giving vibrancy to my appearance. My face—which I kept meticulously protected with sunscreen—was flawless, my foundation seamlessly matching the tanned skin at my décolletage. My yoga-toned shoulders curved pleasingly, my never-nursed-a-baby breasts still as perky as they'd been a decade ago. In every way, I was a portrait of stoic beauty. No one could possibly know that my insides were shaking with fury and shame, that there was a magma chamber of turbulent emotions in the pit of me that only seemed to erupt in my husband's presence.

My appearance was a lie I told without even trying.

What did Edward think he'd find underneath? What would he find if he kept looking?

It scared me that I didn't know the answer to either question.

Having been given no instruction and needing armor, I dressed powerfully for dinner. The dress was ordinary enough—a mid-thigh length black silk slip dress with a racerback. It was a little fancy for our group, but Edward had included it in the wardrobe he'd sent, so that made it appropriate in my mind. The part that gave it power was what I'd put on underneath—sheer black panties, matching garter belt, and thigh-high stockings. Hosiery on the island was completely impractical, even in February, but they made me feel good. Made me feel sexy and potent and charged.

Especially when I added the red satin Casadei plisse high-heel sandals. *Try calling me little bird now, Fasbender.* I was anything but.

Yes, it was a power play, too. An outright opposition to what he'd had me wear the night before. Maybe it was asking for trouble. Maybe I wanted trouble. I didn't really know anymore.

The irony was that he probably wouldn't even notice.

Except that dinner wasn't like the old days.

When I came out, it wasn't the big dining table that was set, but rather the small radial dinette that overlooked the ocean. And it was only set for two. The lights were off, candles were lit. A bottle of champagne sat chilling in a bucket of ice next to a bowl of fresh strawberries.

I heard movement behind me, and without looking, I knew it was Edward. The heat of his presence bounced off the windows and enveloped me. Then his hand was at the small of my back, escorting me to my chair.

"Don't let this get to your head." His breath tickled the hair at my nape. "It's Valentine's Day and Joette has certain notions. It was easier to perpetuate them."

"Easier, yes." As if he'd ever chosen any method because it was easier.

I sat in the seat he offered, placing the linen napkin in my lap as he moved around to take the chair across from me. He was stunning in dark pants and a white dress shirt with black buttons, the top two open. It was a somewhat casual look for him, but not quite as laid back as he usually dressed on the island. And he'd taken the time to style his hair. All to let Joette believe our romance was real?

Maybe.

My breath stuttered when I considered the possibility that it was something more.

Once seated, he leaned across the table to pour the blanc de blanc in my champagne flute. "We can use the opportunity to discuss some rules."

He was so good at plying me with alcohol just before diving into serious subjects. I took a sip of the drink while he poured his own. "Are the rules your response to last night?"

He didn't answer at first, reaching over again to remove the silver cover from my plate, revealing white fish with lemon and capers and green beans with almonds. My mouth watered at the sight. Mateo didn't go out on the boat that often, but all the fish that was served on Amelie came from his fishing trips. Every dish I'd had so far had been incredible.

I didn't wait for Edward to pick up his own fork before diving in. The fish melted in my mouth. Orgasmic.

Distracted by the divine taste, I almost forgot I'd asked a question until it was answered several minutes later. "The rules are not my response," he said, now several bites into his fish. "But you need to know them before we get to that."

I took another sip of my champagne. "I'm guessing that I don't have a choice in whether or not I follow them."

I'd become quite good at considering rules as a challenge. Without hearing what they were, my mind was already preparing to find ways around them if not outright defy them.

Edward smiled, as though he expected my response. "Of course you have a choice. What choices you make determine how quickly this process goes."

"The process of breaking me down, you mean."

"Yes. That." He put another bite of fish in his mouth, and I watched, mesmerized. The way his jaw worked as he took it from the fork. The way his throat moved as he swallowed. The way these simple actions made my pussy clench and weep.

I was really glad I'd worn the power stockings. I needed them right about now.

He rinsed everything down with a swig from his flute. "Are you amenable to me continuing?"

It seemed strange that he was asking. Usually he just did with no regard for my opinion on matters. I understood his motives, understood that this was a test. I knew what answer he wanted and the test was to see if I'd give him that answer or be defiant.

Defiance was my nature with him. My gut reaction.

I forced myself to think first. I thought about how things

had gone so far since my captivity. How the gifts had be-gun when I'd stopped trying to escape. How the struggling only seemed to prolong whatever he had planned for me. How prey caught in the sightline of a predator often froze or played dead.

If I ever wanted to get out of here, that's what I had to do—play dead. "Okay, then. Go for it. Tell me these rules."

It was almost imperceptible—the slight nod of his head, the gleam in his eyes caught by chance in the candle-light. He was pleased.

And then it was gone, his expression once again stoic. "For now, we will only address the rules for our sessions together. There will be more in the future. Do not assume that this is all."

I forced myself to take a deep breath.

"During these sessions," he went on, "you cede your power to me."

I laughed. "I wasn't aware that I still had power to cede."

"Are you sure about that?" He tilted his head, both brows raised. "I'll tell you now that the most important rule is honesty. I expect you to only speak the truth, or the truth to the best of your knowledge. You will not exag-gerate or deflect. Lies will not be tolerated. Withholding information when I ask will be considered a lie."

My body tensed at his bold expectation. He wanted me to lay everything down for him. Everything. I was begin-ning to understand what that really meant. Was I willing? No. But if I thought about it in terms of a longer game, of me playing into his hand until he let me go, then I could tolerate it more.

The real question wasn't was I willing, but was I able?

That, I didn't know.

All I could do is try. "In that case," I said, pushing my words from my throat where they wanted to stay. "I suppose you want me to say that I am aware that I do have some power." He was affected by me—that was power. I had my body. I knew how to play against his possessive nature. I had the ability to withdraw.

They were my only weapons, and he wanted me to put them down.

A sudden rush of bitterness took over my tongue. "Forgive me if I find the power I have left so miniscule that I didn't think it was worth mentioning."

That earned me a leveled stare and the next rule. "You will show respect. Sarcasm and backtalk are not acceptable forms of communication."

"Well, I'm screwed." I grabbed a small strawberry from the bowl and took a seductive nibble from the tip. "We aren't in a session now, are we?"

"Fortunately for you, we are not." He watched me finish it off, his eyes glued to my mouth as I licked my fingers afterward. His eyes were dark, hooded.

Yeah, this whole ceding power shit was going to take practice.

"Normally, whenever we're alone like we are, we would be in session." He set down his fork and picked up a strawberry himself, dipping it in cream before reaching across the table, offering it to me. "But we are just beginning."

I was suddenly very aware of my blood rushing through my body, at the damp spot between my legs. Leaning forward, I let him trace my mouth with the cream before I took a small bite. My tongue swept slowly across my lips.

When I moved in for the next bite, however, he pulled his hand away, popping the rest of the berry in his own mouth.

He sat back then and frowned. "That was a freebie," he said. "Not what you deserved. To receive pleasure, you must earn it."

"Oh, then I'm *not* screwed, you're saying." It was exactly the type of sarcasm he'd said that wouldn't be tolerated.

"Punishments are also mine to dole out as I see fit." The dark expression was back. The idea of punishing me turned him on as much as anything else, I realized.

That was…intriguing/fascinating/scary/hot.

It was a bunch of things all at once that I didn't know how to process.

"No snappy comeback to that one?" He stroked his chin. "Interesting."

"I was thinking."

"Thoughtfulness is good. It shows you're taking this seriously."

Maybe not seriously enough. "Do I get a safe word?"

"You won't need one."

Either that meant he believed his punishments didn't need them or he didn't care if I felt unsafe when he administered them. Both options felt dangerous.

He studied me. "That makes you uncomfortable, doesn't it?"

"You like that it does, don't you?"

He paused then chuckled with a shake of his head. He picked up his fork and resumed eating. It was two full bites later before he said more. "If you feel unsafe, you'll tell me. There doesn't need to be a game about it."

It sounded clear enough. Still, I didn't trust him.

But there was nothing I could say to argue. "I assume that means there won't be restrictions on my speech."

"No restrictions. I do expect you to think carefully before you do—to choose carefully. But no outright restrictions. Half the fun is what you come up with to say."

I rolled my eyes, decidedly disrespectful. It *was* fortunate we weren't *in a session*.

Sessions, he called them. Not scenes like the books I'd read referred to times of kink play. Like he meant them to be therapy.

I frowned realizing that might very well be the case.

I tried not to think about that. "Anything else?"

"Yes. Your birth control shot runs out next month. There will be a nurse brought to the island to administer another."

"Then I *will* be screwed. How fun."

"I did tell you fucking was part of this bargain." He swirled what was left in his glass before taking it back in one swallow, his eyes never leaving mine.

"Just, from everything that's happened so far, it feels like I'm being fucked in a very different way." What was terrifying was how much I still wanted him despite that.

I tossed my napkin on my plate and pushed my plate away, my irritation returning. "Let me guess. This nurse will only speak French."

"Don't be silly. You know French."

"Are you guessing?"

"Fais-je fausse route?"

"*Non*," I said with a sigh. He was *not* wrong. And that irked me more. "Speaking of being fucked over, how is it that you know when my birth control runs out?"

"Your privacy is not a privilege."

"I suppose that shouldn't be a surprise considering the bikini wax." It worried me though, what else he could know. Which of my secrets he could uncover. "Oh," I said, relaxing with my realization. "My doctor sent a reminder email to schedule something, didn't she?"

He ignored me. "My privacy, on the other hand, is assured."

"Of course it is. Is that all?"

He put his elbows on the table, inching his plate away in the process, and clasped his hands together. "Is that all, *sir.*"

"What?"

"When we are in a session, you will address me as sir."

This latest rule sent a shudder down my spine, a flinch I couldn't hide. "I'd rather not," I said softly.

His brow raised in satisfaction. "All the more reason that you will."

I swallowed, my hands sweating in my lap. Memories from another time—another man— flooded me bodily.

"What do you say about my gift, Celia?"

"Thank you, Uncle Ron."

"Thank you, sir."

"Thank you, sir."

I couldn't do it. I *wouldn't*.

Except, it was more important not to let Edward know

how I felt about it. It was not a weak spot I wanted him to know.

I managed to keep from shaking as I picked up my champagne flute. "We aren't in a session right now."

"We are," he said, placing his napkin next to his plate. "Dinner is finished. It's time to go." He stood and circled behind me to pull out my chair.

I finished my champagne and set it down before standing. "Do I need to change into some terribly drab outfit first?"

His forehead rose in a silent prompt.

I drew my hands into balls at my sides and gritted my teeth. "Do I need to change into some terribly drab outfit, *sir.*" I spat the last word out.

His eyes narrowed, and for half a second I thought he'd challenge my tone. But then he looked me over, scanned me from head to toe, as though really looking at me for the first time that night. He couldn't hide that he liked what he saw. "What you're wearing is fine enough," he said, unwilling as ever to give me anything more.

"Careful," I said, smug about my wardrobe choice. "I might mistake that as a compliment." A beat passed before I remembered. "*Sir.*"

TEN

My triumph was short-lived.

As soon as we arrived at the bungalow, he led me into the bedroom. "Take all your clothes off, fold them, and leave them on the chest. Once you're completely stripped, kneel on the floor facing the chair."

Then he disappeared into the front room, leaving me to my task.

He wouldn't see my power stockings after all.

I brushed off my disappointment. It was fine. I'd worn them for me, not him. Mostly.

At least these instructions were familiar. I'd never played the sub before, but I'd prepared for this. The strip and kneel was very basic submissive training. This was something I could do.

I took a moment to scan the room. Again, there were oriental-framed windows looking out to the ocean and bamboo ceilings and tile floors. It was sparsely furnished with only a king size bed, a chest, and a chair. There was no dresser, but there was a closet. There were no apparent kink contraptions. No hooks hanging from the ceiling. No spanking benches.

Not that Edward wasn't creative. He probably didn't need gadgets.

Who had he brought here before? Who had he fucked in that bed? What remnants of other women would I find if I looked?

I'd taken two steps toward the closet hoping to check it out when Edward called out from the other room. "Hurry up about it, please. I expect you ready by the time I come back."

The clink of glassware told me he was fixing himself a drink. That wouldn't take long. I'd have to rush.

Somehow I managed to get the dress off, the garter, panties, stockings, all of it folded on the wood chest, the shoes on the floor next to it, and myself down on my knees just as he walked in.

I kept my eyes lowered, one of the guidelines from my reading, so I could only really see his shoes as he circled around me. Studying me? Whatever he was doing, it made me feel very exposed.

Except when I'd tried to kill him with the shard of glass, I'd never been completely naked this close to him before. I preferred it to the gut-wrenching storytelling from the night before, but on my knees, with my gaze down, felt chillingly different than standing in front of a man, attempting to seduce him. That was a powerful posture. This was pointedly not.

After he'd completed his inspection, Edward sat in the chair. "Eyes on me."

I lifted them and felt my breath speed up when they caught his heated gaze. It was heady, the way he looked at me. Almost intoxicating enough to distract me from the foreign submissive position.

"This might have happened last night," Edward said, sipping his drink casually, as though he wasn't at all stirred by the naked woman in front of him. The bulge in his pants said otherwise. "The second part of the session. We weren't ready to move on, though, so we've divided it."

When he said *we*, I was sure he really meant *me*. But I did recognize it was possible he meant us both.

"I think we should take a moment to recap what occurred last night. Can you tell me succinctly?"

"I believe I can, Edward," I said haughtily, hoping if I "forgot" often enough he wouldn't correct the "sir" slip. "I opened up, told you something personal, became vulnerable like you asked, and you were unappreciative."

The correction he gave was with a glare.

"What?" I asked innocently.

"We won't continue if you won't follow the rules, Celia. And if we don't continue, you'll never get back home." His tone was more matter-of-fact than stern, but it was a clear enough threat. *Obey or else.*

"You were unappreciative, *sir,*" I said, my skin crawling with the simple added syllable.

He nodded. "Because...?"

I had a thousand snappy answers at the ready, but I held back. He'd just given me every reason to play along.

Except, I wasn't so sure of the answer. Wasn't so sure what he wanted to hear. I thought about how my revealing had ended the night before, how, when I'd felt too vulnerable, too raw, I'd tried to counter with my power grab. As he'd so precisely called me on it, I'd been bragging.

I knew the answer. "Because when I was finished, I didn't allow myself to be weak." My eyes lowered automatically, unable to hold his in the admission, then immediately rose again when I remembered he wanted them on him, as hard as it was to keep them there. "I did brag, yes, but if I'd told it differently, if I'd let the truth come out, you would have seen my weakness there too. Sir." I flinched as I added the address.

"Very good. I'm pleased you could recognize your failure. Very pleased."

His praise made me feel sun-touched, like I was glowing in its rays.

"However, as well as you've done now, there must still be consequences for your behavior last night. Let's see what those books have taught you—show me what you can do with that mouth."

He spread his legs, inviting me to fill the space between them.

A mixture of relief and victory and, yes, want, flooded through me. This was my punishment? Sucking him off? This was a cinch. I was good at blow jobs. They were one of the easiest ways to manipulate men, and I'd become an expert. How fucking lucky could I get? How stupid was he not to see that, with his cock in my mouth, I would definitly not be ceding power—I would be claiming it.

And I'd be touching him too, fondling him in all the ways I'd wanted, in all the ways he hadn't let me before now. Moisture pooled between my legs.

Eagerly, I crawled forward and began working on his belt, pausing to stroke my palm along the hard ridge pressing against the pleat of his trousers. He gave a satisfied grunt, and the muscles in my thighs vibrated. Licking my lips, I glanced up at him. I could feel the smile in my eyes. I couldn't help it. I was excited.

He'd seen it, too. The space between his brows creased as though he was just figuring something out, and when I went back to undo his zipper, he caught my hand, stopping me. "I changed my mind," he said, pushing me away. "Get on the bed."

"Uh. Okay." It took me a minute to stand, I was too stunned.

The bed could be good though too. Certainly more comfortable than the ceramic tile.

But if he still had a blow job on the agenda, it was going to be very different from any I'd given before. Because when I got on the bed, he had me lie on my back, my ass at the foot of the bed, my knees bent, my legs spread—a very similar position to the one he'd fucked me in the night we'd married.

Even better.

My stomach flipped expectantly, waiting for him to unsheath his gorgeous cock. Again, though, he surprised me. He got down on his knees.

I clamped my knees together and sat upright, alarm shooting through my veins. "What are you doing?"

"What does it look like I'm doing? I'm going to eat that pussy."

I shook my head, even as new arousal gushed between my legs.

"Why would you want to do that?" I couldn't help the panic in my voice. He couldn't do that. I wouldn't let him. There was no way.

"Because you don't want me to."

The asshole saw everything, knew everything. He'd made a momentary misstep thinking that getting me down on my knees was the way to punish me, but I'd given myself away. This was true punishment. This was true vulnerability. Having my legs open, letting a man give me pleasure—letting myself relax enough to feel the pleasure—that was truly giving up my power, truly giving up control. I'd been there before and never wanted to be there again. The idea was a nightmare to me, and it was obvious in the way I shooed him off, the way I tried to kick him away. The way the sweat beaded on my forehead.

He knew, he knew, he knew.

He knew, and he was so satisfied he hadn't even mentioned my lapse of sirs, a slip that he couldn't possibly have missed.

He knew, and I still couldn't stop fighting him. "That's stupid. What woman wouldn't want a guy going down on her?"

"Good question." He stood again, and my shoulders sagged with relief. He was abandoning this. *Thank you, God.*

After glancing around the room, Edward strolled over to the chest and picked up one of my abandoned stockings. "Excellent," he said, with an almost-wink in my direction. "This will do nicely. Scoot back on the bed and raise your arms above your head."

I did it. Whatever he was planning would be better than what he'd almost done. He came around one side of the bed and positioned my wrists together. Then, after tying the end of the stocking around them, he stretched the hose out and wrapped the other end around one of the slats of the bedframe before tying it off.

"Kinky," I said, my heart still racing from my near escape of orgasm by cunnilingus. "Sir," I added, because I was calmer now and wanted to get back to keeping him pleased.

But then he was kneeling in front of me, spreading my thighs with his hands, and the panic returned with a tsunami-like force.

"I can manage your legs," he said in explanation, "but it was going to be real hard to concentrate on making you come with your hands pushing me away."

His grip was tight and he'd done a good job with the binding, but I thrashed anyway. "No, please! Edward." I sat up as well as I could. "No. You can't."

He paused. "Is this really where you'd like to stop for the night? Because I will, and then we'll have to start all over again another night. When I come back."

Fuck!

I closed my eyes tight and reasoned through my options. It didn't matter how long he'd be gone. If it was two weeks it would be too long. I did not want to start over. I did not want to be stuck here forever.

And I did want him. As fucked up as that was, I still wanted him touching me, still wanted him inside me. He'd fingered me before, and it had been glorious. Would it really be that different if he used his mouth?

"Okay," I said, trying to steady my breathing. "Okay. It's okay. I'll do it."

"Good girl," he said, stroking his hand up my abdomen to fondle my breast. My nipples stiffened and my back arched into him. "I'm very happy with your decision."

He lowered his head then, and ran his tongue up my

seam. "You'll get two."

"Two licks?" I asked, a little delirious from the first swipe.

"Two orgasms."

"Two?!" I yanked involuntarily against the stocking.

"Now it's three."

I clamped my mouth shut, afraid to protest. But three? I was a one orgasm kind of girl. It had been a miracle that he'd managed two from me on our wedding night, and that situation had been entirely different. Then, I'd been in control.

Well, *more* in control.

It wasn't possible. I wouldn't be able to do it.

But I had to let him find that out on his own because there was no way I was going to talk back and get the number upped to four.

He started gently, his tongue teasing my clit with slow, light circles. Then his licking turned more earnest, swiping first this side of my sensitive bud, then the other. I could tell he was reading me, studying my responses. Learning how to give me pleasure, and, despite the tension clutching my back and shoulders, I felt oddly moved by this realization. Even when I reminded myself he was learning me to use his knowledge against me, not because he cared, I couldn't help but think it was one and the same. That everything he used against me was because, at some level, he cared.

That was the way with being caught up in pleasure—it messed with the head. Made the lies I told myself easier to believe.

I was wrapped in that particular lie when the first orgasm grew, sprouting from me like a seedling piercing through the earth, stretching its way through my limbs with a roll so gentle, I wondered if he'd even noticed.

"That's one," he said, lifting up only long enough to say the word before returning to his task.

I breathed easier now, the first one having relaxed my tense muscles. It had felt good—Edward knew what he was doing—and it hadn't felt like I had given up too much to get it. Maybe this wasn't going to be so bad after all.

But he was more aggressive after that, sucking my clit into his mouth, using his teeth, his nips sending megawatt jolts of pleasure through my nervous system, and when the second one came, it had me trembling and gasping his name with shallow breaths.

The third, though—that's when he really went to task. His mouth traveled down my pussy, down along my seam to my wet channel where he speared me with frantic thrusts with his tongue. His fingers entered the scene, dancing over my clit until I was squirming and pulling at the stocking.

I couldn't do it. It was so close, and I couldn't get there. I wouldn't.

The defeatist narrative running through my mind wasn't helping. I struggled against it, tensing up when I should have been calming down, thinking too hard about the man between my legs. Who he was. What he'd done to me.

What I wanted him to do to me.

It was a mess inside my brain, my feelings about Edward, and to top off the confusion, he was giving me the best orgasm of my life. Pulling it from me like he owned it. Like he deserved a piece of me, and I fought, afraid that when he took that piece, he'd take all of me with him.

My eyes were already tearing by the time it finally rushed through me, sweeping me up so unexpectedly, I hadn't been appropriately braced for it. The edges of my vision went black and it knocked the air from my lungs as it took over, shooting bliss through my body like I'd just snorted a line of cocaine.

And then they were done. All three. And I could sigh in relief, boneless. Sated. A survivor.

"One more," Edward said from between my thighs.

I bolted up to protest. "That one was three."

He lifted his head, but left his fingers to stroke against the swollen lips of my pussy. "You're arguing with me?"

"No, sir," I said, defensively. "But that was honestly—"

His expression told me what finishing my statement was going to get me, and I couldn't bear another added to my sentence. I couldn't bear the one he was proposing now.

A tear fell, my mouth quivering. "I'm not trying to argue, Edward. I'm not. I don't want to make you mad, but since you won't let me have a safe word, I just want you to know I can't do it. I can't possibly take one more." It was the most honest I'd ever been. The most raw.

"You will," he insisted, sliding two fingers inside of me to graze against my G-spot.

My hips bucked, my body wanting him inside me despite my head knowing I couldn't take anymore. "You said to tell you," I blubbered. "You said when I couldn't take it to tell you. To not play games, and I'm not playing a game right now."

"Yes, and you are very good to tell me. But I never said

I'd listen." He bent down to add a series of quick tongue strokes against my clit to the deep thrusts of his fingers.

"Fuck, Edward! No, I can't. I can't!" I pulled against my restraint. I pressed my knees inward trying to shove him off.

"Eyes on me," he said sharply, shutting me up. When he held my gaze in his, he touched the tip of his tongue lightly to my most sensitive spot. "You don't think you can take it, little bird." Another soft press of the tongue. "But you can." This time his mouth lingered. "Keep your eyes on me. Relax. Let me take care of you. Let it feel good."

His words were soft and anchored me along with his intense stare, and there, wrapped in the solid promise of his authority, I let myself go. I let him take care of me. I let it feel good.

The orgasm released through me in stages, as though it had been wrenched out of me, leaving parts of it behind that had to be wrenched out as well. It seized onto my limbs, my muscles tensing slowly, slowly, slowly until they were rigid in its grip, shuddering against its ferocity. The world went completely dark. Then spots appeared, dancing across my vision.

And the sound that came from me was foreign and yawning, a jagged moan that stretched and stretched and stretched until my voice was hashed and my throat felt sore.

I lay there after, whimpering, barely aware of Edward coaxing me down, kissing my thighs, running his hands along the sides of my torso, bringing me back to life.

Then, when I opened my eyes again, reborn, I wanted him with a fierceness that I'd never known. Wanted all of him. Wanted his cock buried inside of me. Wanted him shoving against my limp body. Wanted to make him come as savagely as he'd made me come.

He crawled up my body, and I could feel the stiff weight of his desire at my hip as he kissed me, his tongue plunging into my mouth as deeply as it had plunged into my core, the taste of my pussy mixed with the taste of him.

"Please," I begged, unable to articulate my want. "Please, please, please." He'd know. He always knew.

He ground his hips against mine, his fingers threaded in my hair. "You can't possibly have any idea how much I want to fuck you right now," he said against my lips.

"Yes, yes." I nodded, encouraging. Pleading.

He kissed me again, his arm reaching above me to loosen the tie at my wrists. When my hands were free, they flew to his face, gripping his stubbled cheeks as though to hold him in place, as though to pull him closer.

"I want you," he said again. Then kissed me again. "But we mustn't forget that this was a punishment."

He rose and stood over me, his cock tenting in his trousers as his eyes perused me from head to toe. With what sounded like a reluctant sigh, he turned away. "Get dressed," he said, picking up the drink he'd abandoned in favor of eating me out. "I'll be waiting in the living room to walk you back to the house."

And I knew in that moment, without a doubt, that he'd succeed, that he was halfway there already, that he'd completely and utterly break me down.

The next morning, when I came back from my run, I found him standing beside the jeep while Louvens loaded his suitcase into the back.

"You're leaving? Without even telling me?" I sounded hurt when I meant to sound outraged, because hurt was what I primarily felt.

"Not true," he said coming to me. "I was waiting for you to get back so I could say goodbye." He nodded to Lou. "Give me a minute." Then, with my hand in his, he led me off the driveway to the side of the house where we were out of earshot from his driver.

I pulled my hand away from his, trying to find my sense of balance. He'd wrecked me the night before, and after a fitful sleep with dream after dream of his mouth and his tongue and his words—*You can't possibly have any idea how much I want to fuck you right now*—I had a curious sense of attachment.

Was this Stockholm Syndrome? What had he done to make me feel such an intense need?

I pressed my fingers against my eyes and shook my head, as if to shake off the complex emotions stirring inside. "I can't believe you're leaving already," I said softly when I brought my hands down. How long would he be gone? I couldn't bear to ask. I couldn't bear to know.

He reached out to me again, bringing his knuckles to stroke against my cheek. "I almost think you're going to miss me."

"No," I said too quickly, flinching from his caress that I wanted but couldn't seem to let myself have. "Just. How can you break me down if you're not ever here?"

"Play better, and I'll come back more often."

Ouch.

He must have seen the hurt in my expression. Swiftly, he wrapped an arm around my waist and drew me to him, holding me tightly to his chest. "You did very well last night, little bird," he murmured in my ear. "I was very impressed."

I stayed tense in his embrace for several heartbeats. Then, on an exhale, I relaxed into him, taking in his scent of spice and musk and pure man. "Were you really?"

"Yes, really." He pressed his lips to my temple, holding them there, holding me for several seconds before leaning back to look at me.

It had felt good, if I was being honest with myself. When it was all said and done. Except for one part.

I pulled back and wrapped my hands in his shirt. "Edward, I know it's a rule...I know I'm not in a position to ask. But addressing you as sir... please. Is there anyway it could be something else? Master or Your Holiness. Anything else..."

He studied me for several beats. "Is this something we'll talk about in an upcoming session?"

No. No. I did not want to talk about it.

But if he wanted to find out, he would. I knew that now.

"I need time," I said, letting out a shuddering breath.

He considered. I was the one who had wanted things to speed up. There was no way he couldn't know this was something I truly needed.

He gave a quick jerk of his head. "Very well then. You can address me as Edward."

I was so grateful, I buried my head in his shoulder. "Thank you, Edward." It was a whisper, but he heard it.

"I left you something on your bed," he said, when I

pulled away, his fingers once again stroking my face. "A belated Valentine's Day gift. To make the time go by faster."

I nodded. I couldn't speak past the stupid ball in the back of my throat.

"Be good," he said, pressing one more kiss to my forehead then let me go to head back to Louvens waiting in the jeep.

I turned away, and brought my hand to my cheek, pressing my palm against the spot he'd touched as if that could hold the feel of him there longer.

"And Celia?"

When I looked back, he'd paused, halfway in the passenger's seat. I furrowed my brow in question.

"I'm going to miss you, too."

ELEVEN
Edward

"M r. Fasbender?" Astor's tone suggested it wasn't the first time he'd called my name.

I'd been somewhere else. Nowhere. It was easy to get distracted like that sitting in my office now, looking at walls and curtains that *she*'d chosen. Sitting on furniture that *she*'d picked out.

She'd left the desk at my insistence, a heavy dark wood monstrosity that I loved and refused to part with. But now it was the foreign thing in the room, the only thing not touched by her, and I found myself choosing to work from the sofa more and more because of it.

The sofa where I sat now, holding my daily meeting with my secretary and assistant.

I flicked the thoughts of her away, a habit I'd grown accustomed to in the past year as my thoughts were often with her, and gave my assistant my attention.

"The new line-up in Turkey—you're good to make a

statement next Tuesday?"

I'd been vaguely present as he had gone over the bullet points of the announcement regarding the programming changes. These were details that had been discussed by my executives and discussed even more thoroughly by lower-level executives. By the time these matters became of consequence to my direct team, there was little need for my input.

It wouldn't even be me writing the statement that supported the changes. That would be Astor. All he needed was my nod of approval, which I gave him now.

"I'll be sure it's sent immediately to the high-profile media," Charlotte said, making a note on her pad.

"Good, then," Astor said in confirmation. "That's all set."

"Is there anything else?" I was restless, ready to move on with my day. Ready to dive into projects that took more of my bandwidth, left less of my mind free to wander to Amelie and the woman I'd left there. My wife.

The weeks away were agonizing.

I spent every waking minute trying to keep focused. My workouts had doubled in length, pushing myself to the point of distraction. Then I buried myself in business matters, staying at the office later than anyone else, keeping more on my own plate when, in the past, I would have delegated. At home, I drank. More than I'd drunk in years.

It wasn't an entirely successful method of coping, but it got me through the weekdays. Yet, every Friday, as the clock ticked on, and the buzz of work wound down around me, and the long, lonely weekend loomed over me, I'd invariably pick up the phone on my desk and dial the airfield to schedule an impromptu flight to the Caribbean. Every time I'd make it so far as one ring, maybe two, before I slammed the receiver down, wondering what on earth I'd been doing. What I'd been thinking.

I had no sure plan, and that was so unlike me it set a pit of terror in my stomach that grew and grew anytime I allowed myself to ruminate too long. And having no plan, I knew it was better that I stayed away from her. For her as well as for me.

Even though the distance did little to rectify the situation. Wherever I was, I was fucked.

Another flick of the mind, pushing out those thoughts to concentrate on my employees. Charlotte had already begun to gather her things, but Astor sat still, which gave the answer to the question I'd asked without him having to speak.

Whatever he had left to go over was more personal in nature, then. My secretary's presence wouldn't be required.

Charlotte had made it two meters when she stopped. "Oh," she said then sighed. "Warren Werner."

I stretched my neck to the side, trying to work out the permanent kink associated with his name. "He called again?"

"He did. Personally this time. What would you like me to say?"

It might have been less provoking if his calls were regarding his daughter. A handful of short emails sent under her account to his wife seemed to be all he needed to be rest assured Celia was doing well. If it had been my daughter who had wed my business rival, if it had been my daughter who had crossed an ocean and limited her communication, I would not have been satisfied with impersonal messages sent via computer. I would have demanded phone calls. I would have expected a visit over Christmas. If Genevieve had denied those, I would have flown the pond and shown up on her doorstep.

It only proved what I'd always known about Warren, that he was a cruel, heartless bastard.

Because the only reason the man had reached out those several times was to follow-up on the alliance I'd hinted at on the day I'd wed Celia. I'd only dangled the idea to get him calm enough to accept our marriage. It had been an impromptu move on my part. I'd been so desperately close to the end of the plan. I would have said anything at that point, and I did.

And if I'd followed through with the plan as it were, this wouldn't be an issue now. I'd have already buried my wife and any contact from Warren would likely be through lawyers because there was no doubt he'd try to contest the transfer of Werner Media shares to my name. It would be a long and drawn-out process, but he had no leg to stand on, and I'd win. Eventually.

That eventually would never arrive as long as Celia was alive.

"Put him off," I said, rising and buttoning my jacket out of habit. I couldn't be on this couch anymore. I continued as I crossed the room to my desk. "Tell him I've been preoccupied. Long weekends in the islands with my wife. Surely, he remembers we're newly wed."

"Yes, sir," Charlotte said, her mouth set, clearly disapproving. She knew there was something fishy in my marriage. She knew it was odd that my new bride would choose to stay on a small island away from me. She knew how often I flew off to Amelie.

She didn't know how often I thought about it.

I imagined the woman was thoroughly confused. If she'd thought I'd married a woman a decade younger than me for her body, that notion had been dismissed when I'd abandoned her in the Atlantic. If she'd thought I'd married her because of who she was and the connections she'd afford me, then why hadn't I taken a call with Warren yet? If she'd thought I'd married Celia because of love…

Well, bless Charlotte, then, for her ignorance.

It wasn't her job to think anything about me anyway.

I dismissed her now, but she'd worked for me long enough to get away with one more comment. "But I can't put him off forever."

Then she was gone, and Astor was still here to discuss something that would hopefully take my mind off my wife once and for all.

I unbuttoned my jacket and sat behind my desk, motioning for my assistant to join me here. He stood, bringing the chair and his messenger bag with him.

"Mateo has sent over a list of purchase items that need your approval. He says you've authorized a redecorating project?" He set the chair down and sank onto it.

I nearly told him to pick it right back up and put it where it belonged because I was not in the mood for discussing this.

But that wouldn't make the item go away.

"I did," I said, pinching the bridge of my nose. I couldn't even tell myself it had been on a whim because I'd carefully collected the catalogues for her from a variety of stores I knew she liked based on the bookmarks on her computer and then left them on her bed with a note suggesting she fix the room to her liking.

She hadn't mentioned wanting to since we'd first arrived on the island. I'd dismissed it then, convinced that she wouldn't be around long enough for it to matter. Still believing I'd go through with it, that I *could* go through with it, because *that had been the plan*. That had always been the plan.

By giving her this gift, had my mind been made up?

It gave her something to do. It gave her something to keep her mind sharp and her spirits high. It replaced the wreckage from the walls that had begun to break down in our sessions. What was the point if I didn't intend to let her come out of this whole?

The answers weren't at the ready.

"Approve it all," I said, flicking my hand to dismiss the list that Astor had produced. "Whatever she wants, she gets. She has her money." Several months' worth of money that I'd promised her in our marriage negotiations. The cash had been collecting in a bank account, enough to build an entire new building, if she chose. Still I added, "If that's not enough, transfer what else she needs from my account."

"Yes, sir. And the crew that Mateo's asked for? Did you want to bring in islanders?"

At that I shook my head. "Have Mateo find a crew from Mexico. Spanish speaking only." It would take longer to bring one in with that specification, and would cost more too, and I almost second thought the decision. I didn't want to believe that she'd try to escape again, not now. I wanted to believe I'd earned at least the beginnings of what would one day be loyalty if not something else. Something more.

I thought about how her resistance had begun to diminish when I'd been there last. How she looked better than she ever had, her skin supple, her muscles toned. How she'd relaxed enough to let me bring her to climax, not once, but four times. How she'd begged for me to fuck her.

I could still taste her. Could still feel the unrhythmic vibrations of her body as she came against my tongue. Could still hear the catch in her voice when she'd said her parting words—*Thank you, Edward.*

And none of that mattered. I'd imprisoned her. She'd run if she could. Why wouldn't she?

"Yes," I confirmed, for myself rather than Astor. "A Spanish crew."

"Yes, sir." He bent down to reach inside his bag. "Finally, this arrived. The book you ordered. Shall I send it on?"

I took the book he handed me, a scarlet goatskin leather journal with her initials written in gold foil on the bottom. A heart-shaped accompanying gold clasp was a bit more romantic than I'd intended, but it had been the only quality one I'd found that locked.

The lock had been important. I wanted her to feel free to write her soul, to let out what was inside as she had in her second letter to her parents, without worry of what I'd think or do. While I wanted to know with fierce longing every thought of hers, every detail of her imaginings, I preferred that she tell me those things herself. I liked her vulnerable, yes, like I enjoyed all my women, but the point was for her to choose that, not for me to take it.

It didn't mean anything unless she chose.

And if she did choose, then could things be different? Could this really work out another way?

I traced the letters with my finger—CEF. Celia Edyn

Fasbender. I'd taken the Werner away from her when I'd put that ring on her finger—my mother's ring, for fuck's sake. I'd made her mine. She belonged to me now.

Didn't she?

I set the journal on my desk. "Not yet. I'll tell you when it's ready to send. What else do you have?"

The next thing on Astor's agenda was interrupted by the chirp of my desk phone. I hit the speaker button. "Yes, Charlotte?"

"Camilla's on the line for you."

My chest tightened. If the anxiety that was Warren Werner lived in my neck, the emotions I felt for my sister resided deep in my torso, complicated and protective in nature.

But things hadn't been easy between us as of late.

"Tell her I'm in a meeting," I said, tapping the button off with my finger.

Immediately, the phone chirped again.

"She says it's urgent," Charlotte said when I answered.

I should have guessed. Charlotte wouldn't have interrupted in the first place if my sister hadn't pressed. Annoyed, I looked to Astor, as though he could save me from the responsibility of family.

He read my expression wrong. Standing, he picked up his bag. "I didn't have much more. I'll come back." He returned the chair to the spot Celia had designed it to sit on his way out.

I hit line one and put the receiver to my ear. "What is it, C?" I asked, using the nickname that came more easily when I was frustrated. "I was in an important meeting."

It was a bit overstated, but I had a feeling her cry of "urgent" was as well.

"There's a delivery," she said, her tone clipped.

"Then accept it." But I already knew it was more. I'd hoped Camilla wouldn't have been there when it arrived, that Jeremy could have taken care of it all, but she'd canceled her planned photography outing when Freddie had woken up with a fever.

"It's from the States," she went on. "An entire moving truck. And it's addressed to Celia Fasbender. Do you want to tell me what I'm supposed to do with an entire moving truck worth of items? The deliverers are asking."

She was exaggerating. It was a small moving truck. I'd read the manifest before I'd approved the shipping.

But I knew the amount of items wasn't really the concern—it was what they were. That I'd had them shipped at all.

"Tell them to take them upstairs to Celia's room." Jeremy would have already said that. Camilla wanted reassurance from me. "I'll take care of them later."

"But what are they, Eddie? They're her things, aren't they? Why are you bringing them here? Do you realize you called it *her* room?"

"Because it *is* her room." I sat forward, my voice sharp. "There's not anyone else using it. And what would you prefer I do with her things? She's my wife. What would you prefer?"

"I'd prefer that you stick to the plan. You said marrying her was simply a door in. That I would never have to deal with her. You led me to believe that you would be leading very separate lives. Moving her things in is not separate. This wasn't the plan we'd discussed."

"No, it wasn't," I said, but I hadn't been completely honest with her. I hadn't wanted her involved with the gritty details. Camilla was too good. She would have rightly objected, even though it was the surest way to where we meant to end.

I felt guilty about that, more than I wanted to admit. About not being honest with her. About the horrible thing I'd planned to do. About changing my strategy midstream. About getting so fucking twisted by Celia's blue eyes and tenacity and the way she opened up when she began to truly give in.

My guilt made me angry. Angry with myself.

But also angry about being challenged. "Let's not forget that it was *my* plan, Camilla. *My* idea. I'm the one who orchestrated it, all of it. And that makes it my plan to change." Then, before she could argue further, "Let Jeremy deal with the deliverers. I'll worry about the rest. Like I always do."

I hung up before she could say another word. I didn't need to hear what else she had to say. I already knew, already felt the anxiety of having lost control of the reins.

What the fuck was I doing bringing her things to my house? As though she wanted them here. As though she meant to live on with me as husband and wife. As though I planned to keep her.

I scrubbed my hands over my face then held them there. Light slipped in through my fingers, gleaming off the band on my left hand. I pulled them down so I could stare at it. My father's wedding ring, now my own. His marriage had been everything to him. His wife had been his very reason for living. The ring was a reminder of my reasons, why I'd pursued vengeance with single-minded dedication.

But I'd put the matching ring on Celia's finger, and that had changed everything.

That was a lie. *She'd* changed everything. It was why I'd put the ring there, not the other way around.

I reached out and slid the journal toward me. Using the tiny key attached, I unlocked the fasten and opened it to the first lined page in the book. I grabbed a pen and wrote the short note.

Little Bird,

I told you privacy is a privilege. This is yours to keep to yourself. Fill the pages or don't, the words belong only to you. You've earned it.

Edward

I read the words again, disgusted with myself. Disgusted by the flood of warmth that filled my body just from writing my pet name for her. Disgusted that I even purchased the gift and more so that I would still send it anyway.

The plan had always been to ruin Celia Werner.

But she was well on her way to ruining me.

TWELVE
Celia

The first time Edward had left me on the island, I'd been angry. I'd spent the days with him gone trying to smother the fire of rage inside me, or at least trying to tame it down to a manageable simmer. Weeks passed, and by the time he'd returned, the fury had subsided. Still there, but not quite as much of a focal point as it had once been. Still the thing that motivated me, but the flames calm enough that I could concentrate on how to get what I wanted—away from the island—instead of dwelling on the person who had put me there.

It was still what I wanted most. Even as the winter turned to spring and the weather on Amelie blossomed to perfection, even as I felt myself blossoming along with the new season, even as the place felt more like home and less like a vacation spot, I still wanted to leave.

But it wasn't what occupied my thoughts anymore, and the anger had become so distant that I forgot it for days at a stretch.

This time in his absence, my emotions changed. I wondered about him more—what he was doing, what he was thinking, if he was reading before bed or finishing last minute details for work. They were day-dreamy kinds of thoughts for the most part, wistful and curious. Had he gotten a good night's sleep? Was he driving himself to the office or using his driver?

When they threatened to take over, I pushed the thoughts aside by throwing myself into the project he'd left for me—redesigning my bedroom. It had been an unexpected gift, one I should have been allowed to pursue without his permission, but nevertheless I was grateful. It had been a long time since I'd really gotten into my work. It had been an even longer stretch since I'd done something for myself, and it was fun to discover what I liked again and how my tastes had changed. Most importantly, it helped the days pass while also making them remarkable. I began to look forward to what the sun would bring in the mornings. I no longer lingered in bed bemoaning my existence.

It wasn't until I moved out of the room that the jealousy began to trickle in.

The work had gotten to such a point that it was impossible to continue to sleep there. The house had several suitable bedrooms upstairs, and I considered taking one of those for all the obvious reasons, but, in the end, it was more practical to stay on the main floor, near the living areas and the pool, and, frankly, I liked the idea of invading Edward's bedroom, even if he wasn't there. I'd been surprised when, after I told Lou and Joette that was where I wanted to move, they'd actually complied. I'd expected a bunch of hemming and hawing and stalling until the idea was proposed to their boss, but there had been none of it at all. They'd simply nodded and began the task of packing up my belongings and shuffling them to the opposite side of the house.

Of course the lack of argument insinuated that Edward was already fully aware of what I was doing, that he'd possibly suggested it himself, but I tried not to think about that too much. I was successful too, until I was lying in his bed that first night, smelling the decorative pillows for any trace of his scent, and the wondering about him became much more personal. Was he thinking about me? Did he know where I was sleeping? Did he like thinking about me in his bed?

I liked the way these new thoughts made my heart trip and my stomach flutter. I closed my eyes, letting them take me where they would, expecting them to morph into something sexual in nature, and they did, just not the way I'd hoped. Because, a dose of reality seeped in, and all of a sudden it occurred to me to not just wonder what Edward was doing but who he was with.

Who *was* he with?

Was he sleeping alone like I was?

Was he fucking around?

The idea made me sit up with a start and clutch my stomach while wave after wave of nausea rolled through me.

It wasn't just possible he was with someone else—it was likely. In our negotiations before marriage, he'd assured me he'd be discreet, but that he'd have whatever side action he wanted to and that it was none of my business if he did. I'd been bothered by the arrangement, but I'd been more bothered that it bothered me so I hadn't fought it more. Besides, fighting him at all had proved futile. He'd gotten everything he'd asked for in that discussion.

At the time, I'd been determined to make sure he never had need of a side piece. My game had required his sexual attention, but, also, I'd wanted him. More than I had wanted to admit.

I still wanted him. More than I wanted to admit.

And now my game was long over, and I wasn't with him, and he could be fucking anyone and everyone, and I'd never be the wiser.

I tried not to throw up.

After that, a constant ache lived in the pit of my stomach. My mouth tasted permanently bitter, and jealousy shadowed every other emotion that passed through me. I was even more grateful for the design project then, a distraction that I'd come to depend on, but it wasn't enough. So I doubled my time doing yoga. I played more chess. When Eliana wasn't available, I taught Mateo's oldest daughter, Tanya. When Tanya had schoolwork to do, I moved the pieces along the board myself.

Reading was hard. Even when the story engrossed me, there was always something that brought my thoughts back to him, back to who he might be with. Any book with any sort of romantic storyline was impossible to get through, but even the others would catch me off guard—an orphaned character, a misunderstood hero, an asshole of a villian. Soon, I was as scared to pick up a book as I was to be alone with my own thoughts.

Then, the diary came.

It was the last thing I needed, and I definitely didn't trust it, even with the two keys and the lock and his promise inside not to read it. The lock could be easily picked or busted, and Edward's word felt as unreliable as the wind. Though, he hadn't really lied about anything so far.

Tricked me, deceived me, but hadn't quite lied.

But I'd always had a thing for blank lined paper, an itching desire to fill the pages with whatever words came to mind. I'd kept a diary all through my youth for that very reason, and then later, when Hudson had invited me into his experiments, I'd taken over recording the observations. He'd been quite scientific with his journaling before I'd come along, referring to people as subjects and proposing an expected outcome from the beginning. Mine were more story form. While I'd kept Hudson's name out of them, referring to him only as A—because it was the first letter of the alphabet, and he was definitely the alpha of the games—I'd mentioned our victims by name and noted and evaluated their emotions in prose.

I missed that, I realized. Not the playing of the games, though maybe I missed parts of that too, but, more, I missed the telling about them.

And so, six weeks after he'd left, when I was bored out of my mind and unable to ignore the thoughts in my head and the journal on my nightstand, I picked it up and began recording him. Began recording everything I'd had planned for him and how my game had come about, sure to include every one of his nasty assholish quips and misogynistic demands. If he picked it up and read it, he could hear about how much I hated him. How terrible he was. How easily I'd schemed against him. I wouldn't care. In fact, I hoped he did.

But the writing morphed as I went on, and I found it impossible to write with the detached voice that I had in the stacks of journals sitting in the closet of my condo back in New York. Edward had stirred too many emotions. They'd leaked through small punctures in the Teflon walls I'd so carefully built inside. Punctures I hadn't known he'd made. Emotions I hadn't known still existed. I had a lot of feelings about my parents, apparently. I missed them, but not as much as I thought I did. I resented them. I wanted their approval. Their affection. I hated them a little, too.

And there were other feelings, about other people. Hudson, his father, my uncle Ron.

Edward.

So much about Edward.

Most of the emotions were still shapeless blobs, too complicated to call one color or another, but they were there, oozing out of me. They trickled out into my words even as I tried to hold them back, and soon I wasn't just telling about the devil who'd inspired me to play him and then took me into captivity, but the man I'd begun to glimpse underneath. How he affected me. How I longed to affect him.

How I suspected I *did* affect him.

It was cathartic to have a space to pour it all out, a place to line up the stray feelings and examine them properly. It was like he'd chipped away at a big stone wall inside of me, with his demands and his smirk and his *I'm-gonna-break-you* sessions, and now I was collecting the pieces, attempting to figure out the picture they made if they were whole.

It gave my life meaning. Not because it was one of the only activities available to me on the island, but because of how it let me look at myself. It didn't just give meaning to the life I lived here but to the life I lived before. I began to understand things about myself, things I'd never known, things I hadn't wanted to know. Like how much I enjoyed the power struggles. How they made me feel alive, even when it was exactly that type of struggle that had landed me captive on an island by a man who easily dominated me.

I liked that too. Being topped. Being cared for. Being seen.

There was more he brought out in me, and writing about it, I started to become more comfortable with those feelings—the desire, the anger, the longing, the jealousy.

I found myself in the words. Things I'd buried, I wanted to uncover. Things I'd held back, I wanted to share. Things I'd suppressed, I wanted to feel.

The most shocking part was how much I wanted those things *with* Edward.

Because he'd started this whole journey, probably. Because I associated this self-reformation with him. Because I was lonely and confused, and he'd brainwashed me. That was likely too.

It was part of his plan, I was sure. Little by little, he was breaking me down, like he had been all along, like he was still doing from afar.

Only difference from before was that now, I wasn't just letting it happen.

Now, I wanted it to.

THIRTEEN

I consciously fought not to hold my breath as I watched Edward move around my bedroom. It was the beginning of May, almost three months since he'd last been on Amelie, which had been just enough time to have the new design of my bedroom implemented. It had been finished so recently, in fact, that I'd only slept in it two nights.

Like before, Edward had shown up without any warning. One minute I was capturing Eliana's queen, and the next, my husband was standing over us, criticizing my winning move.

I was so excited to see him, I hadn't minded. I'd jumped up, given him a kiss that he might have assumed was for our guest, then tugged him out of the library to my bedroom to show off what I'd done. There was a momentary coldness before he accepted my grip around his hand, a split second where he'd felt cut off and callous like he'd been when he'd threatened to kill me instead of the coy and almost charming man who'd said he'd miss me, but it disappeared so quickly, I decided I may have imagined it.

And then I forgot about it entirely because I was too eager for him to see my room.

It didn't make him special. I'd cajoled everyone on the island into coming by and seeing the finished product three days ago. That was half the fun of completing a design project—showing it off.

I hadn't been nearly as nervous when any of the others had checked it out though. Maybe because everyone else had walked around with smiles on their faces, complimenting each and every detail.

Edward strolled through silently, tracing the beading on the plush gold settee as he walked by it, studying the mural behind the bed and the newly plastered walls. His expression was stoic, his lips drawn in a tight line, his eyes guarded.

"The curtains are purposefully heavy," I said, as he lifted a panel from the ground, as though testing the weight. "It adds drama to the room."

He nodded then sauntered over to the antique curtained yellow and filigree cabinet. He fingered the curvature of the cutout without saying a word.

"It's Louis XV period. Some of the metal adornment has tarnished, but I really wanted an authentic piece in the room."

Again he nodded.

The knot in my chest tightened as I thought about the small decorative decisions I'd implemented in his room. Would he hate those too? Would he tear down the tufted wall I'd added behind his bed? Would he get angry when he smelled me in his bedding?

The last one was stupid. He probably wouldn't even recognize my smell, and surely Sanyjah had changed the sheets on his arrival.

Edward continued on to the other authentic piece in the room—the bronze gilded writing desk I'd discovered in one of the antique catalogs he'd left me. It was small and ornate, and it locked and had been exactly what I'd been looking for when I'd found it.

It was quite unlike anything that had been in the room previously.

"I suppose I have different tastes than Marion," I remarked when my husband had almost made a full circle of the area and still hadn't said anything. His last wife had decorated the space, or rather, stuck furniture in the room and called it good. It was possible the changes were a shock.

I stared at his profile as he carefully examined the rope molding I'd added along the top of the walls, expecting to see him nod again.

"Better taste," he said, surprising me.

His voice was even and his posture unremarkable, and the only reason I noticed the subtle twitch of his eye was because I'd been staring, which meant he hadn't wanted it to be seen, but I *had* noticed it.

And I wondered what it meant.

Then I was sure I knew. He'd never talked to me about his former wife, but Blanche Martin, a woman I'd involved in one of my cons who had also once worked for Edward, had told me he'd been heartbroken when Marion left him. Devastated.

I tried to ignore the pinch of envy and concentrated on what this might feel like to him—another woman coming in and changing everything up, ruining fond memories, of-ficially ending an era. "Does it bother you a lot? That I changed it?"

He jolted, swinging his head to look at me, his ex-pression telling me I'd surprised him with the question. Shocked him, even, by thinking to ask it.

Quickly he schooled his features, and I expected him to deny or ignore, but he didn't. He stuck his hands in his suit pockets—he must have flown directly from work again—and stood next to me, gazing out over the room.

"It doesn't bother me as much as I thought it would," he said thoughtfully. "Perhaps because it's as stunning as it is."

His off-hand compliment made my skin as warm as if he'd kissed me.

"Or maybe it's because I was rarely ever in here any-way. There's nothing that I should have been attached to. Still...I thought that I might have been."

It was the most he'd ever shared with me, and the shar-ing was even better than the compliment. He'd said he would tell me things, that he'd be honest and exposed with me the more that I was with him, but I hadn't yet seen it, and I'd never quite believed it.

And he might not have let this out purposefully, but he *had* let something out, and I was startled to find how much I liked it. How I wanted more. How I wanted to collect his bits of honesty and hold them to myself like I'd collected his notes in my drawer.

"Tell me about her?" I asked with quiet hesitation, afraid to spook him.

For a fraction of a second, he seemed he might say something else, something meaningful.

Then he gave me a sharp, "No," spinning on his dress shoes back toward the door he'd come in. "We'll meet after dinner for a session. I have things to do in the meantime."

It was maddening to be so close to him after so long, more maddening that I cared to be close to him at all, and I told myself firmly to let him go, that this was a reminder of what a shithead he was and to stop romanticizing the goddamn asshole who'd kidnapped me and threatened me with death because wanting anything from the monster was the real definition of insanity.

But I *did* care.

And after weeks of writing about all the ways I cared in the diary that was right this very moment double locked in the writing desk across the room, the intricate details of those feelings were at the surface and ready to launch off my tongue.

"Have there been other women?" I asked, stopping him at the door. If he wouldn't tell me about his past, fine. But I sure as hell deserved to know about his present. Especially if he expected to take me off to his fuckpad later.

God, I hoped I could call it a fuckpad later.

He didn't turn around. "Other women since Marion?"

"Since me." As reasonable as it was for me to need to know, the simple statement felt like I was giving too much away. Revealing too much.

But wasn't that what he wanted from me? For me to expose and reveal while he gloated in my discomfort of the baring?

He swiveled to face me, a smirk dressing his lips. "I believe you said it wouldn't matter if there were."

It was a gut punch. Because I hadn't meant it when I'd

said that, and he knew it as well as I did.

But he'd said things too, things that he also hadn't meant.

"See," I took a step toward him, "but you said you wouldn't be fucking me. And now you have. And you've alluded to doing it again. So, if you're going to be putting a cock that's recently been exposed to another woman's pussy anywhere near me, then it does matter."

Before the words were out of my mouth, I could see his next potential move, could see him taking away sex as an option between us all together, and it would kill me if he did. Literally kill me.

But the jealousy that had taken root inside me was on its way to killing me as well, so the words came out and now I had to face the consequences, whatever they may be.

He assessed me for a beat, his gaze brushing over my features with familiar tendrils. "It's not a concern," he said finally.

Which wasn't a fucking answer. He could be saying he hadn't slept with anyone or that he'd been recently checked for STDs or that he always used a condom or that the sex he'd had didn't warrant worry or that he just didn't care about what affect his sex life had on me at all.

"Does that mean—"

He cut me off. "It means it's not a concern. Don't push me further on it right now. I give what and when I'm ready to give. Your job is to give always. Do you understand?"

He expected an answer. He expected respect. "Yes, Edward," I said.

His smile appeared and vanished so quickly I wasn't sure if it had existed at all. "I'm having dinner with Joette and Azariah. I'll set out clothes for our session beforehand. Be ready by the time I return."

This time I let him leave. I didn't want to know that I couldn't stop him again if I tried.

FOURTEEN

"Whenever you're ready," Edward prompted, making himself comfortable on the sofa across from me. He hitched up the leg of his linen pants and crossed his ankle over his knee, draped an arm over the couch back, and took a swallow of his cognac. Except for the more casual attire, he appeared exactly the same as last time.

Everything was the same as last time, actually.

I wore the same white dress, the same boring underwear. He'd walked me down the same path, ushered me into the cabana in the same way. The only difference so far had been that, instead of offering me a drink, he opened a bottle of Petit Verdot and handed me a glass.

It tasted of plums and figs and spice and couldn't have been a better choice if I'd selected it myself.

He was beginning to know me, really know me. I was already so vulnerable with him, and he wanted to crack me open and bleed me more? I wanted it and I didn't all at the same time. Parts of me were ready to pour forward, like water through a sieve, but other parts—larger, bulkier pieces of past pain—strained against the netting, dislodged by the movement of the liquid, but unable to follow the same path.

I pinched the skin of my forehead and tried to find my balance. "The same as before, Edward?" I asked, when I felt more solid. "Tell you something that makes me feel exposed?"

"I'm surprised you don't have several anecdotes at the ready. You've had nearly three months to prepare."

I couldn't help glaring. "Was that why you stayed away so long? So that I'd have time to decide what to tell you? It would have been nice to know I had homework."

My irritation slid off him like water. "The length of time wasn't meant to be anything but time. Distance, I've learned, can be very valuable. And homework or not, you can't tell me you didn't think about it, that you didn't peel away layers and find more that you could share."

I suddenly felt a strange urge to cry.

I rarely cried. For sure I didn't cry in front of people. Not because I tried not to, but because I just couldn't. There wasn't enough emotion inside of me to need to get out.

Until now. Until Edward.

Just as suddenly, the urge went away. I took a sip of wine. "Yes, I did think of things I could tell you. Some of them even true." I smirked at him like a smartass because I couldn't help myself, but I quickly dropped the expression because it wasn't who I wanted to be all the time anymore. Not with him.

"I thought of things," I said, honestly, "but I didn't prepare them because I figured there was zero chance in hell that your next session would ask the same thing of me precisely because I had three months. You've always preferred to keep me on my toes. Edward."

My breath shuddered through me as I waited for him to respond. Sincerity was foreign to me, and I didn't know how to wear it. It felt as unusual on my tongue as the cotton panties felt against my skin. Both should have been more comfortable than they were. I wondered if either would ever feel natural.

"It seems I've kept you on your toes once again, then, doesn't it?" His tone was authoritative but not malicious. His own brand of sincerity. "Unprepared is exactly as I prefer, but I'm also glad that you've let yourself think about things you could talk about. I'm sure the right account will present itself now."

I already knew which one it was. There was only one that I was even close to being ready to discuss, and it was going to be a bitch to tell. I'd even tried to explore it in my diary, but couldn't get myself to recount the details—the parts that mattered. But I'd wanted to. For the first time ever, I'd wanted to. And I wanted to now.

God, this was exactly like therapy, wasn't it? I supposed it was beyond time.

I pulled my knees up and bent them to the side underneath me as I searched for where to start. "After..." I paused, wondering if it was best to stay far away from the story I'd told last time since he hadn't approved of the ending, but there was no way around it. That ending was this beginning in every way, shape, and form.

I looked Edward directly in the eye. "Okay, it was a shitty thing I did—sleeping with the guy's dad. It was vengeful and disgusting, and I knew it, even as it was happening. It wasn't comfortable or even fun. It definitely didn't make me feel sexy or wanted or like I'd won anything, but I'm not going to expand on that or try to make myself a victim with that part—even though, let's be real here, the guy had been around me my whole life. I'd been friends with his kids. I should have been like a daughter to him, and when I showed up at his door, it did not take one tiny bit of convincing for him to try to get in my pants." In fact, Jack probably even thought he'd been the one who seduced me. "Which is kind of disgusting all on its own level and somewhat predatory, but my point is, I was culpable, and I was of age, so it was what it was."

"Just because you put yourself in the situation doesn't mean that you have to carry all the blame. It certainly doesn't mean that you shouldn't be allowed to have feelings about it."

His words surprised me so much that it had to be written on my face.

Edward dropped his arm from the couch and leaned forward, and I knew it was a cue to listen, to *really* listen to what followed. "Last time, I didn't approve because you told me this only to boast," he explained. "You wanted to shock me. You acted proud, and we both knew that wasn't honest. *This* is honest. This is what I want you to talk about."

Who was this guy?

I stared at him incredulously. "But you think that fucking him made me a slut, right?"

His cheek ticked at the word *slut*. "It doesn't matter what I think. It matters what you think."

Classic. Turn it back on me.

"Did you really want to be a psychologist instead of a businessman?"

"No."

"Could have fooled me." Not for the first time I wondered what he was getting out of all of this. He wanted to break me, sure, but that was as much a part of his rivalry with my father as it was about me, and he'd suggested he liked to do this with other women too. Did it turn him on to watch women examine their wounds? Because he liked being a sort of hero to them? Or because he wanted to use their pain against them later?

There was a possibility it was both.

It made it hard to want to continue on. What if I bared my soul to him, and all he did was hurt me with whatever he learned? I could feel iron walls threatening to close around everything inside of me, pushing him out.

The thing was, I already expected him to use my pain to hurt me. To break me. He'd not only told me he would, but he'd also admitted to being sadistic. And he'd wanted to kill me. This wasn't supposed to be an easy alternative—it was supposed to be terrible.

I expected it, and I'd accepted it. And maybe I was a bit of a masochist, because I wasn't completely opposed to taking the ride.

So, here I was, buckling in, preparing for the roller coaster.

"Well, I did think it made me a slut. I felt dirty and... used...and...stupid." I'd never articulated the words, and they came slowly as I began to understand the blob of feelings that had painted this time in my life. I had a sudden flash of me on my knees, taking Jack's cock in my mouth while he spouted on about my lips and my eyes and my breasts. "Cheap. I felt cheap. But also like I deserved it because I'd done it to myself."

I shook my head, throwing the memories of the night

with Jack out of my head. "I carried all of that with me when I went back to Berkeley. Dirk was there, wanting to talk, maybe even get back together, and that just made me feel worse so I—"

"Why?" Edward interrupted.

"Why did it make me feel worse?" It was another blob I had to examine. This one was particularly hard to look at. "Because I didn't deserve that. I'd dumped him. Over the phone. For no reason other than that I thought my old crush liked me. And then, instead of trying to repair my relationship with him, I went and fucked an old guy. He'd been nothing but decent to me. Decent and kind. The first guy who ever had, really. When I was with him, he'd made me think that maybe I was better than the way other people before him had made me feel, and then one summer away from him, I proved that I was exactly what I'd always been told I was—only worth the value of my body."

"That wasn't what the summer proved." He let that sit in the air for a minute. "I'm curious to know why men before him led you to feel that way, though."

"I'm sure you are, but that's not what I'm talking about right now, Edward." It came out more defensive than needed, but he didn't call me out.

I thought about the other thing he'd said. "I guess the summer hadn't proved that. It had been one night, but the baggage from that felt heavy, and I hated it so much—hated myself so much—that I couldn't even look in the mirror anymore. I certainly couldn't put that on someone else, someone good. So I avoided him, and threw myself into things that made the self-loathing more tolerable. Random hookups. Drugs. I did a lot of coke. Some ecstasy. I drank. A shit load. I was smashed all the time that semester. I don't even know how I passed any of my midterms."

Actually, I did know how I'd passed some of them. I'd paid a girl to write my papers for western civ and I'd let my economics teacher masturbate on my breasts. Thinking about it now made me feel nauseated.

"Anyway, it wasn't pretty for a good two months or so. And then…" I could still remember the moment I realized it clearly, walking down the Walgreens aisle to grab some condoms and passing the pregnancy tests and coming to a halt because I hadn't had a period in ages and I knew, I just *knew* that I was pregnant. I'd bought a box and taken the first test in the store. Then, when it turned positive, I'd taken another one right after.

"And then?" Edward prompted, softly as though he were interested, not as demanding as usual.

"Then I found out I was pregnant." There was weight to that statement. It was obvious I didn't have a kid now, and so there'd be assumptions. I imagined Edward was thinking them through, trying to guess—*did she have an abortion? Give it up for adoption? Where was the birth control?* It was impossible for him not to form a judgment, and I ached to know what he was thinking so I could judge him back.

But he sat silent, waiting for my tale to unfold.

"It's funny, I'd imagined saying that before. I don't know when—in my play. In my fantasies. I didn't even want kids necessarily, but the notion of being pregnant always held drama. 'I'm pregnant', I'd say to the imaginary whomever in my head, and damn, did that get the attention I wanted. It's a heavy phrase, you know? 'I'm pregnant.' 'I was pregnant.' You immediately know something intimate about the person—that she's had sex. Sometimes you even know whom with. And when she doesn't have a husband or a boyfriend, you start wondering who the father could be, and then you also know that she was careless. That she was irresponsible. That she's easy."

Edward looked about to say something, but I waved him away. "Whatever you're going to say, it's true. People think those things and sometimes even say them out loud, and it shouldn't matter what other people think, I know, I know, but those things do matter. Especially when the things they were thinking were true. I was careless. I was irresponsible. I was a slut, and sure, power to a woman if she wants to sleep with lots of men. I'm all for that and fuck everyone who puts her down for that, but that wasn't who I was in that moment. In that moment, I had carelessly gotten pregnant from something that had made me feel shitty and slutty, and those words people said mattered. Because I was already saying them about myself."

I'd meandered. None of this was where I'd thought I was headed. The painful part was coming up, but in telling these parts, I remembered they'd been painful too. I remembered it in my muscles, in the way my hip suddenly ached and my shoulders tensed. In the twinge at my neck. These things had lived inside me, stuffed into the fascia of my body, breathing and festering, and all this time I'd thought there was nothing there.

And now? Could I finally let it go?

I'd been silent for several minutes when Edward asked, "Are you sure it was his?"

He didn't need to frame the question any other way. I knew who he meant, and it was obvious that was where I was going.

"Yes. The dates matched up, and when I did the ultrasound at Planned Parenthood, that matched up too. I'd been on birth control, but I wasn't always that diligent about taking it, and he was the only one I hadn't doubled up with a condom." Which was stupid. Which was why the whole thing had left me feeling stupid.

"Stop judging," he said, sternly. Also, ironically since that was exactly what I was silently pleading from him. "Stop judging yourself and just let it be what it is."

"How do you—?"

"It's written all over your face. I'm not judging you either, for the record, though that shouldn't matter."

He'd set his drink down and folded his hands in his lap, and with the way he was angled and the intensity of his stare, I could feel exactly how much of his attention was devoted to me. All of it. Every single speck of focus was on me.

It should have made me feel more exposed.

Somehow it made me feel more safe.

It didn't make sense. None of it. Why he wanted to know, why he cared. Why he was so rapt. "If you're not judging, what are you doing?"

A smattering of seconds passed before he answered. "I'm listening." He startled me with a smile. "Now go on."

"You're really that into this? You want to hear what happens next." I chuckled as I drank my wine.

"I think you want to tell it." He said it so it was clear when he said *think* he meant *know*.

And that knowing made me feel safer too.

I set my glass down. "Well, I immediately got my act together. Stopped the partying, did better in school, took prenatal vitamins. I didn't know what I wanted to do about it yet, but there was only a couple of weeks until Thanksgiving, and I was going home, and I could talk to my parents about it then. I didn't know about timelines for abortion so I figured it would be fine to wait until then."

"Did you expect them to be supportive?"

I shook my head. "It makes me feel guilty to say that when you already detest my father as you do, but it's honest. He didn't expect much from his only daughter, but he certainly expected her to stay classy."

"As fathers do."

I'd forgotten that he was a father. Or, not forgotten, but the fact hadn't seemed relevant, and now I realized how relevant it was. His daughter, Genevieve, was as old now as I'd been then. He had to be thinking about her, comparing us.

It took all my strength not to ask him about that. He'd tell me if he wanted me to know, and he'd been right—I wanted to finish what I was telling.

"It turned out it wasn't as bad as I'd expected."

"It never is."

I started to agree then stopped myself. Experience had told me better. "No, sometimes it is. But this time it wasn't, because I told…" I hesitated. I'd specifically left Hudson's name out of the first story. He was a prominent businessman, someone who Edward would probably work with eventually if he hadn't already, and I owed too much to Hudson to be the one to soil his name and turn his past against him.

So I left his name out again.

"I told the guy before I told my parents. The guy who I'd liked. The one who slept with my friend."

"And you told him the baby was his father's?"

I nodded. "He decided to claim the baby as his own, and that made telling Warren and Madge a whole hell of a lot easier because who the fuck cared what trouble Celia had made because now she was going to have a very wealthy baby! I mean, it hurt. It hurt knowing their reaction was only what it was because of what it gave them, but at least I didn't have to get the tight-lipped, cold-shoulder treatment. So, you know. It was going to be okay."

Edward sat forward, his finger up to stop me. "Hold on a moment—the guy who'd been an ass before now out of the blue decided to claim it was his?"

Up until then, he'd been almost soft—well, soft for Edward—but there was something distinctly biting in his tone.

"He wasn't always an ass," I said defensively, knowing that wasn't the most important part of his question. "But, yes. He stood up for me. We told our parents together."

It had been tense—all four of them and the two of us, half of us knowing that Hudson was definitely not the baby daddy, the other half ecstatic. My mother and his had immediately begun planning the wedding even though we'd made it perfectly clear we were not getting married. Then, while the others were talking about baby names, there'd been the moment between Jack and Hudson, a moment no one else saw but me. An eyebrow raise from the older, a terse statement from his son. *This baby is mine now. I'm doing this, and it's mine.*

That had hurt in its own way. I'd believed Hudson had volunteered to be dad because he'd felt responsible for the position I was in. He also hadn't wanted his mother to find out what his father had done, cheating on his wife with a woman half his age. But his words to Jack felt like they were only protecting my baby, his little brother or sister. Where did I belong in all of it?

"Why did he do that?"

I furrowed my brow, and since Edward couldn't know what I'd been thinking, I didn't know exactly what he was asking.

"Why did he choose to tie his whole life to yours?" His expression was as accusatory as his tone. "He didn't even want to date you for a summer and now he wanted to be linked to you forever?"

"Uh...kind of harsh, don't you think?" It was actually a valid question, though. One I hadn't spent a lot of time thinking about when it had happened. I'd been too relieved and grateful to have him step up and save me.

And maybe I'd hoped it would turn into more. Eventually. If I was honest with myself.

Maybe letting Hudson pretend it was his wasn't one of my finer moments.

"I only meant that it was a fast turnaround. He went from not caring about you to caring enough to make a terrible situation better for you. Why would he do that?" Edward had backed down, but his critical gaze continued to drill into me.

Why *would* he do that? "He didn't want me ruining his parents' marriage, that's for sure. Though, honestly, I was not the reason there were problems in their marriage."

"That's a hell of a sacrifice to save a parents' marriage." He leaned forward, his elbows on his thighs, his hands clasped together. "He didn't think it was his? You didn't *tell* him the baby was his?"

"No. I didn't sleep with him, remember?"

"There could have been a part of the story you'd left out." He ignored the way I bristled at the accusation. "Was he in love with you after all?"

I could feel a muscle in my neck tick. "Were you listening last time? He knew sleeping with my friend would hurt me, and he didn't care. He most certainly didn't secretly love me."

"Did you have something over him? Was it blackmail? Did you trick him?"

A cold chill ran down my spine. I hadn't done any of those things, and the accusations had me seeing red.

But they were too close to things I *had* done to other people, and that made me feel guilt along with the rage. But how did he know? How could he possibly know?

I swallowed hard before responding. "I don't know what you're trying to get at, but no to all of that. He felt responsible, I think. Because he *was* responsible, in a way, and maybe I was the asshole because I let him do it, because I thought he owed me, but I didn't trick him into it. It was all his own choice."

We held each other's stare for several breaths. Finally, he sat back into the sofa. "He stepped up. That's admirable, I suppose." There was no trace of apology on his features, but he was calm again. "I can't imagine Hagen ever doing something like that."

"I can't imagine you getting in the position where he'd have to, especially after you assured me that you knocking up a mistress would never happen." I frowned because now I was remembering that conversation, the same one where he'd declared he would sleep with whomever he wanted, when he wanted.

"You're right. It wouldn't. You may continue."

He was so bossy, so arrogant. It infuriated me. I was opening myself up for him and he could still remain so closed off. I was half tempted to stand up and stomp my foot and demand that he share too, that he open up and become vulnerable, that he give me something. Anything.

But I didn't have the power in the room. Throwing a tantrum would gain me nothing. My only play was submission.

"Thank you, Edward," I said, as politely as I could manage. I'd intended to go on after that, but I'd lost the momentum and couldn't figure out where to pick up the thread.

"You decided to keep it then." He was gentler now. Encouraging. "How did you feel about that decision? About bringing a child into the world."

The prompting helped. All I had to do was answer honestly, and I did. "I was excited, actually. For lots of reasons that weren't just about having a baby. I'd struggled with an identity for so long, and this felt like such a *good* identity to have—mother. Respected. Loved. I think it was the time in my life I was truly happiest."

It was *too* honest, too raw of a thing to say, not just to Edward but to myself, so I rushed past it as if it hadn't been said at all. "But I was worried too. I hadn't spent much time dwelling on it when I figured I'd probably end up having an abortion, but now that I was going to keep it, I had to face the fact that I'd partied hard. Drugs. Alcohol. In the earliest times of development. There was a good chance I'd already fucked it up, and I spent the next month fretting over every terrible thing I'd done. I was truthful with my doctor, who wasn't helpful. She just said we'll have to watch and see. I was so anxious all the time, my nails were bitten to stubs."

Edward's shoulders sagged then, ever so slightly, but it was enough to tell me he knew where this was going, and that he found it disappointing. "How far along were you?"

"Eighteen weeks. It happened just before Christmas." I hadn't told anyone this, not anyone. Every person important enough had lived through it, and there'd been no one to talk to about it after. And I hadn't wanted to, until now.

I wasn't even sure I wanted to talk about it now, but the story poured out as thick as the blood had gushed out from between my legs. "It was more blood than I'd ever had during a period. And the cramps were the worst. The absolute worst. Like something was trying to tear its way out of me. They had to give me morphine because I was screaming in the emergency room.

"And then I went into shock. I was so cold. The nurses brought three microwaved blankets to wrap around me, and I couldn't stop shivering. The cramps kept on and on while my body pushed out this thing inside me, this dead thing that I'd centered my identity around. This thing that I'd killed with my irresponsibility." My throat was tight, and I had to pause to swallow. "It hurt, it fucking hurt physically. It was basically labor, and labor has a bad rep for a reason, but the actual pain eclipsed what it should have been. Every part of my body ached. For days. My muscles, my skin. My face. I didn't want to feel. I didn't want to live. I didn't know what there was to live for."

It was there in my hospital room that I'd begged Hudson to teach me how to be like him, how to bury emotions, how to become cool and aloof and heartless like he was.

He must not have felt completely heartless because my pleading had won him over, and he taught me The Game. And from then on, I worked not just to bottle and suppress my feelings but to dissolve them with acidic behavior. I annihilated every pain that dwelled inside me by giving pain to others. It had worked for so long.

And now...

Now I was realizing I'd been wrong. That it had never worked at all. That everything I thought I'd killed still remained, and when it finally came out of slumber inside me, it could very well destroy me. Especially if it wouldn't let its grip on me go, and this one wasn't letting go. I felt a need to cry, this pressing need against my chest. But it stayed there, tight between my ribs, unwilling to move higher. Unwilling to come out, even though I had the distinct feeling that it would feel so much better if it would.

It would feel validating, too. Tears. It would prove that I really felt this big, terrible pain, that I wasn't faking what it was or what this experience had meant to me.

But there was nothing. My eyes were dry. My nose didn't even run. The pain wouldn't budge from its prison. Was this supposed to have made things better? What was I supposed to do with this now?

I looked to Edward, silently begging him to tell me what to do.

He sighed, a sympathetic, compassionate sigh, and stood up. He moved to me, stopping in front of me, his body slightly offset from mine. He reached down and stroked the back of his hand along my cheek, a gentle caress.

"My children are the joy of my life," he said, softly. "To lose them would be to lose everything. You are human in this moment. This pain is human. But it's not something I can replace. The only way over this is through. Just know you'll be someone different when you get to the other side."

Fuck you.

I wanted to scream it at him. How was that helpful? Oh, sorry you feel like your heart wants to rip out of your

*chest, but not really sorry because I'm the one who made
you talk about it in the first place.*

If my eyes were weapons, he would have been dead for
all the daggers I shot in his back as I watched him cross
over to the bar and refill my wine glass.

And what the hell did he mean by "replace"? It seemed
obvious that this was his response, that his response was
to pat me on the head and move on, but if I'd told him a
different sort of story, what had he intended to do to "replace" it?

I was confused and mad and beat up by the time he
returned the glass to my hand. I was also tempted to hurl
it at him.

But then he cocked his head, bringing his tumbler to
his own lips and taking a sip before he asked, "Were you
told it was your fault?"

The question jarred me. I hadn't expected it. "The miscarriage?"

"Yes. Did anyone tell you that you caused it? Could
it have happened anyway? Maybe it was something completely unrelated to your actions. Is that possible?"

The glass dangled from my fingers as I thought about
it. "I didn't tell them at the hospital in New York. Didn't
tell them about the stuff I'd done. My doctor back in California was the one who knew, and I saw her a month later
for follow-up." I tried to remember if she'd ever told me
specifically I'd caused the loss of the baby. Tried to remember if I'd ever asked.

She hadn't.

And I hadn't either.

I'd just assumed. I'd always just assumed.

Edward seemed to understand without me saying it. "That's an awful lot of blame to assume without confirmation. Doesn't seem like you."

I almost snapped back that he didn't know me, but I stopped myself. Because he did know me, better than I wanted him to. Maybe better than I knew myself.

But also, he was right—it wasn't like me to assume something big like that at all. I was too practical for that bullshit. Too intellectual.

So why had I let that be a weight I carried around for so long? Didn't I have enough baggage without it? Didn't it feel better to set that particular piece down?

It was a lot to think about, a lot to process, but as we walked back to the main house in silence, even though the emotions of the evening still pressed heavily against my chest, it did seem like they were a bit lighter than they had been before.

FIFTEEN

The next day carried out very similarly to most of the days when Edward was on the island, but there were some noticeable differences. He still left me to myself, as usual, but instead of disappearing, he hung around. He left the library door open while he worked, and I could hear him tapping away on the computer as I ate my breakfast in the radial dinette. Occasionally he'd record a message for himself, a reminder to *"follow up on the numbers from Turkey"* and another to *"see about purchasing that Jan van Bijlert that went up for auction."*

Later, I caught him looking at me as I returned from a walk to the beach and again as I sat outside by the pool. He met my eyes that time and made no effort to hide that he was indeed spying. Warmth rushed up my neck and into my cheeks. He was distant and aloof, as always, but there was a new weight in his gaze that kept me pinned down, and surprisingly, I liked that feeling. Liked the way it pulled me together and anchored me. I'd needed it and hadn't known it. How had he?

After the session from the night before, I'd woken up

somewhat frazzled. This large thing that had happened in my life, this event that held such enormity, had finally been unpacked, and it was impossible to shove it back inside me again. It didn't fit into the box I'd put it in before. I couldn't completely let go of the blame I'd put on myself for my miscarriage, but I couldn't hold it in the same way either. I could breathe around it now when once upon a time it had suffocated me. And I could feel it breaking up further, slowly dissolving into a new shape as I wrote about it in my diary.

I was changing. I was becoming something new, and it scared me, but it felt good too. Thrilling, almost. Especially when Edward looked out across the patio and regarded me with that intense stare. Part of me couldn't believe he could stay so distant after everything I'd said the night before, but a bigger part of me liked that he did. Was grateful. I needed the space to process the revelations. It was almost as though he could see what was happening inside me, the good and the bad, the breaking apart and the pulling together.

And of course he could see it—he'd orchestrated it. I just couldn't figure out why.

After lunch, Marge showed up unexpectedly to give me a massage.

"It's not our usual day," I said, not actually protesting. Honestly, a massage sounded amazing right about then.

"Mr. Fasbender requested it," she said. "He said you'd had a rough night. Let's see if we can get that worked out of you."

Stunned, I followed her out to the pool house, and when I glanced back toward the library and caught Edward watching us at the window, I smiled.

That evening, everyone came for dinner and stayed to socialize after. The men didn't separate like they sometimes did, instead joining the women in the courtyard. A tense game of poker commenced using poker chips in lieu of actual money. Eliana played savagely, which wasn't at all surprising, though Edward won almost every hand, also not surprising. What was somewhat astonishing was the way Joette cursed and swore like a sailor when she got a bad card. The woman had zero poker face and was the source of many laughs. Even my usually stoic husband spent much of the game with a grin on his face.

There was no session with him. I'd barely spoken to him at all, in fact, and yet he was foremost on my mind as I went to sleep that night. He fascinated and intrigued me, and as much as I still hated him, I also didn't. There was chemistry between us that I couldn't deny, and I wanted him, and it wasn't just Stockholm Syndrome or the common situation of falling for my therapist, though it was definitely those too. But it was more than that. It was that unique feeling of being known in a way that no one else knew me. It was the sense of being cared for, actually *cared for* rather than just groomed. It was the interest of someone in me for something other than my body, someone I hadn't manipulated into giving me his attention.

I'd never had a relationship like that with a man. I'd never had that sort of relationship with anyone. I yearned for it to be real and not just one-sided, but like everything with Edward, I knew there was nothing I could do to influence what happened between us. He would feel what he felt, and if I was ever to be privy to what that was or what went on his head, it would only be when he determined to share it.

Of course, I also couldn't forget that I was his prisoner, that he'd told me he'd kill me if I didn't comply to his whims and fancies. Even though he hadn't done anything particularly terrible to me, hadn't hurt me physically or starved me, he had still taken power over me, and I battled with myself over how to feel about that. Could I ever forgive him? Why should I?

And the biggest question, the one that consumed me, made me toss and turn, made me sigh with longing—did he even want my forgiveness?

That answer alone might change everything between us, if I could just figure it out.

The next few days repeated in the same way—the looks from Edward, the writing in my journal, the massage from Marge, the evening gathering. His stare was always on me, always heated, but there was a dark undercurrent of hesitation that I couldn't understand. At times I'd find him near me, reaching out to brush a hair off my face, then dropping his hand, stepping away. Something was holding him back, and the more he pulled away, the more he drew me in. I had to force my own restraint, knowing I was to take my cues from him.

I hated having to give him that, having to hand over my power so completely.

But maybe I didn't hate it that much. Instead of having to stay ahead of the game, constantly scheming and planning, I got to sit back and relax. There was freedom in his control that I never knew could exist. Never knew I could like. Love, even, maybe?

Maybe.

Monday, I was surprised to find he was still around. I was half afraid to ask, sure he'd leave as soon as I voiced any interest in how long he'd stay. The other half of me tried to embrace the anxiety of not knowing. I meditated on it during yoga, opening myself to his whims, letting his power soothe me instead of rattle me. He'd taken care of me so far, hadn't he? Giving me massages and space and yoga and chess games. He'd tell me when he needed me to know, not a minute sooner.

That night was Joette's birthday. Dinner was moved out to the beach. Tents were set up, and tables brought out. The entire family had joined us, even the children and Azariah, and that might have been an excuse for Edward to act more husbandly, to put on the happily married show, but I'd seen that show before and it was different. He'd stand next to me then, touch me a lot to prove his ownership of me.

This wasn't that at all. He sat away from me all night, rarely getting closer than a foot or two, but always, always, his eyes were on me. Every time I glanced at him, there was his gaze. It was so hot and fierce, I could feel it, even when I wasn't looking in his direction. It made me squirm. Made my thighs tense and my pussy clench. Made my dress feel too hot in the cool night air.

After dinner, champagne was opened and a bonfire was lit. Tom made a Bahamian rum cake that was a family favorite, and Joette wore a paper crown that one of her grandkids had made. Louvens lit fireworks, which dazzled the night sky, but scared Marge's nine-month-old baby, Liam. Erris was too busy with their older son who was delighted by the noise and lights, and Marge had spent the entire evening with the baby, so, somehow, I found him snuggled up in my arms.

It was strange holding a child, and such a young child as that. I'd never been around children. I'd never babysat, never had friends with kids. The closest I'd been to a baby was feeling the tiny feather movements of my own before it had bled out of me.

Now, here I was, days after opening myself up to that loss, and a tiny creature was clutching onto the strap of my dress, trying to snuggle in tighter at each loud boom. He was heavy in my arms, heavier than his twenty pounds should have felt. But the smell of him was sweet and precious, and the brush of his tiny fingers against my skin sent warmth down my limbs.

"See how pretty," I cooed to him, turning my body so he could see the spray of colors in the sky. "It's okay to be scared. Just don't be so scared you miss out on the good stuff."

When Marge came a little while later to retrieve her son, my body missed the weight of him, oppressive as it had been only minutes before. I was empty now. Too empty. And alone.

Except, not alone.

As soon as I turned to scan the crowd, Edward's gaze caught mine. The way he looked at me, I could tell he'd been looking for some time. He held me like that, several feet across the sand, just with his eyes.

He broke the connection first. At my husband's bidding, Mateo had brought out a box of cigars. Nice cigars. The kind people spent real money on. I watched as Edward lit one for the birthday girl then stowed two more in his pocket along with a lighter. Next, he grabbed an unopened bottle of champagne, and he walked over to me.

For the first time all night, he touched me, lacing his fingers through mine.

"My wife and I are going to call it a night," he announced. "Please, everyone, continue celebrating as long as you'd like."

My pulse sped up as he led me toward the house. As emotionally draining as sessions were with him, I was curiously keen to have another. I hoped that was where we were headed.

"Do I need to change?" I asked, eagerly, when he took the path around the house instead of going into it.

"No." Reading my surprise, he added, "Just keeping you on your toes, little bird."

At the cabana, he surprised me again, leading me out to the deck overlooking the ocean rather than having us take our usual seats in the main room. He gestured for me to sit on one of the lounge chairs then turned on the gas firepit before sitting on the chair next to me.

"Want one?" he asked, holding up a cigar.

I hesitated. "I've never had one before. But sure."

He bit off the end, puffed on it until it was lit, and handed it over. "Have you ever smoked a cigarette?" he asked as he watched me delicately put it between my lips.

"No. I've smoked a joint, though."

"You don't need to inhale this. Draw it in like you're sucking a straw. Puff every minute or so."

I did as he instructed, coughing a bit until I got the hang of it. When I realized he'd frozen in place, his own cigar hanging loosely from his lips, I became self-conscious. "What?"

"That's extraordinarily sexy." His voice was deep, vibrating in his chest.

My skin felt hot, everywhere. "That's...surprising."

"Please. I've told you on several occasions how attracted I am to you."

He had. I had memorized every mention. While many men had told me I was beautiful, the few times that Edward had said it seemed to hold greater meaning. He was too honest to not mean it and too rich and spoiled for good-looking women to inspire his notice.

Not that his notice had meant much. "You have said it. But actions speak louder than words."

He chuckled. "Yes, they do. I'd never intended to fuck you at all. Remember?"

My breath shuddered as I inhaled. "I think you've shown an admirable amount of restraint. Not that I'm one who admires it."

He grinned. "I'm sure you haven't. But perhaps you have yet to learn the joy of delayed satisfaction."

"Says the man who has a plethora of women at his fingertips back in London." I couldn't just be happy with the confirmation of his attraction, could I? I had to mention his possible trysts.

"Jealousy only makes you look sexier."

"Whatever, I'm not jealous." I was *insanely* jealous.

"We're supposed to be honest here, Celia." The stern reproval didn't help my withering self-confidence.

"All I'm saying is that it's easier to have restraint with me if you're getting it somewhere else. Perhaps I need to jump Louvens the next time he's working in the house without his shirt on."

"Every man—and woman, for that matter—on this island knows the entire family will be fired and banished from Amelie if they touch you. Just remember what you'll be destroying if you go that route."

Before we'd married, he'd encouraged lovers for me,

said he'd help me find one if need be. That had obviously changed. So I still didn't know if he'd wandered into other beds, but now at least I knew that jealousy looked good on him too.

He stood and disappeared into the house, coming back a moment later with two champagne flutes. In my periphery, I saw his eyes rake over my body once more. Then he shook his head and sat down.

I stretched my legs out in front of me, reveling in the attention. I didn't know how to get back to the sexy banter, though, not without dwelling too much on the information that he refused to give me about his fidelity, so I dropped the subject and let my mind wander elsewhere.

"My grandfather used to smoke cigars," I said, savoring the taste of cedar and nutmeg. "They always make me think of him."

"The grandfather who died when you were six? You were close to him?" He spoke around his own cigar as he wrestled with the cork of the champagne.

I remembered the way he'd dismissed me the last time I'd tried to talk about my grandpa Werner. I could sense now that he expected me to tell him how much I'd loved him and how it had been my first brush with death and how I'd cried for weeks.

But the profound effect his death had had on me wasn't in the way I'd missed him, but in how my life had changed with his passing. And, as much as I was intrigued by this process of breaking down, I wasn't ready to talk about that.

I threw the ball back at him. "I'm sure it's nothing like having your parents die when you were only thirteen."

"I'm sure that's true," he said, offering nothing more.

So much for getting him to share anything.

The cork popped and champagne bubbled out all over the sand, barely missing Edward's sleeve. Looking smug, he filled both glasses, and handed one to me then sank back in his chair, looking out over the ocean as he puffed and sipped.

I relaxed too, following his lead when the ash grew too long at the end of my cigar and knocking it off in the sand. It was nice—the crash of waves on the shore, the nostalgic scent of the cigar. The company.

But after a stretch of silence, I grew antsy. "Should I figure out another woe-is-me story to feed you, Edward?"

He shook his head. "Not this time. Tonight, I'm going to probe one out for myself."

I raised a brow.

"Keeping you on your toes."

"Keeping me on my toes," I repeated, my breath quickening. I wasn't sure if I liked the surprise element of dealing with him. On the other hand, I wasn't sure that the surprises weren't my favorite part. "Just let me know what I'm supposed to do."

"All you have to do is answer my questions. Answer them honestly." He considered momentarily. "What was your first period like?"

"Oh my God!" I couldn't help laughing.

"After everything else between us, that is the last thing I would expect for you to find embarrassing."

"It's not. I don't. But if you're looking for past trauma, that's not where you're going to find it."

He gave a one-shoulder shrug, an uncharacteristically casual gesture for him. "Let me be the judge of that."

"I was fourteen. It started when I was at a friend's

house, and that was the best place it could ever have started because Felina had already had hers and she had an older sister who was much more supportive and helpful about it than my mother would have been. She even taught me how to use a tampon."

A glint appeared in Edward's eyes. "Did she demonstrate?"

"No, you pervert." I took a sip of bubbly and remembered the details of that milestone moment, knowing he'd want more. "I hadn't been looking forward to it, honestly. I was one of the last in my friend group to get it, and it seemed like a bunch of fuss and pain and humiliation."

"Hm." He puffed on his cigar. "I was around for both Camilla and Genevieve's first period. Except for the fact that I had to be involved in the purchasing of necessities, both of them seemed rather ecstatic about it."

My skin tingled with his words. There were very few times he shared with me, and these details, tiny as they may be, left me elated. I wanted more, wanted to know everything about him.

I also knew not to push.

So I gave him more of what got me what he'd given. "Yeah. Most of the girls I knew had been excited, too. I guess…" I'd never really examined why I'd felt the way I had, and as I realized the reasons now, I struggled to articulate it in a way that was honest but didn't give too much away. "I wasn't ready to be a woman, I think. There was a burden that came with that. I'd already gotten a lot of attention over my body from leering older men, and I was caught between despising that and how it made me feel and wanting more of it from the boys I liked. If I'd been given a choice, most days I would have wanted to stay a little girl. Having my period meant the decision was made for me."

Edward's head tilted one way then another as he processed this.

"But it wasn't traumatic or unusual to feel that way, I'm sure. Lots of women struggle with not wanting to grow up and wanting to be an adult at the same time."

"Men, too," he remarked, with an empathetic tone.

I studied his profile. He'd been so young when he'd been orphaned. Then he'd lived for years in foster care before he was old enough to care for his sister. He had to know more about becoming an adult too fast than I could even imagine, and I ached for him without even knowing the story behind his simple words.

A beat passed.

"Your first breakup," he said as the moon came out from behind the clouds. "How did that go? That wasn't Dirk, was it?"

I shook my head. "But Dirk was the first bad one. I had a few boyfriends before but none that were really serious. Each time we either drifted apart amicably or—"

"Or you broke their heart before they could break yours?" There was a hint of accusation, that made my gut drop. Isn't that why I'd played people for so long? So their pain would eclipse mine?

"Something like that," I said, hugging my arms around myself.

"How about when you lost your virginity?"

I almost stopped breathing.

"What exactly does that mean these days?" I asked when I found my voice. "The first time I was penetrated? The first time I sucked a dick? The first time I had an orgasm?" Two of those stories were not ones I was prepared to tell.

His eyes were glued on me, as always, and I was halfway sure he knew exactly what I didn't want him to ask, but then he said, "Let's go with the traditional sense."

"That was fine," I answered, relieved. I hadn't thought about it in a long time, but it hadn't been a big deal when it happened. "Over and done quickly. Nothing to tell Dr. Edward about."

"Uh-uh. That's not adequate. Tell me what happened."

"You're a little horny bugger tonight, aren't you?"

"You wish. Stop stalling. Tell."

A breeze blew a strand of hair across my face. I set my flute down in the sand, making sure it was balanced before I gathered my hair in one hand and pulled it over one shoulder, and angled my body to face him. "It's not a grand tale of erotica, so don't get excited or worry about memorizing it for the spank bank. Okay." I took a deep breath, trying to remember just how it had begun. "I was almost seventeen. It was October. In the fall we spent a lot of weekends at the country club upstate. Dad called it father/daughter time, but, really, he'd play golf, and I'd hang out at the stables. Which was fine. I didn't have much interest in spending time with him anyway. I mean, I was a teenager."

I was twice that age now and still didn't want to spend time with him.

"Anyway, John was a security guard, and when I came back from riding, he'd often be—"

"Pause a second. He *worked* at the club? How old was this John?" Edward had the tone I'd seen him get with his daughter, protective and possessive. It wasn't a tone I'd heard often from my own father.

"He was twenty-seven," I admitted.

"Celia." Edward looked at me sharply. "He was ten years older than you?"

"You're ten years older than me."

"You're thirty-two now, not seventeen. Not almost seventeen. That's rape."

I waved at him dismissively. "It wasn't rape. It was consen—"

He cut me off again. "It doesn't matter if it was consensual. He knew how old you were, I'm guessing. If you weren't yet seventeen and he was an adult—"

It was my turn to cut him off. "Fine, it was illegal. But I was two weeks away from my birthday. It wasn't ideal, and he knew my age, and, yes, that was bad, and I am not at all minimizing the impact of rape on a woman's life, but this did not have that effect on me. He was just a guy, and he'd noticed me, and I wanted to get it over with, and I didn't want it to be stupid and juvenile, so John seemed like a good choice. *Dad*."

Edward was quiet, his jaw clenched.

I waited to see if he was going to say anything more, if I was going to have to defend the situation further.

Then, in the silence, I wondered why I was trying to defend the situation at all. "Maybe it was a big deal. I don't know. The whole thing was just so anticlimactic. Literally. There was a utility shed that he took me to with cement floors. He took his jacket off and laid it on the ground for me. Then he helped me pull down my riding pants and told me to lie down. He unzipped his slacks and put on a condom that he'd had stashed in his wallet. Then he laid down over me and pushed himself in. It didn't really hurt, and I didn't bleed. I'm pretty sure my hymen had been broken a long time before that. It wasn't comfortable, though. I wasn't wet. He didn't kiss me. He held my hands over my head, which, nowadays I think is pretty hot, but with John I felt...restrained. And then..."

I trailed off, trying to remember the details, the slapping of his belt against the cement floor, the smell of his breath, the strain in my thighs as I tried to keep them open with my pants still wrapped around my ankles. "My brain shut down. I think it went on for a while, but I don't remember much after that. Just, eventually, he was done and tying off the condom. Then he was helping me to my feet and making sure my hair wasn't a mess before sending me out to meet my father. It happened a couple of other times, exactly the same way. I'd thought it would get better, and it didn't so after the third time, I found excuses not to go to the club anymore and that was that."

Edward's features had relaxed, but his expression was still grim. "He didn't force you?"

"No." Though, there had been a part of me that had felt like I hadn't had a choice. Not that I could explain that, because I certainly did have a choice. He hadn't bullied me. There had been plenty of chances to walk away.

"Why did you do it?" he asked, voicing the question I hadn't been able to ask myself.

I shrugged.

"Not good enough, little bird."

I puffed on my cigar a few times, thinking. "I wanted to get it over with. I know I said that already, and it's true. All my friends had boyfriends. Everyone was fucking. Everyone wanted to be fucking. I don't know that I was especially eager to, but it felt like my virginity was more of a liability than an advantage, if that makes sense. When a guy found out I hadn't done it yet, that's all they cared about. I was tired of always having to protect that virtue. Also, when the right guy came along—because yes, I still believed in that whole right guy thing back then—I didn't want to be inexperienced.

"But if you're asking why John...that's harder to answer. He was always around, saying things. Dirty things. About how pretty my cum would look on his dick and how much better I'd feel with him between my thighs than a horse. Maybe if that had been the first time I'd heard a man say those kinds of things to me, I would have run off and told someone. Made a complaint. But it wasn't even the third time I'd heard them. Not even the thirtieth. I'd been told for years by so many men in so many ways that my value was in getting men off. And since I'd never been fucked, I guess it felt like I wasn't even living up to that."

My mouth felt dry after all that. I picked up the champagne and finished it off in one swallow, then returned the glass to the ground and stared out at the ocean, the light of the moon reflecting on the ripples. "So it was fine. It wasn't awesome, but it wasn't the worst. Do I wish it had been different? Yes. I was a sort of romantic girl. I wanted the dream scenario. The boy who loved me, a boy I trusted. There'd be rose petals laid out and candles burning and soft piano music playing, and I'd be so turned on that I'd be wet before his dick got anywhere near me, especially because he'd give me three orgasms before his pants ever came down. But things rarely happen like the dream, and I didn't see any way the dream was going to happen for me, especially when..." *When Hudson hadn't looked at me twice in any way that wasn't sisterly.*

I let the thought fade off in the wind.

Edward didn't let it go, however. "Especially when the boy from the other story wasn't showing any interest."

"Yeah. So what was the point in holding out this false hope? It was better just to kill the dream before it got out of hand." I cringed, visibly. "That sounds way more dramatic than it was. Teenage girls have crushes. Unrequited love isn't unique; it's a fact of life."

"It doesn't mean it didn't hurt to live it."

I sighed. "I suppose."

Abruptly, Edward got up and sat down on my lounge chair, straddling it as he faced me. I pulled my knees up to my chest to make room for him, but he pulled my legs out one at a time to rest on his thighs.

"I'm going to need a day or two to respond," he said, taking my cigar and putting it out on the sand next to where he'd disposed of his. "But I'm very happy with you."

"You are? I didn't do anything special."

"Exactly." He ran his hands up my bare legs, letting his fingers drift under the edges of my dress. "You didn't put on a performance. You were honest. You were vulnerable."

There was pride in his voice, and I felt my chest and cheeks get warm with the praise. Or maybe it was the way he was touching me. That was heating me up awfully quickly too.

"What would you like?"

"A present?" I tried to lessen my smile, make it more seductive and less sloppy grin. "Can I fuck you?"

"Try again." His hands were now massaging my thighs, speaking a very different language than his mouth.

"Will *you* fuck *me*?"

He shook his head, but he smiled at my attempt.

"Can I blow you?" Another head shake. "Watch you jerk off?"

"My cock is staying where it is."

A glance down at his crotch said that was going to be awfully uncomfortable for him.

"So what you're saying is this gift can't be sexual?"

"It can be if you choose to have your pussy eaten." He pushed my skirt up, letting me know it was already decided. This would be the present I got, whether I chose it or not.

I was okay with that.

"Ohhhh," I laughed, my panties now flooded. "That was a punishment last time. Now it's a present?"

"I think you've learned to feel differently about it." His lips came down against the panel of cotton covering my damp heat, and I let out a hiss.

"Yes, yes," I said, arching into him. "I feel very differently about it."

I stretched my hands up over my head and abandoned myself to his mouth and his fingers and his tongue, and it wasn't until three orgasms had passed, when I was boneless and seeing stars that I realized, despite knowing how he'd answer, it hadn't even occurred to me to ask for the gift of going home.

SIXTEEN

"Have you ever tried role play?" Edward asked as he led me into the cabana two nights later.

The days between had been lighter than any I'd had since arriving on the island. While he continued to be stoic and aloof, he did it in close proximity. He'd invited me into his library while he worked. He'd dismissed Eliana and played chess with me himself. He accompanied me on my morning run. Heated glances had turned into subtle caresses, brushes of skin, a few stolen kisses that I'd given willingly. His moves still felt calculated, but there was an organic rhythm to the way we danced around each other, a natural ebb and flow that drew us to each other for heightened moments before we'd part and drift away.

Always, the drifting felt initiated by him. There was something he was hiding—*a lot* that he was hiding—and whatever secrets they were, they held him back. More than once, he seemed to start to say one thing then said something else instead. It often felt like a question was ready at the tip of his tongue, waiting for the right moment to be asked.

Was this the question he'd been hesitant to ask?

It didn't seem powerful enough to give him pause, yet, at the same time, the question felt significant.

"I can't say that I have," I answered. But if role play was what he was after, I was down for it. I could be his naughty secretary, his sassy nurse, his frisky maid, his slutty nun.

Damn, role play sounded like a lot of fun, actually.

"Never? Never put on another persona just to see what it felt like? Just to see if you could pull it off?" He walked behind me, his fingers sweeping across my bare shoulders.

I shivered, but not just from his touch. Everytime he said something that sounded like it could be a veiled reference to The Game, I got cold. I was paranoid, I knew that, but Edward was the kind of man who made it easy to be suspicious.

I considered how to answer. I'd devoted myself to being honest with him and that meant not tiptoeing around truths just because I didn't want to deal with the fallout. The Game, though. Talking about that wouldn't be exposing how others had hurt me, but rather how I'd hurt others, and I wasn't ready to let him see that side of me, not when he seemed to be starting to like the me that he had seen.

I decided to circumvent. "Is that a loaded question? You know I tried to play you. So you already have an answer."

He circled around in front of me, his fingers wandering over my collarbone before skirting the top of my bodice. "This was an excellent choice, by the way. Quite appropriate. You're stunning in it, too."

I glanced down at what I was wearing. It was an Oscar de la Renta strapless gown with metallic leafing and lots of tulle. It was pretty and poofy and made me feel younger than I was, like I was dressed up for the prom. The dress had been one that Edward had sent earlier in the year, one of the items I'd scoffed at because where in the hell was I going to wear something as formal as that on this stupid island?

But tonight, when his instruction for clothing had merely been, *"Dress like you want to be seen,"* I'd decided why not?

When I'd stepped out of my room and found him waiting for me in an extremely well-tailored three-piece suit, I knew I'd chosen right.

I put a palm on his chest and tugged at his tie with my other hand. "You don't look so bad yourself, Mr. Fasbender." Maybe precocious schoolgirl was what he'd like. I could do that. Look at him coyly underneath my lashes and ask for help with my grades.

He continued his circle around me, the tie falling from my grip as he rounded my side. His lips kissed along my shoulder and up the side of my neck. "Here's what we're going to play—young sweethearts. We've been together for quite some time, but you've never let me have my way with you, and believe me, I've tried. Tonight, though, you're finally ready."

"To have sex with you?" My words came out breathy.

"To give me your virginity."

My stomach dropped. At the same time, goosebumps scattered down my arms. How was it possible to feel both excitement and dread at the same time? I didn't know, but that's exactly what I felt.

"This is because of what I told you the other night," I said stiffly. "Are you mocking me?"

He chuckled, which only increased my skepticism. He found pleasure in my discomfort. He'd never tried to keep that a secret, and so what else would I expect from him now but to twist and turn the private admissions I'd shared with him, using my words against me as I feared from the very beginning.

But his laugh died quickly, and then he was sucking on my earlobe, sending sharp bolts of lust to my pussy. "Does it feel like I'm mocking you?"

"No."

"How does it feel?" He swept my hair off my other shoulder so he could give the same attention to that side as he had to the first.

"It feels like you're trying to be nice," I admitted. "But it's hard to trust you. Especially when I don't know what your motives are."

Swiftly, he turned me to face him. "Trust is the one element here I can't reproduce. You'll either believe me or you won't when I tell you that my motives aren't diabolical."

"Then why? Why do you want to do this?" I wasn't even sure what *this* was, if it wasn't mocking.

"Because once upon a time, an asshole who was a decade older than you took something precious from you without acknowledging how beautiful and precious it was. You were honest and open about that. You gave me what I asked for and this is how I'm moved to respond—with a reward."

"And my reward is another decade older asshole who recreates the whole thing?"

He lifted my chin up with two fingers and stroked my jaw with his thumb. "Not recreate. Replace."

The muscles in my shoulders relaxed ever so slightly. There was a nice sentiment there, if I believed it. I wanted to believe it.

Could I?

"I don't know if this is going to work if it's only about me. I need to feel like you want this too." My heart tripped in my chest. Of all the vulnerable moments he'd pulled from me, that confession was one of the most raw.

Instead of answering with words, he bent his head down and kissed me. It was slow, at first, his lips moving, not with caution, but with self-control. I sighed into it, opening my mouth for him, and his tongue slipped in, probing tenderly at first then more aggressively. His hand cupped my jaw, angling my face the way he wanted it while his other arm wrapped around my waist and pulled me flush against him where I was met with a very thick, very hard bulge.

"Does it feel like I don't want this?" he asked, pulling back just far enough to speak.

"No. I can't say that it does." I wanted to say more, something that would make me feel less unguarded, something that would help me gain my footing.

But he was kissing me again, more eagerly than before, and the thoughts and doubts disappeared from my mind replaced by the captivating sensations of his teeth and tongue, nipping and licking along my lips, along my jaw, down my décolletage.

I was dizzy and disoriented when he finally pulled away so he could tug me toward the bedroom. After pushing the door open, he stepped aside for me to pass ahead of him. I walked in and gasped.

The bed had been made up with luxurious satin bedding. Plush pillows were piled at the head. About a dozen candles were lit around the room, champagne sat chilling in a metal ice bucket. There were four separate vases with bouquets of roses, and, the best part, red and white petals were scattered across the bed and floor.

Behind me, piano music began playing softly, and when I turned back to Edward I discovered it was coming from his phone. He set it down on a side table and removed his jacket, his eyes never leaving mine.

My breath caught between my ribs. There was gravity in this moment. Romance and affectionate gestures were not his style. Even when someone else had thought of them, he was not the type to carry them out, and seeing him now, witnessing what he'd done for me was both overwhelming and confusing.

I shook my head as he strode toward me, unsure how to process any of it.

When he reached me, his hand once again cradled my face. "Do you want this?"

It was the first time he'd ever made me feel like I had a choice. Four simple words, and for all the ways he'd held me captive, his asking made the entire scene everything that my first time hadn't been. Then, I'd felt trapped. What happened with John had seemed inevitable. Like it was what I was destined for, to lie down and be quiet. To be a good lay.

Now, with Edward, a man who never asked permission, who took what he wanted and gave even less, his offer of a choice was an enormous gift.

And yes. I did want it. More than I could bear.

"I'm going to need you to say it," he prompted when I hesitated too long in answering. "Nothing happens without your consent."

I stepped into him, brushing my lips against his. "Yes, please, Edward. I want this, please."

He devoured me. He worshipped my mouth, his hands raking through my hair, occasionally pulling too hard, the sting of pain making me wetter than I already was. It was a relief to have the rough mixed with the soft, to know that the man I was kissing was still really Edward and not just this persona he'd invented for this game, not just the guy he thought I wanted.

Because that's what I really wanted—him. Only him.

Kissing led to groping, and when I'd managed to wrestle both his tie and his belt from him, he broke away to lead me to the bed. With the flat of his hand at my back, he pushed my torso down to the mattress.

"Stay," he said before dropping to his knees where he took off my shoes, kissing the instep of each foot as he did. Then his hands stroked up my legs, pushing them wider apart as he settled between them under my skirt. My thong was quickly removed, and then his mouth was there, licking my clit.

He teased me with his tongue, spiraling me up with flat brutal passes over my bud, making me pant when he followed with featherlike flicks with just the tip. The first orgasm came quickly, like a gut punch, the full force of it felt on the onset. If I hadn't already been doubled over, the climax would have taken me to that position.

Edward stood and lay his torso on top of mine. I could feel the ridge of his cock pressing against my ass as his breath blew hot at my ear. "I cannot imagine a better taste than your pussy. My favorite flavor."

Heat rose to my cheeks, and my chest tightened, wanting to believe it. Not sure how much of this was an act.

"Do you mean that?" I asked, unable to help myself.

"Only honesty, remember?"

My cheek was still pressed into the mattress, away from him. He couldn't see the doubt on my face as I echoed him. "Only honesty."

Was that really what this was? Honesty? It felt too good to be honest.

His hand worked the zipper of my dress, pulling me to a standing position when it was all the way down so that it would fall to my feet. I'd gone braless, and my muscles tensed with the realization that I was now naked while he was still almost fully clothed. It made me feel off-balanced. Defenseless. Vulnerable.

But that was always the tilt of power between us, whether I was nude or not, and as disarming as it could be, I was beginning to learn that there were benefits too. *Don't be so scared you miss out on the good stuff,* I'd said to baby Liam.

I could have been saying it to myself.

With the next breath, I let the strain release from my body.

"That's it, little bird," Edward said, turning me to face him.

Even his pet name for me made me feel small. Was that really so terrible? To be littler than him? For him to be able to manage me?

As he tossed me swiftly to the bed, I decided maybe it wasn't terrible at all.

He crawled up over me, spreading his body along mine before taking my mouth in his. He tasted like me—his favorite flavor—and another wave of lust rushed between my thighs. Soon, he moved down to suck on a breast, tugging roughly at my nipple until it was a sharp peak.

"These are mine," he said, lifting his head to hover over the neglected breast. "You know that, don't you? These gorgeous tits only belong to me."

"Yes, Edward." He'd told me that specifically as he'd fucked me over his desk, months ago. He'd been in a rage then, but the words were the same. There was something strangely thrilling that his possessiveness remained at his core, no matter what mood he was in.

His fingers moved down to the space between my legs. "And this too. This cunt is mine."

I cried out as he plunged two fingers inside me, demonstrating how much "mine" it was. The second orgasm followed soon after, brought on as much from his claiming words as from his ministrations on my body.

When I came down from that one, I came down impatient. I jerked at the zipper of his pants, wanting access to the big secret he was hiding inside.

"Three orgasms before my pants come down, Celia. I'm trying to do right by you, but you're making it hard. *Very hard.*" He bucked against my hand, his hardness evident.

It took a minute to remember that I'd been the one who'd specified three orgasms when I'd told him my dream virginity-loss scenario.

"That was greedy on my part. Two is more than fine. I need you inside me." The last words came out ragged, too true to be spoken without emotion.

"How about this—you make yourself come again while I'm undressing. Shall we see who can finish first?"

I was no more comfortable playing with myself in front of him than I'd been on our wedding night, but the prospect of seeing him naked was enough to let those inhibitions go. I'd never seen him completely naked. He'd never let me get that close to him before.

God, the thought, the relevance of this one thing, stripping in front of me—I'd come again before he was even halfway done.

"Fuck," he growled when the orgasm ripped through me, my limbs quivering with the ferocity. "You better treat my cock as good as you treat your fingers." There was a warning in his tone, as though he meant to punish me if I didn't come as easily when he was inside me as I had when he was watching.

It was so Edward, so the man I was used to, and seeing him appear, even just the glimpse of him made me deliriously happy.

"I'll treat you better," I said, sitting up as he approached the bed wearing absolutely nothing, his cock jutting out in front of him with pride.

My pussy clenched at the sight of him. He was chiseled and lean, but not too lean. There was a bulk to him, too. His pecs were man pecs with dark hair scattered across them and down his stomach, which was flat, but not concave. His thighs were long and strong.

And his cock…

I hadn't had much of a chance to admire it before. I'd known it was big from the shape of the bulge in his pants and the feel of it inside me. I hadn't known it was also beautiful. Hadn't known there was such a thing as a beautiful cock until there was his, long and fat with a gorgeous smooth head.

I was speechless.

"Do you want to touch me?" He was already touching me, stroking his knuckles along my jaw.

"Yes, Edward." It was a moment of him handing over the reins. Letting me behind the wheel for even the briefest of minutes couldn't be easy for him. I wanted to respect that, so I watched his face as I reached out to grip him, looking for any signs of misgiving.

But then he was in my hand, and I couldn't think about his face because his cock!

"It's so big," I said, mostly to myself. "How the fuck does that fit?"

"You're really good at the virgin routine," he said, his words ending on a moan as I palmed his crown.

"Not a routine. This is honesty. Remember?"

He stared at me for half a beat before he was pushing me back down, kneeling on the bed between my thighs. He lined his head up to my entrance. "I wish I really had been the first person inside you." It was said so low, I wasn't sure I was supposed to hear it. I definitely wasn't supposed to respond, because he thrust inside of me, all the way with one stroke, and I couldn't speak, couldn't think, could only clutch onto his arms and trust I'd come out of this in one piece.

But if I could have spoken, if I'd been able to say the truth right then, I would have told him he *was* the first person inside me, truly inside me. In all the ways that mattered.

It was a good thing, then, that I'd been rendered speechless. Giving away that truth would have been a far more precious gift than my virginity had been.

He wasn't as vicious with his fucking as he'd been in the past, each stroke didn't tear me apart and blind me with sensation like the previous two times, and for that reason, I knew he was still holding back, that he was giving me what he believed was the ideal lover.

Even restrained, he was magic.

He propped my feet up on his shoulders and lifted my hips to meet him as he pumped into me with vigor. When he was sure I was balanced and wouldn't drop my ass to the bed without his support, he stretched one hand up to plump my breast. His blue eyes were eclipsed by his large pupils, and they swept over me, studying every inch of my body, as though memorizing it. Revering it.

I'd never been looked at like that before. There had been plenty of men who'd seemed to worship me, but they'd only honored the idea of me, the brainless, beautiful woman who let them stick their dicks in her hole. When Edward looked at me, he saw everything that went with the pert breasts and flawless skin and narrow waist. He saw the things hidden underneath. And I knew he saw those things because he'd specifically gone looking, needling my secrets out of me in his "break-you-down" sessions.

How could he see me like that, all weak and impotent, and still look at me like I was something to be admired? Still fuck me like I was someone to be enjoyed? How could he ruin me so completely and also be the only person to make me fully whole?

My eyes smarted with tears, and I could feel another orgasm coming, but I wasn't entirely sure that was the source of the weeping. A feeling of desperation gathered inside me like a cyclone as my pussy tightened around him.

"Is this real, Edward?" I needed to know. I needed to know what this was, if it was all an act, if it was everything it seemed to be. If *he* was everything he seemed to be.

His hands rushed back to my hips, holding them in place as he struggled against my impending climax. "Does it feel real, little bird?"

God, yes. For me, yes. It was the realest I'd felt in my entire life.

Stars shot across my vision, blinding me. My body strained and trembled, and then the devastating flood of euphoria spread through my limbs, leaving me slack and exhausted. My legs fell from his shoulders. Edward lowered me to the bed, never disconnecting from me. He stroked into me long and leisurely.

"What do you want, little bird?" he asked, his lips hovering inches above mine. I'd been thoroughly fucked, and he could do whatever he wanted with my limp body, and still he was seeing this fantasy through. Making sure it was everything I needed him to be.

I could easily curl up in a ball and go to sleep, I was so wasted on him. But I wanted to feel him come, and I wanted it to be real for him when he did. I wanted him to let down his walls the way he'd made me let down mine.

What did I want?

"You," I said, not sure he'd understand but unable to articulate it any clearer. "Just you."

He paused for only a moment before he swiftly gathered my wrists together above my head with one hand and pushed my knee up to my shoulder with his other hand, pressing down on my bent leg with his body. In this position, he was so deep inside me, so deep I felt him at the end of me, and still there was the barrier of my leg between our torsos, that last little obstacle he wouldn't allow to be removed.

Without warning, he smacked his hand across my breast, so hard I yelped. Then he began driving into me with brutal blows, pounding without mercy. It hurt and the hurt was wonderful. It was good pain. Pain that made me want to feel more and more. I knew this was him, the real him, fucking me with such cruelty it was hard to believe he was the same man who'd been so reverent only moments before.

But his eyes...his eyes still looked at me the same, and that's what gave him away.

He came inside me, the first time that he ever had, grunting and rutting into me, milking every last drop of his cum before he pulled out and I collapsed in an almost fetal position on my side. He fell behind me, and I could hear his breaths, heavy and fast, evening out as the minutes passed.

I closed my eyes, afraid of what came next. Nothing good, I imagined, since the last two times we'd fucked the aftermath had been shaky at best.

Which was why I jerked when he curled up behind me, wrapping his arm around my waist.

"Were you not expecting cuddling?" The amusement was evident in his tone.

"I never know what to expect with you," I said sincerely.

He nuzzled into my neck and sighed softly. "That's fair," he murmured. He fell quiet, and I wondered if he was going to sleep.

"I was thirteen," he said, his voice startling in the silence.

I didn't move, not sure where he was going with this beginning, but somehow sensing that it was meaningful.

"My parents were both dead, and I was angry and destructive, particularly to myself, but also to those around me. Pilar was my foster sister. She was not a virgin and was seventeen, and before you ask, yes, that's illegal in the UK, but, honestly, she probably left the situation feeling more violated than I did. I'd bullied her into it, though technically it was consensual, and she was good about taking care of herself so she had more than one orgasm. But we went for a long time, and I hadn't come. Couldn't come. It felt good, certainly better than jerking into my own hand, but it wasn't happening, and I really needed it to happen. Being with an actual person, I realized, wasn't the same as doing it on my own. By myself, I'd imagine one of a thousand discomforting situations, and I'd release, no problem. Pilar underneath me, grinning with the delirium of her own orgasms, that wasn't inspiring. It was too easy. I wanted her to be nervous like she had been when I'd come on to her. That's what had been attractive. Her unease.

"So I bent down close to her and whispered in her ear, told her that I had a camera secretly filming us and when I showed it to our foster parents she'd be kicked out. She might even be arrested. None of it was true, but she became quite upset, squirming and struggling to get away. Panic was written all over her face.

"That did it. I came, and it was everything everyone said sex was—amazing and overwhelming and powerful. And from then on I knew who I was, who I am. What kind of a man I am."

A devil. He didn't need to say it for the meaning to be clear. There wasn't any apology about it, no shame. It was just fact.

My stomach felt heavy. His story had been dreadful, but along with that heavy feeling there was something else, a warmth in my chest, growing and spreading through my torso. I was drawn to the devil in him. Edward Fasbender fascinated me and captivated me and it certainly wasn't because he was an angel.

But more important than his confession itself, was that he'd confessed anything at all. He'd shared something with me, something I had a feeling he didn't tell many people. He'd opened up. He'd let me in. After everything he'd done that night, this was the thing that held the most meaning.

I turned toward him, needing to see his face. "Why did you tell me that, Edward?"

He traced his finger along the line of my lip. "You told me something honest. I told you something honest in return."

"Why do you care about my honesty? Why do you want to know all of my secrets? Why does it matter what I have locked up inside of me?" They were the questions that had troubled me for months. His motives. His reasons. It was killing me not knowing, and I doubted he'd tell me now, but if there was any chance at all, I had to ask.

His brows furrowed as though he was confused why I'd even have to ask. "It's the only way to have you," he said.

I held onto those words, let their meaning seep into me well after he'd blown out the candles, pulled the covers up over us, and fallen into the rhythmic breathing of deep sleep. If my vulnerability was all he needed to own me then he owned me, full and clear.

But he'd shared too, he'd been vulnerable as well.

Did that mean he wanted me to have him too?

SEVENTEEN

I woke up in the cabana, and before I even opened my eyes, I knew I was alone. I lay there for a long moment, letting the lingering memories of the night before to fully absorb before I officially woke up and let them go. I'd never had such an incredible sexual experience, one where I'd been pampered and adored, made love to. As it was happening, I'd known it wasn't real. Edward had clearly said we were role-playing, and yet there'd been a sliver of myself that had believed it could be something more.

He was good with his games, that way. He had pried into my head and then twisted what he'd found, made it physical, planted his "replacement" deep in my body and my soul. There were pieces of me that belonged to him now, and the longer it continued, the more of me he'd own, just like he'd said.

The worst part was that I loved it as it occurred.

But after…

Today was after, and I was alone, naked and sore, in a room that smelled of sex and vanilla candles, and I couldn't begin to fathom how I felt beyond confused.

And well-fucked. At least there'd been that.

I finally opened my eyes and stretched, squinting against the sun streaming in through the windows. I turned away to look at the empty bed behind me. The sheets were still tangled from where he must have thrown them off of him. Had he spent the night? I'd gone to sleep in his arms. Whenever he'd left, it had been after that.

I rolled over and buried my nose in his pillow, dawdling in his scent before throwing my legs over the side of the bed. I paused then, my eyes catching on the robe laid out on the armchair. *My* robe. A comfortable yet luxurious piece that Edward had sent earlier in the year. A scan around the room said my clothes and shoes from the previous evening were gone. He—or someone—had been to my closet and brought the robe and a pair of flip-flops to wear instead.

Still confusing, but the disappointment I'd felt at my husband's absence lifted ever so slightly. Whatever he was thinking, wherever he was, he'd at least had a passing thought about me, even if it was just to tell Tom to bring the items for me.

God, I was hopeless. Clinging to the scraps given by a man who'd imprisoned me. Making me feel a sense of romance about him. Making me want more.

I'd said it before, I'd say it again—he was good.

The layout of the clothes, besides being a thoughtful and practical touch, also seemed to be an order of sorts. *Put these on, come find me.* The unspoken command was clear in the appearance of flip-flops instead of slippers. The shoes were meant for walking. For that matter, if he'd wanted me to stay put, he'd probably have taken everything and left me naked.

Or maybe I was reading too much into it.

But this was Edward—was there anything he did or said that wasn't calculated and precise?

A stubborn bit of me wanted to rebel. Maybe walk to the main house naked, or not return at all until he came looking for me, but I forced myself to behave. I was adjusting to the man who kept me, learning to acquiesce to his demands. Bowing down to someone else's authority, though, had always been tough for me, and the tendency to force against it came naturally. In some ways, that made the giving into it all the more freeing.

I let that feeling of unconstraint envelop me as I wrapped the robe around my body, momentarily letting go of my worries and fears. I was confused and didn't know what today would bring, but I'd had a wonderful, memorable night, and Edward had thought of me, and wasn't that worth holding onto for a little longer? As unreal as all of it had been to him, it sat real in me, and for now, that felt good. So fantastically good, that by the time I arrived at the main house, I had a smile and a hum on my lips.

"Someone had a good night's sleep."

I stopped, stunned out of my daze by Edward's uncharacteristically charming timbre. My heart beat a little faster at the sight of him, fully dressed and sitting at the small dining area, two settings placed, as though he'd been waiting for me.

"I did, actually. Slept very well. And you?" I felt my breath still as I waited for his response. Whatever he said next would set the tone of whatever followed, and I was eager to know what that tone would be.

He considered quickly, his expression telling me his answer surprised him before his words did. "Despite being unused to sharing my bed space, yes, I did sleep quite well."

So he had spent the night!

My smile grew as I pulled my robe tighter, suddenly bashful. "Good to hear, Edward."

His eyes glinted at my use of his name, and when I started over to the chair opposite him, he shook his head. "Come here." He scooted out from the table, making space for me to sit on his lap.

Years ago, there was a moment, when Hudson's lips met mine, when it seemed like this man I'd been wanting and wishing for so long had finally opened the door for us to be more than what we were. That moment had felt like blossoming. Like being a flower left in the dark for so long that it had stopped believing in the sun, and then, when the rays fell from the sky and nature awoke, that flower opened up and became the beautiful thing it had always meant to be.

I'd felt like that, blissful and fervent and exuberant in my skin until Hudson revealed I'd just been his test subject, and I never let myself blossom like that for anyone again.

Until now.

Now was like that moment, and as I sat on Edward's lap and he wrapped his arms around me, I lifted my petals toward the man I'd married and woke up. The world became vibrant. The colors of the greenery out the window, the blue of the ocean meeting the horizon in the distance, the aroma of roasted coffee, and the warm wall of man at my back—my senses were flooded with an effervescence that had gone unnoticed. Was this what normal people experienced all the time? Was this what it felt like to be alive?

He nuzzled into my shoulder, sending a zing of pleasure through my limbs. "You've been such a good little bird, sharing everything I've asked from you."

The praise brought on a sort of orgasm, my entire being lighting up with euphoria.

His mouth moved up to suck on my neck. "We have a trust between us now, don't we? You've learned the reward of confessing your secrets, haven't you?"

"Mm hm."

His lips continued up to nibble on my earlobe. I could feel the pleasure sting of his teeth rumble between my legs, and I was suddenly very aware of how naked I was below my robe. "Now," he said, his breath hot on my skin. "Tell me about The Game."

Darkness fell like a veil over my vision, a darkness thick enough to permeate all my senses. I clawed my fingernails through the cotton material until I felt them dig into my thighs, bracing myself. Holding myself together.

Then I took a breath, and the haze began to clear.

I was overreacting, like I always did when I heard the term. He hadn't actually made the capital T and the capital G. I was sensitive to the phrase and tended to hear what I feared most.

"What game?" I asked when I had my voice, certain he meant my latest chess match with Eliana or some other benign activity.

But he brought his hand up to grip my chin, hard, holding it in place. "Don't do that," he fumed at my ear. "Don't pretend you don't know what I'm talking about."

The hair on the back of my neck stood up, straightening my spine. Embracing the lie was the best way to pass it off, a lesson I'd learned quite well, though for half a second, the tiniest fraction of time, I considered laying everything out and giving this to Edward too.

Then the second passed. "That would be easier if I actually did know what you were talking about. And I don't."

"You don't." It sounded less like a question and more like an incredulous clarification of my last words.

Still, I answered it. "No, I most definitely do not." Then I held still, my breaths shallow as I waited out his skepticism.

He dropped his hand from my face. "Your determination is almost admirable. I'd be impressed if you weren't such a bold-faced liar. And there's nothing I hate more than a liar."

My stomach plummeted. A minute ago, I'd been glowing in his praise, and now I wanted to crawl under the dining table where I could hide under the long tablecloth.

At the same time, my feathers were ruffled. Being called out irked me, even when it was deserved, because he couldn't *know*. It was impossible. He would have confronted me with it long before, and while he'd acted somewhat guarded around me on this visit to the island, what could have happened while he was gone that would fill him in on the truth?

Nothing. There was nothing.

He couldn't know. He *didn't* know, and I wouldn't stand to be accused. I started to get up so I could face him with my indignation, but his arm around my waist tightened, holding me to him.

"Shall we go about this a different way then?" his voice was controlled and confident. "Who's *A*?"

And then my stomach dropped again, hitting the floor this time. Dropping lower still. That simple question proved he *did* know, as well as told me exactly *how* he knew.

"You read my journals." It was the only place I'd referred to Hudson as A, afraid someone would find them accidentally and discover who they were about. There was nothing to protect me, though, when they'd been found in my own possession.

Fuck, if he'd read those...he knew everything. Every terrible thing.

"I read some notebooks, yes," he confirmed. "Filled with some very interesting things, I might add."

And this was what had bothered him over the last few days. He'd been waiting to bring this up, looking for the best moment to destroy me with the information.

"Things that weren't for you to see." I cursed silently. Then I cursed out loud. "How the fuck did you even get them?" I'd left them in the closet of my condo back home, boxed up so no one would find them.

"I had my wife's belongings sent from her residence in New York to the one we share in London." His breath at my neck had been arousing before. Now it felt menacing, as he surely meant it to.

"Oh, fuck you. The house we share in London?" The house I'd never lived in with him as husband and wife. The house he didn't seem to ever intend to bring me back to. "Fuck you."

I pushed my elbow back into his torso, hoping to throw him long enough to loosen his clutch on me, but my jab didn't even make him wince, and he moved his hands to hold me at my forearms.

"You're welcome," he said with no hint of exertion despite wrestling with me. "It was rather thoughtful on my part. When I was unpacking your items, I came across a box full of notebooks. I had to see what they were to decide where they should be kept."

"Sure, sure. That was why. Not because you're a nosy asshole who doesn't know how to mind his own business."

He brought his face forward so his cheek was next to mine. "You are my business, Celia. Don't ever doubt that."

His words and inflection were so chilling, yet, also, somehow inviting. There was a part of me that wanted to tell him. Wanted to finally confess everything and maybe, *maybe* then I could begin to pay penance.

But I didn't know how to say it. Didn't know where to start, even when he'd given me the opening.

I shook my head, denying him once again. "They were fiction. Stories I made up. That's all. No one was ever meant to see them."

"They weren't fiction. They were real."

"Bullshit. You're guessing. And you're guessing wrong."

"I can tell when you're lying and these were honest. I don't have to ask how long you've been doing this manipulation of innocent people—the dates were clearly written, which I found particularly helpful." He barely hesitated, but when he spoke again, his words were raw. "Was that what I was to you? Another game?"

My eyes pricked. It was the first hint he'd ever given that he might have some sort of feeling for me, and it was revealed in an accusation of betrayal.

This couldn't be happening like this. There was no way

this could be how last night ended up.

"You already know what you were." A tear fell down my cheek. I didn't try to wipe it away.

"No." The word was sharp and enraged. "I had a perception of the situation based on your deceit being a singular incident. These journals note that I was only one of a long list of lies."

I craned my neck, turning toward him as much as I was able. "Is that what bothers you, Edward? That you weren't unique?"

The eyes that met mine were hard and mean. "There is a hell of a lot that bothers me, and that's not anywhere near the top. If you start explaining your gross form of amusement, perhaps I can point out my grievances as you go."

I ground my teeth. He'd already judged me. Of course he had, and why shouldn't he? I would have told him eventually, probably. Possibly. If things had continued the way they were. But not like this. I didn't want him to know like this.

I looked forward again, unable to stare at those vacant eyes another second. "Is this a session? I'm supposed to tell you things freely in my own time. This is coercion."

"You get to tell me your vulnerabilities when you're ready. What I read aren't accounts of your vulnerability—they are accounts of your cruelty."

Every pore in my body oozed of shame. And that's why he was wrong. This was the *most* vulnerable thing about me. It was the worst part of me, the worst things I'd done, the actions that no one would ever forgive. The reason I would never be loved.

How could I not be more exposed than that?

With a sudden surge of adrenaline, I yanked myself out of his grasp and stumbled to my feet.

Throwing my shoulders back, I threw him a bitter, forsaken scowl, and started to my room.

He was on his feet in a heartbeat. "Don't you dare walk away from me. We are discussing this now."

I swung back around. "This isn't yours to have! We never bargained for this."

"Clearly you weren't paying attention because my bargain demanded everything."

He'd told me he would break me down and that I would be his, and, if for a second I thought that hadn't meant giving him everything, I couldn't doubt it now.

But what was it all for? Give him everything so he could hate me? I already hated myself enough for both of us.

"Who's A?" He was relentless.

I shook my head. "It doesn't matter."

"He sure seems to matter, considering how long the two of you played this game of yours. Did he know about this one? Is he waiting in the wings for an update?"

Oh, the irony of that accusation. Hudson had been the one to leave The Game—The Game that *he'd taught me*—and found the incredibly impossible person who could love him despite everything he'd done. Then, in a fit of envy and disgust and loneliness, I'd obliterated any future for our friendship by playing a scheme on him.

And what exactly was it that Edward was doing with me?

I pointed an angry finger at him. "What about *your* games? This shit you do to my head. The way you pretend you care and that these sessions mean something to you and then pull the rug out from me when I react to that. What about those fucking games?"

"This is not the same."

He began to slowly circle around me, and I moved with him, keeping him in front of me. "Right, right, because you're above scrutiny."

Abruptly, I was caged against the table, his arms on either side of me. "This isn't a game between us." His mouth was so close I could kiss him with only a tilt of my chin.

My heart pounded so loud, I could hear it in my ears. "Are you certain about that? It sure feels like a game, and, believe me, I ought to know."

His eye twitched as it glanced quickly at my lips then back again. "Tell me, or I'm leaving."

He thought I was cruel? That threat was the cruelest of them all.

It was tempting. I wanted my freedom so badly that at times I was tempted to do anything to get it.

But the truth was, my telling him what he wanted to know wouldn't change anything. He might even leave faster if I did. "You're leaving anyway. Eventually."

His lips pressed together in a tight line. A beat passed, and I could hear the gears whirring in his head, deciding his next move.

Finally, he stepped away. "You're right."

He turned around calling Tom out of the kitchen where she likely heard much of our argument, but showed no sign of it when she appeared. "Tell Lou to arrange my flight out today," he told her, then, without giving me another glance, he strode toward his office.

With the decision made and announced, I felt the sharp sense of loss. What if he never came back? What if we never got past this? What if he never tried to have me again?

I tripped after him. "This wasn't a session. You said so yourself. You can't hold this against me."

"Can't I?" He didn't turn around.

"No. You put out the rules, and I followed them. It's not fair for you to change them on me just because you don't like something you found out. You have to still play." *Please, please still play. Please come back for me.*

He spun around then, so quickly, I nearly collided with him. "There is no fairness here, Celia. You still think this is a game? That one of us is going to lose and one of us is going to win? That's not how this will go. I will win. I will win, no matter what you do or say or don't say. The only thing yet to be determined is how badly you lose."

A chill ran down my spine, and this time when he stalked away, I didn't follow.

EIGHTEEN

"What's all the activity about?" I asked Tom as I came back from my weekly massage in the pool house. Usually it was just her and Joette in the main house on a Thursday, unless Eliana was over to play chess or Lou was there to do some repairs.

Peter and Sanyjah usually only cleaned on Monday, Wednesday, and Friday, but here they were, bustling around with the vacuum and duster, and Erris and Marge were trimming the bushes in the back, something they typically only did in the mornings when it was cooler.

Joette stepped out of the kitchen at the sound of my voice, and Tom turned her eyes toward her, questioning.

All the walking on eggshells made the answer clear before Joette said anything. "Edward arrives today. I wanted to tell you, but…"

She trailed off, so I finished for her. "But you aren't supposed to give me a heads-up on these things, are you?"

Her smile was apologetic. "His plane is landing shortly. Mateo just left to pick him up at the airstrip."

That was more warning than I'd gotten any other time, and, for that, I tried to be grateful. It wasn't Joette's fault I was married to an asshole. No, that blame lay solely on me.

"Thank you for telling me." I forced the words out, hoping that she'd try to share more in the future if I were appreciative. Then I took off for my bedroom to change into something less grungy.

After tearing off my shorts and tank, I hesitated at my closet door, deciding I needed a quick shower since I was covered in massage oil and sweat from my earlier workout. Once that was taken care of, I put on a simple sundress, threw my hair in a bun, and applied a swift coat of lipgloss.

"He doesn't deserve this," I told my reflection. Because he didn't. After the way he'd left last time, he didn't deserve my dressing up for him at all. Especially when he'd stayed gone for three months. Three goddamn months. He'd sent gifts as he had before, nothing personalized, things that helped keep my mind occupied, the biggest being permission to redecorate the upstairs rooms and remodel the pool house, a task I'd undertaken with gusto. I loved the work. It was invigorating to have something to do, something I was passionate about.

But no matter how much I enjoyed it or how much mental energy it required, it hadn't taken my thoughts off Edward entirely. He'd left, and I was pissed. He'd told me I couldn't walk away, and then he had. He'd told me if I opened up to him he'd come back sooner, and then he stayed away three fucking months.

I'd been so angered by his absence, I'd mentally given him ninety days. If he wasn't back by August fourteenth, I'd told myself, I was done. I was going to get myself off the island, whatever it took, even if it meant taking a rowboat out on the ocean alone.

But here he was on August thirteenth, as though he could read into my mind, and I was both relieved and devastated.

More relieved than devastated, if I were being honest.

And because he'd shown up within the time frame, I planned to be exactly that—honest. With myself, and also with him. I'd had plenty of time to think about what I wanted to say to him, what our next session would entail, and by God, he was going to hear it, whether he wanted to or not.

Now *that*, he deserved.

I made it to the front of the house where Joette and Tom had gathered to greet Edward just as Mateo pulled the jeep into the driveway. My pulse picked up, and I suddenly wished I'd had more time to do makeup, that I'd picked something less plain to wear. Despite his unworthiness, I had a sick desire to please my husband.

Even more base than that, I wanted him to notice me, which felt ridiculous under the circumstances.

Still, standing with the two other women who'd become my family over the better part of a year, I suddenly felt like I was the stranger. It wasn't an unreasonable feeling considering his close relationship with Joette's family, but it was hard to grapple with all the same.

Mateo had parked with the passenger side toward us, so it was Edward's long, lean body and devilishly handsome face that I saw first. My breath caught—every time, he stole it from me. It was impossible to get used to how attractive he was, even dressed down in a polo shirt and white jeans. His hair was longer than when I'd last seen him, and a bit unruly from traveling. He still wore the facial hair I'd suggested he grow, and my fingers itched to touch it. His blue eyes were hidden behind his sunglasses, but I could feel them sharp and focused as he scanned his welcome committee. As they landed on me.

Just as quickly, they were gone, and he was opening the door behind his, reaching in. From around the back of the vehicle, a figure appeared. A brunette woman also in sunglasses wearing linen pants, a large brim hat, and a long-sleeved sweater over her camisole.

My body felt immensely heavy, like it was being pulled into the earth, and my ribs felt tight like they were being crushed.

He'd brought a woman. A gorgeous, sophisticated woman to the island where he kept his captive wife.

If I weren't so heartbroken, I'd be seeing red.

But then Edward pulled something out of the back seat—some*one*—and I realized I hadn't looked closely enough at the woman. It was his sister, Camilla, and the small boy he'd lifted into his arms was his nephew.

Damn, he looked good holding a child.

I'd seen him before with the kids on the island, seen him tease them and sneak them cookies behind Joette's back, but this was different. He'd pushed up his aviators, and I could see the pure devotion in his expression as he looked at Freddie. It was knee-weakening. Panty-melting. Ovary-exploding. Men didn't look at kids like that, not generally, and seeing it from Edward was especially astonishing. And poignant. And overwhelming.

It didn't help that the little boy resembled his uncle so entirely with the dark hair and deep-set blue eyes. I could imagine it then, what he must have been like as a father when his children were young. What he'd be like with a baby. What it would be like to have a baby with him. The power of those images was so startling and compelling, I almost forgot I hated him because of how badly I wanted to love him.

They started toward us, Camilla smiling at Joette and Tom, which threw me momentarily. They were *my* people, not *hers*, but of course she'd known them first. The master upstairs was clearly the one she stayed in when she visited, a crib and play area set up in the adjoining suite. I'd just never thought about her actually being in the space that I'd come to think of as mine.

I slunk back in the shadows as she removed her sunglasses and greeted the women, watching as they embraced and gave cheek kisses before they moved past her to help Mateo with their bags.

Which was when she finally laid eyes on me.

Her brows rose, clearly startled by my presence, and for half a beat I wondered if she hadn't known I was there. What on earth had Edward told his sister about me? Surely not the truth.

She turned to face her brother as he strode up next to her. "She's staying in the *main* house? Are you kidding me?"

Somehow I'd forgotten she disliked me.

"Where else would I stay? I'm his wife." She'd had plenty of time to get used to the idea. I had zero patience for her ire.

"You're a *Werner,*" she said with such disgust I could feel how sour the name felt in her mouth. "Anything else you are bears no meaning next to that."

So maybe disliked hadn't been a harsh enough word. She detested me. Because of the rivalry my father had with her brother? It was beyond ridiculous.

I shot a look at my husband who hadn't spared me more than the first initial sweep of a glance. He didn't return my look now either, remaining focused on his sister. "She'll stay out of the way," he promised, as though he had any power over that.

My lips flattened into a thin line, my hands curling at fists at my side. Every rage he'd inspired in me over the last year was newly ignited. He'd put me on this goddamn island. It was mine now. He'd forced it on me. Like hell was I changing my routines for his sister who had the freedom to come and go as she pleased. Like hell was I going to be swept under the rug.

But I wasn't going to throw a fit in front of a two-year-old. Three-year-old now, likely, though I hadn't been aware of his birthdate.

Keeping my teeth gritted, I stalked several feet behind them. I continued to hang back as more greetings were exchanged. The staff was just as warm and casual with Camilla as they had always been with Edward, sharing private jokes and knowing what to inquire about back home. Apparently the "August holiday" was an annual event, which meant everyone had known their arrival was on the schedule for some time. Everyone but me, that was.

I shoved every pang of irritation and jealousy into the pocket of anger I intended for Edward. Not that I needed any more fuel than I already had.

Eventually, Freddie became restless and Camilla announced that she was taking him upstairs so they could both have a "bit of a nap." With her disappearance, the staff scattered, and Edward headed, as typical, to the library.

I was right on his heels.

"When I said you'd stay out of the way," he said callously, "I had meant you'd stay out of my way as well."

They were the first words he'd said to me, the first real acknowledgment he'd given to my presence, and I was fuming. So much so that I was momentarily speechless.

"Go on then. What is it you need? Don't be all day about it." He leaned against his desk and gave me a bored stare.

I took a beat to steady myself before responding. "I was going to ask you why your sister hated me so much, but now I think the better question is why do you?"

"I am not in the mood for one of your tantrums, Celia."

"Well, that's too bad, because I'm throwing a big one. Unless you want to be a decent person and sit down and have a civilized conversation, in which case I am perfectly willing to calm down and do so."

"Please. As if a civilized conversation would get us anywhere. We both know that nothing that comes out of your mouth is to be trusted."

There it was. The reason he'd been so angry with me before. I'd wondered many times over the summer what exactly had infuriated him so much about the games I'd played in the past. They hadn't affected him, and he certainly hadn't shown himself to be some moral pillar that couldn't stand unscrupulous behavior, but now, with these words, I understood. Part of it, anyway. All the time he'd spent "breaking me down" had also been about earning his trust, and when he'd realized how easily I lied, he'd doubted his tactics.

Another me, a before-Edward me, would have considered that the very definition of victory.

But I wasn't that me anymore. Whenever it had changed, I wasn't sure. Incrementally, most likely, bit by bit as I'd lived on Amelie and formed real relationships. Most of it, though, because Edward had forced me to knock down walls, not only did he see what was behind them, but so had I, and what I'd found had altered me so much that I couldn't be who I'd been before. I honestly believed that.

Now, the only victory I could imagine would be one where Edward believed that about me too.

There was only one way to fix it. "You know what? You're stuck on what I didn't give you last time so let's just get past that." I stomped over to his wet bar and poured cognac into a tumbler then brought it back, shoving it into his hand before sitting in the chair facing him.

"What are you doing?" His tone was more annoyed than curious.

"We're having a session. I meant for this to all be said later, but if this is the only way you'll hear me, then this is where it will have to be said, so sit your ass down and listen."

"Sessions aren't on the agenda for this visit. Go and—"

I popped to my feet with fury, cutting him off before he told me what I could "go and" do. "No, no. You don't get to say that. You do not get to cut me off from this arrangement." My anger crescendoed, and I pointed an accusing finger at him. "You said that if I played well you'd come back sooner. I played well, and you stayed away. You say you want honesty? Then be honest with your negotiations. Sit down and give me what I deserve, Edward."

His expression guarded, he straightened. His eyes were on me, and behind them I could see him considering. Deciding. After several heavy seconds, he crossed around his desk and took the seat I'd demanded he take.

I managed to sit back down too, though I felt a bit like I was floating.

He swirled his drink and threw back a swallow. Then clapped the glass down on the desk. "Whenever you're ready." He was taking charge.

Or he wanted me to believe he was in charge. But now I knew one of his secrets—that my confessions made him vulnerable too, and that gave me power. A lot of power.

It wasn't power I intended to wield lightly.

"I played games," I began, prepared for this. "I've played them for almost fourteen years. I began playing them when I was in a dark place, right after my miscarriage—you know who I was then. I needed an outlet. I needed something else to occupy my mind, something that wasn't centered on my pain, and someone I knew stepped up and gave me a tool."

I paused only long enough to be sure I had his attention. The slight tensing of his jaw said I did.

"They were never just games, but I told myself they were. It was easier to justify the entertainment value, I think, when I called them that. And, they were games, in a way. They required strategy and foresight. I don't need to tell you what kinds of situations we set up—you read the journals. You know they involved manipulating other people's emotions. That they were centered around guessing how people would behave when they were forced into crisis situations. We got good at predicting. I got very good, and when the other guy decided to abandon the games, I kept at it. Because it was the only thing I had, okay? There wasn't anything else in my life but this."

I closed my eyes, forcing myself back from the path of

justification. That wasn't what I wanted this to be. I was not the victim here, and I wanted to own that. For myself, as much as for Edward.

I really should have poured a drink for myself as well.

Or maybe it was appropriate to face this completely sober.

Taking a deep breath, I opened my eyes. "The things we did were terrible, I admit that. I've never not known they were cruel and devastating. That was the appeal. In no way is this an attempt to validate, but I want you to know my reasons, which, to be honest, I'm still trying to figure out myself. I was so consumed with not feeling all the things that I was feeling—I didn't want to feel anything at all—and I realized that other people's pain was quite distracting from that.

"Having learned that, what I should have done, was volunteer for a homeless shelter or a soup kitchen or a crises center, but, I don't know." This was the newest discovery I'd made, the part I was still sorting through. "I was immature, maybe. Self-centered, definitely. My family has always been involved with charity organizations, but the motivation was always about status, not actual giving, and the idea of helping other people was not one that came naturally, and, also, I didn't want to think for myself. I couldn't, at the time. I needed someone to hold out a hand and invite me in, and the only hand I saw to grab pulled me in this direction, and *it worked*. Little by little, I stopped feeling. I went numb, and the only emotions that existed were outside of me, in these people's lives I destroyed. It was quite habit-forming—watching the world blow up outside of me instead of inside. Maybe that's why so many angry people are drawn to destruction, because the ruin of others minimizes the ruin going on in your body. It's a distraction.

"Perhaps that's why people bully too." I gave him a hard stare, in case that resonated. "You want to destroy me. That's what you've said, not in those words, but similar, and I can't begin to know your motives since you've never shared them with me. All I can do is compare it to what I know from my own life, and I can't help but wonder if your reasons aren't the same as mine."

He started to open his mouth, but I put my hand up to stop him. "I don't want to talk about that right now. This is about me. This is about my truth, not yours. You were a game too. You know that you were, and yes, you were at the end of a long list, and maybe that offends you to not be a singular incident, but if you were hoping to be unique, then you got your wish, because you are the only person who has ever given me a reason not to play anymore. The only person who has made me feel my own feelings without wanting to demolish everything and everyone around me.

"You want to know why I didn't want to tell you about the games? Because I actually care what you think of me, for some insane reason. I care that you know that I've done terrible things and that I'm a shitstain on the foot of human existence, because you are the first person who has truly looked at me in a lifetime and made me feel like I wasn't those awful things, and I knew that telling you about this would take all that away. You want vulnerability? You want honesty? This is me being honest. This is me being completely exposed.

"And here's where this is also about you." I sat forward, needing him to listen particularly close to what I said next. "This is about you because you made this happen. You reached out your hand and said 'break down for me,' and I grabbed it, because maybe I need someone to lead me more than I like to admit, or maybe just because I was so fucking tired of being alone. Or maybe because you didn't leave me a choice, but here's the thing. I *do* have a choice. I could lie to you and feed you whatever bullshit you wanted to hear, or I could clam up and say nothing no matter what you did to me, but *I'm here for this*. I am all in. I committed to your fucked-up offer, and I know I have no rights as far as you're concerned and that there is no such thing as fairness, but if you don't show up and commit to this as well, then you might as well just kill me like you planned in the first place. You say I'm going to lose, then let me lose. Give me that chance to lose everything. You might even realize I already have. Because I have nothing except what you give me. If you're going to give me nothing more, then I might as well already be dead."

He was silent, his gaze unwavering, his face hard. He'd never let me say so much without interrupting with questions, possibly because he wasn't actually giving what I said a chance, but he'd heard it. I knew he'd heard it. He'd sat and listened and now the next move was on him.

I'd learned a thing or two from him about processing time, though, and I didn't want his response to be rash. I stood. "I'm asking Tom to help me move my things to the cabana for the week. I'll take all my meals there. I will stay out of your way. I am not moving out for your sister, though you're welcome to tell her that's the reason. God knows you'll tell her what you want to anyway. But between you and me, let's just be clear that the reason I'm moving out is one hundred percent because of you.

"When you're ready—if you're ever ready—you know exactly where you can find me, Edward." I turned and walked away then, without looking back, with all my cards laid out on the table. I should have felt powerless, but for the first time since I'd met him, I believed I held the upper hand.

NINETEEN
Edward

*S*he wasn't supposed to be like this.

The thought repeated in my head over and over as my eyes followed the line of the beach, wishing I could see past the outcrop that met the rock wall above and hid the cove where the cabana was neatly tucked away.

As my wife had promised, after sufficiently chiding me, she'd stayed out of the way. Thirteen days had passed, and I'd only caught glimpses of her from a distance. When she emerged to attend yoga or walk around the island, she'd avoided the main house. Tom and Peter brought her all her meals, remaining with her in the evenings when everyone else gathered for dinner. She was being looked after, even without my directive. Which was as it should be.

And I missed her.

How the fuck was it possible to miss her? To have gotten close enough to her to regret her absence? It hardly seemed feasible.

The plan had been simple enough. I had never expect-ed it to be easy to execute, but it had been straightforward. There was a clear path to those shares, and while that route required hideous action, I knew I was a man worthy of the task. I'd proven it before, hadn't I?

That plan had assumed Celia was either a shallow rich girl princess or a knock-off of her malevolent father. Both versions of character had their challenges. I'd mapped out all the possibilities, drew up contingencies. I'd been pre-pared to handle whichever woman it was that I met the day I'd asked for the meeting. Initially, she'd seemed like a mash-up of both.

She had been neither of those things in the end.

Yes, she was calculating and manipulative, more so than I'd even guessed until reading those journals, and she was very spoiled about getting her way, but that was all surface. She was an onion. There were layers and lay-ers underneath, parts of her that she held away. Parts she showed no one. For whatever reason, I'd caught sight of what she kept hidden, whether she'd meant for that to hap-pen or not, I couldn't be sure. Regardless, I was captivated. There was so much to see there, so much to take down. So much of her to know and own and destroy and redesign, and like an old habit, I couldn't break away.

She was an addiction, and I wanted to feed on it. She wasn't supposed to be like that.

She wasn't supposed to want to bend to my whims. She wasn't supposed to open up and give what I asked for. She wasn't supposed to be so eager to take what I gave her. She certainly wasn't supposed to see past my own curtain, wasn't supposed to ask to see more.

I'm here for this, she'd said.

And for thirteen days, all I could think about was how much I wanted to be *here for this* too.

So why was she still there, and I, standing here, hoping for impossible glimpses of her in the distance?

"I have to admit, I like this. Love it, actually." Camilla's voice behind me pulled my focus from the woman hidden in the horizon to closer surroundings. "This was all *her*?"

My sister was referring to the newly remodeled deck on top of the pool house. It had been nonexistent on my previous trip to Amelie. Now it was the highlight of the building. Celia had kept the design minimal with only a four-piece furniture set and a granite fire table, but the stone tile flooring and the ability to see so far along the coast made it a spectacular addition. It was a compliment I knew I should deliver myself.

I also knew I wouldn't.

"It was," I confirmed, wondering if my tone sounded with the pride I unexpectedly felt.

"Hm." The reverberation came out tight behind pursed lips. She wrapped her arms around herself, despite the unusual heat. The long-sleeved shirt had to be a burden on days such as this, but Camilla was more tied to her secrets than to comfort.

I loathed what she hid underneath. I despised how her secrets had come about. I wanted to protect and avenge her more than I wanted to exist.

Or I *had* wanted that. I'd wanted it for so long, I didn't know what it felt like to want something different. And I still *did* want it.

Only, I wasn't sure it was all I wanted anymore.

I turned so my entire body was facing her, annoyance

at my inability to stay the course bleeding into my words. "If you love it so much, why have that tone?"

"Because you let her do it in the first place. And I can't begin to understand why." She was frustrated and it showed in both her posture and her expression.

She had a right to be frustrated. She couldn't understand because I hadn't told her much about my plot with Celia at all. It wasn't the first time I'd kept her in the dark. I was almost more father figure to her than brother, and I took that responsibility gravely. I tried to shield her as much as possible, never bothering her with the darker details. She'd had enough darkness to last several lifetimes. She didn't need more.

But now she was asking for more, and I rarely denied her when she asked.

When I didn't say anything, Camilla prodded me. "Are you going to let it sit like that or are you even going to try to explain?"

I couldn't. That was the problem. I couldn't even explain to myself why I'd deviated from my plans, why I'd kept Celia on this island, why I'd taken to giving her gifts and wheedling out her demons and caring.

I had nothing for my sister. I turned my gaze back to the ocean.

Camilla sat down on the wicker love seat, the furniture scratching as it adjusted to her weight, informing me of the action. "What I've been wondering most is what does she get out of this? You married her to get access to her father's company. I didn't approve, but I can understand that. I see the logic, though how *her* shares give you access, I can't quite fathom. I'm not the business-minded of the two of us. But why did she agree to marry you? And why is she living out here? Why is she redecorating and remodeling and making herself comfortable on your island? I can only think that...that..."

"Think what?" I swiveled my head toward her, pressing when she didn't continue.

"Either you've trapped her into this arrangement by some dubious means or you've fallen in love with her."

Camilla was more perceptive than I'd given her credit for.

"Which would be worse, in your opinion?"

"If you didn't already know, you wouldn't have asked."

And that was why I was still standing on this rooftop after thirteen days of wanting to be elsewhere. Because I *did* already know which Camilla felt was the worse of the two options.

I almost believed she'd feel the same if she knew the original plans for my wife had included murder.

"Have you even made any move yet to infiltrate Werner Media?"

She knew the answer. What she wanted to know was why I hadn't.

"It's not the right time," I said with finality.

"Bullshit."

She was right, but I started to defend the decision anyway, only to be cut off. "I've never needed this like you have, Eddie. What's been done has been done, and I don't believe seeking retribution will change any of the ways I've been damaged, but you have. It's been the only thing in your sightline since you took me in. And now? What's going on with you?"

I felt the scowl pulling my lips downward despite intending to remain emotionless. "Nothing's going on with me. My goals haven't changed."

"Then why take this detour?" She sat forward, her hazel eyes pinning me in place the way our mother's used to. "Look, I'm not going to hold anything against you if you abandon your plan. If you were doing any of it for me, it's not necessary. I don't need that. That said, I'm not able to sit back and watch you get in bed with the enemy. Either she's part of your plot or you have nothing to do with her."

"Is that some sort of ultimatum?" I could feel the thrum of my pulse in my veins.

"I suffered, Eddie. I wear the scars like tattoos. Scars in the shape of cigarette butts and hot pokers."

"She's not the one who put them there."

"I wouldn't have been put in that situation if it weren't for—"

"Weren't for *him*," I finished for her, in case she was going anywhere other than the truth with the statement. "Not *her*. She's not who we want to ruin." The words surprised myself because the plan all along had been to ruin *him* by ruining *her*.

Had that changed?

Camilla stood up and crossed the short distance between us. "I can't separate them like that," she said, her shoulder practically touching mine as her gaze drifted over the ocean. "I'm astonished that you can. 'We inherit what's been done to those before us.' Those are your words. If that's true then it stands to reason that we inherit the sins of our ancestors as well."

Did we really, though? Weren't we flawed enough carrying our own sins, and we had to answer for others as well?

"I'm not sure I want to believe that." But I'd been carrying the weight of my father's wrongs for more years than I hadn't.

"You might not *want* to believe it, but you do," she said, echoing my thoughts.

A squeal of laughter drew my eyes over the roof wall to the patio where Freddie played with Joette. She dragged him around, pretending to not be able to find him, with him clutching onto the back of her leg. She'd filled the role of grandmother, a role he'd desperately needed. I smiled despite myself, glad he was here. It was good for him to be here.

"Divorce her," Camilla said, a thick cloud covering a lone ray of sun. "Walk away. From all of it, even your revenge scheme. We win if we're still standing, and we are right now. I'm not sure you will be if you pursue this further."

I couldn't tell her that it was too late, that I'd already said and done too much to be able to divorce my wife without repercussions. Celia would never let me walk away now.

I definitely couldn't tell her that I wasn't sure I wanted to, even if I could.

It was less than twenty-four hours later that I made my way down to the cabana. The flight crew had already arrived, and the plane was being prepped for take-off. This couldn't be delayed any longer, whatever this was. I'd spent half the night tossing and turning, trying to figure it out.

I felt caught.

Caught between Celia's lies and her brutal truths. Caught between my sister and my wife. Caught between a past that deserved retribution and a woman who could be...

Could be...*what*? A future?

It wasn't as laughable as I would have once thought.

But there was too much to be sorted in the present to think about anything beyond, and the only way to sort through the present was to speak to Celia.

I hesitated at the door, wondering if I should knock. Then, reminding myself that it was *my* property and that I was the one in charge, I walked in.

She was stretched out on the sofa, her hair up in a ratty ponytail, wearing only a thin camisole that highlighted the beads of her nipples and shorts that made her legs go on for miles. Even lounging around, she was the most beautiful thing I'd ever seen.

Someone had given in and brought her one of the kids' portable DVD players, or she'd stolen it on her own. I'd left specific instructions that her entertainment be restricted to not include screens, and my orders were generally followed, but even Joette had made her disapproval of my treatment of Celia known over the last two weeks, so anything was possible.

The small player sat balanced on her stomach, and I watched silently over her shoulder as Moana sang about how far she'd go, the movie only recognizable because of the countless times Camilla had played it for Freddie. Celia gave no indication of having heard me come in, until, without turning her head, she said, "If you came to tell me you're leaving, that was unnecessary. Tom already told me you'd be gone today."

"That isn't what I came to say." Though it had been the excuse I'd planned to tell her for coming over in the first place.

She paused the show, and spun her head toward me. "You're not leaving?"

The note in her voice was so purely recognizable as hope, I hardly dared to answer.

"I am," I said, after a beat, and before I could say more, she turned her focus back to the movie, hitting a button to resume play.

"What I meant…" I trailed away when it was obvious she wasn't going to pause the show again.

Stalking behind the couch, I pulled the plug from the wall, praying the machine didn't have batteries. Instantly, the picture disappeared from the screen, and she glared in my direction.

At least I had her attention.

"What I meant is that's not all I came to say."

She pulled her knees up and crossed her arms over herself. "Go on then. What is it you need? Don't be all day about it."

They were the same prickish words I'd said to her two weeks ago, said in what she must have thought was a British dialect.

I had to fight a grin at her paltry attempt.

And then I remembered that I hadn't yet worked out what I meant to tell her, and the urge to grin disappeared entirely. "I came to tell you that I heard you," I said, managing to sound sure of myself through the earnestness of the words.

Her arms relaxed and her expression softened, urging me on. "I heard what you said, and I want you to know that I'm willing as well. I commit to this. I'm determined to give you..." *Everything.* I bit back the word, surprised it had even entered my head. "More," I said instead.

Fuck, even that...what was I intending with her?

Celia's eyes glossed over, but she quickly blinked the hint of emotion away. "But you're not staying."

"No, little bird. But I'll be back."

She shook her head dismissively and put the DVD player down on the couch before standing up and spinning to face me. "Your words have zero bearing without something to back it up, Edward. I put myself out there. I waited for you for three months. Add two more weeks on top of that, two weeks where you were five minutes away, and you couldn't bother to stop by, not once."

Her hurt was evident, and I was torn between shame for inflicting it and awe at her willingness to let me see it. I also wanted to touch her, more than I'd ever wanted to touch anyone in my entire life.

"I don't have energy to give you another three months on top of that," she went on. "I deserve more for what I've put into this."

"You do," I agreed, wishing that there wasn't a couch between us or a sister waiting at the house or a business to be run across the ocean. "I'll make up for it. I promise. But I can't right now. This visit has been what it's been, and it's done now. I can't change that, and I have to be on that plane in thirty minutes. All I can do is promise that next time will be different."

Her thigh bounced as she considered, her brows knit tightly together. "Thirty days," she said finally.

"Excuse me?"

"You have thirty days to come back."

I nearly laughed. "Thirty days isn't possible."

"I have nothing left to say to you then." She picked up the player, pulling the cord with it and turned as if to find another outlet to plug it in.

"Two months," I said, refusing to let her shut me out. I'd booked my calendar months ago with quarterly visits worked in. Two months would be difficult, but I'd make a weekend happen.

"Thirty days."

"Six weeks."

"Thirty days."

"Two months, and I'll give you an entire week." I could see my schedule in my head, see how impossible it would be, even as I offered it.

She wasn't budging. "Thirty days."

"I'll give you two weeks." And I smiled, because in all our previous negotiations, she'd been easy to bulldoze. She'd stood up for herself, certainly, but always stepped away when I pushed.

She *had* changed. And it was a good part because of me.

"Thirty days," she repeated. "One day longer, and this whole deal is off."

There were too many important meetings on the books. A gala and a wedding and a critical trip planned to Turkey. "I'll see what I can do," I said, knowing that I'd just agreed.

Knowing it too, she beamed.

There was a field of energy between us, a magnetic pull that wanted me to go to her and draw her into my arms and scandalize her lips.

But there was another force, equally strong, holding me back. A force comprised of promises and blood loyalties and stubbornness and habit and the matter of the sofa between her body and mine. And I was still who I was, and she was still who she was, and the only thing that had been sorted was that there would be more between us, and that was enough to send a flood of relief coursing through my veins.

It was with a lighter step that I started toward the door. "But when I return, you participate," I said, turning back. Needing to have another word. The last word. "No passive-aggressive punishment for wrongs you think I've committed against you. No hiding. No petty stories. No games."

Her body had rotated as I had, and while she still stayed standing in the same spot, she also still faced me entirely. "We aren't a game," she said fervently.

In three strides, I was in front of her. I grazed my knuckles against the side of her cheek and pulled her in with my other arm. My lips hovered above hers. "No, we aren't," I agreed.

Then I kissed her, and while the kiss on our wedding day had been sincere, this one sealed us in a way that one hadn't, and for the first time since we'd married, when the plane took off over the island, I ached. No matter what my sister understood, I wasn't leaving behind Celia Werner.

I was leaving behind my wife.

TWENTY
Celia

His shadow hit me first, the shade stretching over the catalog full of baby decor that I'd been perusing. Marge's baby Liam was only just over one, and she was already four months along with another one. She'd returned from the doctor in Nassau only the week before with the news that it was a girl this time.

Of course I'd offered to design the nursery. Though I'd never designed anything for children of any kind, it would be something new and the challenge was welcome.

Right now, however, with the fall of his shadow, my interest in the task was eclipsed. My heart all of a sudden felt like it was in my throat, beating a thousand times per minute, and I couldn't look up at him for fear of what my expression would show.

I threw the catalog on the table in front of me and glanced, instead, at the sky. The sun wasn't even directly overhead yet. My guess was closer to eleven a.m.

"You must have left at the crack of dawn," I said, still not able to look directly at him.

"I would have left last night at the end of the business day, but I wanted to cut it close."

And close it was. In two hours it would be thirty days exactly since I'd last seen him.

My gaze shot to his, and I caught the gleam in his eyes. He was teasing, but not really. He wanted me to know his position in this relationship still stood, that even though I'd been granted a moment of strength with his adherence to my demands, he still held the power.

As if I could forget.

As if I wanted it any other way.

"You're a dick," I said, fighting the smile that wanted to burst out on my lips.

"But I'm here."

He was here and I felt all sorts of things about that. I'd believed he'd come back in the time frame I'd given him. Our last encounter had felt too real for him to not. Then, as the days had passed and got closer to the thirty-day mark, I began to doubt. I'd expected him to reach out with some confirmation that he was returning, not that he'd ever shared his plans before. Just, he'd said he committed, and that was new, and because it was new I'd thought everything would be different.

And then everything was exactly the same, and I wasn't so sure about what had occurred between us anymore. It was possible he'd been fucking with my head. It was *likely*, even. Wasn't that the best way to destroy me? Let me believe what was going on between us was genuine, and then pull the rug out from under me. Wasn't that how I would have chosen to do it?

It would have been a fitting sort of karma.

So even as I believed he'd come back by today, I'd held space inside for the possibility that he wouldn't.

Now, with him here in front of me and two hours to spare before the deadline, I could let that space go and all the emotions I'd crammed into a dark corner now had room to stretch and show themselves and there were so many. Apprehensiveness and happiness and desire and disbelief and gratitude and humility and a little bit of suspicion and panic.

Mostly, though, what I felt was relief.

He pulled out a chair next to me and sat, and I hurried to gather up the notepads and catalogs that had been strewn over the table, both an anxious gesture and a show that I was ready to give all my attention to him.

The movement, though, caught his interest. "What are you working on?" he asked, his eyes already scanning the catalogs and notepads.

"Nothing important."

"I say what's important. If I ask, I want to know."

Another display of his dominance, and my skin vibrated in tune with the show. His authoritarian arrogance was annoying on many levels, but there was something soothing about it too. And arousing.

Still, I always had to take a beat and decide if I wanted to fight him or submit.

I decided to lean in. "Marge asked me to design a nursery for her," I said, bending the truth a bit. I assumed he knew about her pregnancy, since he knew everything. He didn't communicate with me during his absences, but he sure communicated with someone, telling staff what gifts and allowances to bring me and how to orchestrate my days.

"She asked or you offered?"

He nodded and reached for my sketch pad, and I forced myself not to make excuses about the rush the drawings had been made in or the quality of the ideas. As if I weren't already nervous.

After he flipped through all I'd drawn so far, he made a low rumble of appreciation in his throat that echoed between my legs, then put the pad carefully back where he'd taken it from. "I'm glad you're doing this. I like to see you using your talents."

I was simultaneously giddy over his approval and indignant that he didn't deliver more effusive praise. Brusqueness won out, as I recalled the negotiations we'd had over our marriage. "Oh, yes, hobbies are fine as long as it isn't a career. I remember now."

"Did I say that?"

"You did."

"And you agreed to it." His smirk was so charming, he was nearly forgivable.

"I wasn't planning to be married to you for long."

"Neither was I." The smirk disappeared with the gravity of his admission.

It hit me in the gut, the severity of who he was and what he'd planned. My little game seemed petty in contrast, and a wave of bitterness swept through me, threatening to sour all the pleasant feelings his arrival had unleashed.

"Wow." I put a hand on my chest, as though to keep my heart from pounding out of my ribcage. "This is a lot of honesty right off the bat."

"It's what we agreed to, wasn't it? Are you still here for it?" He looked down at my other hand, resting on the table. Then he placed his palm on the surface and swept it toward me until the tip of his pinkie finger was nudging mine.

That simple touch was enough to ignite a nuclear explosion inside me.

"Yes," I said, breathless from the effort. Definitely yes. I twisted my hand and pushed it closer so that our little fingers rested against each other entirely.

I studied them together, the way his dwarfed mine, the variances in our skin tone, the heat that emitted from his. I'd never studied his physical characteristics with such depth, and suddenly there wasn't anything I wanted to do but examine all of him, from head to toe, leaving none of his body unexplored.

"How long do I have you this time?" However long it was, it wouldn't be enough.

He paused, and the pause was enough to draw my eyes back to his. "Let's not ruin the beginning by worrying about the end."

"That long, huh?" I was sure he could hear the ache in my voice.

I swallowed it away. "I suppose we shouldn't waste a single minute then." There were things I had to say, things I'd held in too long. In the month he'd been away, I'd come to terms with the fact that, if I really wanted to be in this with him—whatever this was—there were things he had to know.

Things that could end whatever this was.

Things that could get me killed.

"We should go inside," he said, seeming to understand.

"Can we only do this in the cabana?"

"Sessions? No. We can have one anytime, anywhere, but a session wasn't what I've been thinking about nonstop since I left, and I'm not about to let our staff witness the things I want to do to you."

A shiver of want ran through me, and I blushed. "I haven't earned anything yet. How are you so sure I'll deliver?"

"I'm sure." He beckoned me with a jerk of his head. "Come here."

God, I wanted to. I wanted to crawl over the table and straddle his lap and let him carry me inside to show me all the things he'd thought about doing to me. Without even knowing what they all were, I was sure I wanted them twice.

But that secret that pressed heavy on my back had to be set down first.

"I can't, Edward."

His brow raised at what he could only assume was a challenge. "You seem to have forgotten who's in charge here, little bird."

"I haven't at all. You've demanded honesty, though, and I don't think you'll be happy with me if I let anything else go on between us without giving you some truth."

"That sounds ominous."

"I was going for transparent."

"I approve of transparent." But his hand had moved away from mine, and his guard was up, and I couldn't blame him because what I had to say to him was going to be the worst. Not the worst thing for me—those things would come out too, eventually—but the worst thing for him.

He leaned back and crossed his ankle on the opposite knee, pushing his chair back a bit as he did. It could have been accidental, but I was certain it was purposeful, an attempt to mimic the parameters that typically accompanied our sessions. The distance between us. The space to lay out my confessions and for him to process what I said.

I took the cue and withdrew as well, dropping my hands in my lap where I could wring them out of sight under the table. "I know you've done your research, and some of this might be old news to you, but since I don't know what you know and what you don't, I'm going to say it all."

I'd had a script planned, and already I wanted to jump from it. So I did. "First, though, I need you to know— I could have told you this earlier. Maybe I *should* have, but…" I shook my head. "Well, you'll understand when I'm done. I just need you to know what it means that I'm telling you now."

I wanted him to realize how defenseless this made me. I needed him to see that by telling him now, it proved how committed I really was to this. To being his.

"Go on," was all he said, refusing to give me the acknowledgment I wanted until he heard for himself what it was.

Leaving me even more vulnerable.

That seemed about right.

I took a breath and plunged in, beginning with a history lesson. "Werner Media was founded in nineteen thirty-five by my father's father—Jessop Werner. There were some friends involved in the actual work of it, but it really all belonged to Jessop because he had the start-up money. It was old money that had dwindled a lot when the stock market crashed. He seemed to realize what he had wasn't going to last without turning it into something big, so he went all in on the newspaper business, and obviously the gamble worked. The company grew and expanded to magazines. Then TV stations. Then TV programming. I'm sure you know all that better than I do.

"Anyway, when Jessop died, he gave fifty percent of the business to my father, who was the oldest of his two sons, and the one most interested in running things. The one most capable. He left my uncle Ron with thirty percent, which was overly generous considering that his only interest in the business was flaunting the wealth and power it gave him. The remaining twenty percent of the business was divided in two percent increments between Jessop's extended relatives."

"And then those extra shares got sold and bought a bunch of times and divided and diluted," Edward said, almost bored. "And Ron sold his thirty percent to Glam Play and your father sold ten percent to Pierce Industries so now Warren owns only forty percent, which he put in a trust for you to inherit at the date of your marriage. They've already been transferred to your name. I've checked."

"I'm sure you have." I wasn't so sure he meant the threat in the subtext, but it was there all the same. "Did you also know about the conditions Ron sold his shares? He wanted the money, but he also wanted stability, so in exchange for a secure top position in the company, my father required Ron to include certain terms in the sale to Glam Play."

"Ah." His eyes lit up, and finally I'd told him something new. "So that's why they're required to vote along with the majority. It kept your father in control of the company, even with less than fifty percent of the shares."

"Right."

"I'd wondered how that occurred. It's a good strategy."

"Until Glam Play gets sold. And then the terms are null and void." I carefully studied his reaction, trying to feel him out before getting to the blow.

But his response was dismissive. "They aren't selling."

"You've tried to buy them?" I almost chuckled, because of course he had. Of course marrying me wasn't his first scheme to get into Werner Media.

"Yes," he said, slowly, aware of what he'd given away. "I've tried to purchase from them numerous times."

"Because they've already been sold." There. It was said. Easy as that.

But the burden wasn't in the actual saying—it was in surviving whatever he said next.

I watched him as the words sank in, as he absorbed the meaning. If Glam Play wasn't required to vote with Werner Media, then forty percent of the shares wasn't enough to hold a true majority.

His body stiffened, his eyes grew cold. "You're lying."

"You know I'm not." He'd told me he knew the difference between when I was and when I wasn't, and maybe it was naive to actually believe that, but I did.

He didn't refute it, but he was still unsure. "How is there no record of a sale?"

"That was part of the terms of the new deal. The sale happened in complete darkness. No one knows it's been purchased, not even my father. The shareholder votes are to continue to align with the majority unless..." I trailed away. This part was hardest to tell, because the entire strategy had been executed because of me. Because Hudson had needed something to hold over me, and this was what he'd found.

"Unless what?" Edward prodded.

Unless I tried to interfere with Hudson's life again. If I did, he'd destroy Werner Media.

But that wasn't the most important part of this confession. "I guess unless the new owner decides otherwise."

Edward dropped his foot to the ground and pulled at his chin, thinking. Calculating. "That's only thirty percent. Pierce Industries always votes with your father. There's no reason to be concerned about losing Glam Play." The assurance was for himself, not for me.

"Except that Pierce Industries is who bought Glam Play. They also managed to buy out two percent from another shareholder along the way. Technically, Hudson Pierce owns forty-two percent of Werner Media."

I'd held the secret for so long now, carried the weight of it alone, and even though the reality of it was awful and hard to look at, I could breathe deeper than I had in years from the sharing.

But after that breath, I had to face the facts. My father had been usurped of his legacy, and it was my fault. He never had to know for me to feel the shame of that. It was overwhelming.

"How do you know all this?" Edward asked, still unaware of how humiliating this was for me.

He would though. Before this was all over, he'd know.

"Hudson told me," I answered softly.

"Why would he tell you this? Why does he want to own a controlling interest and yet do nothing with it?"

"He wanted power over me."

A beat passed, and his face hardened, and he knew. I could see that he knew.

"What did you do to him?" he asked, crudely.

The disgust in his voice made me shrink inside myself. The sun was beating down as it approached mid-sky, and I was so very cold.

"Does it matter?" I asked, blinking back tears.

"You played him." It wasn't a question. "His names weren't in the journals."

"I didn't record what I did to him."

"Why not?"

Because it hadn't been a game. It had been my reaction to what I had perceived as betrayal. It had been unhealthy and destructive and unplanned, and a million times I'd wished I could take it back. Wished that I had been someone different than I'd been.

Than I was.

Again I shook my head, searching for a simpler answer. "It was a confusing time for me. It was the first time I was playing on my own."

"What did you do to him?" he asked again.

This time I answered. "I tried to break up his relationship with his girlfriend. His wife, now. Obviously, I failed."

"You failed, and he wanted insurance that you wouldn't fuck with him again."

I nodded.

"You'd think you would have learned your lesson about playing powerful men." There was no hint of teasing in his statement.

"You'd think."

He held my stare for several heartbeats, hostility radiating off him as hot as if he were a furnace. It hurt to have him look at me this way, but I forced myself to bear it.

It was he who broke away first to stare vaguely into the distance. "You knew that this undermines my entire strategy of controlling Werner Media through your shares."

I did.

But I searched for optimism all the same. "It doesn't have to mean that. Glam Play could still continue to vote along with you. Unless you tried to do something that would destroy the company from within."

His eyes came back to mine, as though to stare down my naivete. What else had he been planning to do with my shares but destroy the company within? If I'd thought his motive was simply to move his own company into the U.S., I was wrong. He meant to bring my father down.

"Why do you hate him so much?" This was beyond business. This rivalry was personal.

He ignored the question. "You didn't tell me because you saw it as a worst-case scenario way to make sure I still got fucked over in the end, even if you weren't around to see it. You were hoping if I did anything detrimental with those share votes, Hudson Pierce would use his control against me."

After everything, the accusation still stung. "I couldn't possibly have been looking to protect my father," I threw back sarcastically. "You might hate him, but he's still my family."

"So it was still a game. All along."

I slammed my palm on the table so hard it stung. "No, goddammit. It wasn't a game, because that wasn't the reason I didn't tell you, you condescending asshole. I hadn't even thought of that, which is stupid, because I clearly *should* have thought of that. Maybe it was the threat of death that threw me off my game."

I cringed as soon as it was out of my mouth. Not the best choice of words in the moment. Not when Edward had already decided that was what this was all along.

"Look," I said sitting forward, taking a breath to make sure my next words came out clear. "I didn't tell you because it was obvious you were after controlling interest, and this information would let you know that this plot of yours was futile."

"That makes no sense. If you'd told me that your shares wouldn't get me control, what would be the point in killing you for them?"

I flinched at his openness.

"You'd already told me that was your plan," I said, avoiding words like *kill* and *murder.* "Like you were just going to let me go after that. 'Oh, I guess that's not going to work, you can go home now.' Yeah, right."

I gave him a second to face the validity of that before going on. "Letting you believe I still had something to give you was the only thing that kept me valuable."

His features softened momentarily, and I almost believed he was going to deny it, that he was going to say I had value beyond what I knew or who was my father.

But the moment passed, and he went back to glaring into the distance. "Warren doesn't know your family no longer holds control of the company," he said, as though he had to say it again to believe it.

"He doesn't." It would kill him if he found out. Edward could destroy my father with that information alone. Did he realize that?

Apparently not because his next words were, "This entire scheme was all for naught."

I nodded, too unsure of the menace in his tone to say anything else.

His serious expression vanished abruptly as he broke into laughter. Deep, bellowing laughter. It stunned me. He rarely laughed at all, and I'd never seen him laugh so heartily. It was almost frightening in its intensity. I wasn't sure if he'd truly found the humor in the situation or if he was going mad.

It *was* kind of funny, actually. How much work he had done for nothing. Maybe the only option was to laugh.

Then, just as suddenly, he was done.

He shot up from his chair and held his hand out in my direction, his face again solemn. "Come with me."

I hesitated. Despite the moment of humor, he was angry. That was apparent. And maybe a little crazy too. "Where are we going?" I asked, trying to decide if it was really a good idea to be with him right now.

The smirk was back. "Wherever I say. Do you not trust me?"

"Should I?"

"I'm not entirely sure."

It was the most honest he'd ever been with me. And for that reason, because in this moment he was *all in*, I reached out and put my hand in his.

TWENTY-ONE

A little over an hour later, with a cooler filled with bottled water and a lunch packed from Joette, I found myself in the middle of the ocean on a boat manned only by my husband.

Sailboats made me nervous anyway. Alone with a man I didn't trust brought an entirely new level of unease. My hands ached from the constant wringing, and my sundress was wrinkled from the amount of times I'd balled it into my fists, only to smooth it out a moment later with my sweat-soaked palms.

It didn't help that the boat's name was *Vengeance*.

"When you said we were going somewhere, I thought you meant to the bedroom or the cabana. I would have changed my shoes if I'd known we were doing something sporty." Not that I was doing any of the work. Honestly, if he'd told me, I might have fought him on it, and fighting him was nearly always a losing battle.

This time I had a deep fear that not fighting him may have meant I'd lost the battle as well. Alone on the ocean... what did he have planned for me?

I shivered at the possibilities.

"What you're wearing is fine," he said without looking at me. "Slip them off if you'd prefer to go barefoot."

I kept them on, not wanting to get too comfortable.

"I thought all sailboats this size had motors," I said, subtly expressing more of my concern. "How do you even manage this thing out here without one?"

"Are you worried about it?" He turned his eyes from the sail to tack me with his gaze.

Yes. I was very worried about it. And for so many reasons, the most concerning being that my skipper had shared his nefarious plans for me on more than one occasion.

But I was trying to play it cool, so I pressed a smile to my lips. "Just curious."

His expression said he didn't buy the act, but he answered all the same. "Purists prefer to sail without an engine. It makes the experience more authentic."

That was Edward—always concerned with authenticity.

I studied him as he fiddled with the boom and jib, terms I'd only just learned. His chambray shirt, in a color that could only be referred to as pink but was too masculine to say out loud, was rolled up to his elbows, showcasing the sculpted muscles of his forearms. When he lunged to get a better angle, his thigh pressed taut against his white linen pants, and I had to swallow and look away.

Even with dread nestled in the center of my belly, the man was still the sexiest thing I'd ever come in contact with. Watching him use his hands and body to steer our boat only made him hotter. And our chemistry wasn't one-sided. There was a blanket of tension that stretched and pulled in waves as unpredictable as the water beneath us.

Once happy with the direction we were headed—how he could even know since there weren't any maps around, I had no clue—he took a seat on the bench across from me and retrieved a container of cold roast chicken from the cooler.

"No, thanks," I said, when he handed it out to me. My stomach was already complaining, either from the motion of the boat or anxiety, I wasn't sure.

He reached again into the cooler and brought out a bottle of water and a loaf of french bread. "Nibble on this. It will help."

Reluctantly, I took both from him, setting the water to my side and tearing off a piece of bread that I ate in morsels.

We were quiet for a while as he ate and I pecked, and the sun moved farther west in the sky and the boat sailed farther from land. I kept reminding myself to relax my shoulders and breathe. There was definitely an aura of calm out here with the rhythmic lull of the sea and the wet, salty air. Serenity rolled lazily underneath the apprehension, and I could almost give into it. But not quite.

Eventually, Edward put away his meal and sat back with a bottle of water, his foot resting on the cooler. "Tell me about your relationship with your father," he said, his attention solely on me.

The tension that I'd managed to release came back in a rush. "Is this a session?"

"No. Just talking." He brought the bottle up to swig, his throat stretched and exposed as he swallowed.

The casualness of it felt dangerous. Staged.

But also not. Also it just felt genuine. Like a question someone you'd known for a while— had sex with, married—might ask.

Whatever was going on out here, whatever this sailing trip was about, there wasn't any benefit in me going backwards.

So I went forward and stayed honest. "We're good, I suppose. Not particularly close, but most of the kids I grew up with weren't close to their fathers either. They all worked too much. Had too many affairs. Weren't around. Mine wasn't any different than the others, except I think the only mistress he had was golf. I'm his only child, and that matters to him. He loves me as much as I think he loves anyone, though he doesn't really know me. At all. Doesn't even try. I don't really try with him either, anymore."

I considered the distance between my father and me, how it hadn't been there when I was young. How we'd grown apart when I was a teenager and why. The afternoon that had changed it all.

The story of it pressed at the back of my throat until it was snaking through my mouth and out my lips. "He was never a corporal punishment kind of guy. That was his father's style, and whenever I was in trouble as a kid, he made sure that I knew that if he'd been *his* father, I would have had my ass whipped.

"I'm not even sure he knew most of the times I got in trouble. That sort of stuff was usually handled by the nanny or, on rare occasions, my mother. But sometimes it was bad enough for him to get involved."

"You were a naughty little girl?" The gleam in Edward's eye caused goosebumps to chase down my skin.

"Not particularly," I said, smiling. "That came later. But there was this one time, when I was thirteen. Almost fourteen. I'd told him…" I paused, deliberating how much of this I wanted to share in the moment, deciding on sticking to the tale on hand and not branching off to the other. "I'd told him something he didn't believe, and it made him very angry. He accused me of lying. Told me to take it back, and I considered it. He was so mad, I actually considered it.

"But I'd been telling the truth, and—don't laugh—that was important to me back then. So I stuck by it. And then, at thirteen flipping years old, he turned me around, pulled down my leggings and spanked me raw. It hurt, I mean it really hurt. I can still remember spending the rest of that weekend on my stomach with ice packs on my ass, but the physical pain was nothing compared to how much it hurt to not have him believe me. I don't think our relationship ever recovered after that.

"I think that was also when I began to realize that there wasn't much value in honesty. If truth was so hard to believe, what was the purpose in it?"

The edges of Edward's mouth turned down. "The lessons from our parents are the hardest to unlearn, aren't they?"

"Yeah. I think they are." My body felt lighter, and, even as I wondered what hard lessons his parents had taught him, the tranquility of the sea beckoned me to embrace it and I found I was closer than I'd been before. Closer to peace.

"There is purpose to honesty, you know," Edward said after a beat. "With the right person. A person who will acknowledge and support your truth instead of admonish it."

"Yes. I've been learning that. New teacher."

"*Better* teacher?" He almost smiled, and I wondered if we were flirting.

"Much better teacher." I leaned my elbows back onto the hull of the boat and stretched my legs out in front of me, the knot in my stomach finally uncoiling.

"If this were a session, I'd respond to this tale with a lesson in a different kind of spanking."

"I think you've already taught me that lesson." My core clenched at remembering being bent over his desk, at the heat of his hand against my ass, at the delicious pleasure of his pelvis thrusting against the raw skin as he thrust his cock inside me over and over. I hadn't even thought of my father's punishment while Edward had been spanking me, I'd been too entirely wrapped up in the moment. In him.

Now I'd go so far as saying I liked being spanked hard. It was possible I only liked being spanked hard by Edward.

"That was a good lesson," he said, his eyes shining like he could read my thoughts, and this time he was definitely smiling. "I wouldn't mind giving it again sometime."

A promise of a future? I wouldn't let myself get too snagged up on the thought.

Another silent spell passed.

"What was it your father hadn't believed?"

I sighed, scanning out into the distance where the ocean met the sky. I'd known he wouldn't let that slip when I chose to say it, and yet, briefly, I'd thought he had.

"I'll tell you," I said, sincerely. "But I'd rather it not be here. My stomach's already fighting the waves. I don't want to push it."

When I returned my gaze to him, he was staring, and I could sense how badly he wanted to press. If he did, I'd probably tell him, though I really didn't want to.

"What about *your* relationship with your father?" I asked, hoping the change of subject would force him to move on.

It took a minute, but then he followed where I'd steered. "He's the reason I like sailing."

"He taught you?"

"Some. I was still young when he died. Thirteen." The nod of his head acknowledged it was the same age I'd been in the story I'd just told.

Thirteen had been such a transformative year for both of us. It wasn't significant, necessarily, but it felt binding. Like, I could see him a little more clearly for it, for what had happened to him and what had happened to me.

"He never set out to really teach me, he just liked it. We spent several vacations on the water. We sailed everywhere—the Lake District, the Channel. The Mediterranean. It was the only downtime he took, because my mother liked it so much, I think, and he wanted his leisure to be completely wrapped up in her, and sailing was something we could all do together.

"I had good memories of it, and so, when I had the means, I learned officially. Marion and I sailed a fair amount when Hagen and Genevieve were young."

My jaw went rigid. "You sailed with Marion?"

"Are you jealous?"

He was so handsome and so smug and so right, I had to look away. I wasn't used to being jealous. It prickled inside me like I'd swallowed a porcupine, and the only thing that would make it worse would be to admit it.

"Just trying to understand your relationship," I said,

nonchalantly.

"I've gone sailing now with you, too."

I fought a smile that he couldn't see, sure that he'd know even though I wasn't looking at him. He was trying to comfort me, and that did all sorts of delicious and strange things to my insides.

And it did comfort me, because I was out here on the ocean with him, and where was she?

Still, the reality of why and how I was with Edward was unsettling. "I'm not really sailing. You're sailing, and I'm trying to survive it."

"You're surviving just fine from where I'm sitting. So far."

His addendum set off another roll of nausea. I studied the water, trying to convince myself he meant I'd managed to not throw up as of yet, which was accurate, and there was still a possibility that I might.

But maybe that hadn't been what he meant at all.

The poke of a fin above the surface just then sent a chill down my spine. Was it a dolphin or a shark? Was this a safe venture or a dangerous one?

"My relationship with Marion seemed complicated from the outside," he said, drawing my attention back to him. "But very simple on the inside. She was a submissive—a true submissive. She lived to bend and serve and please me. With my help, her entire life was orchestrated so that she could immerse herself in that lifestyle, that's how much she enjoyed it."

The porcupine was back, wriggling in my insides, loosing needles into my ribs. "I enjoy it, too," I said with a pout. "Sometimes."

He laughed, not as deep as he had back at the house, but a sizable laugh at that. "You like it when you finally surrender to it. I'll give you that. You just fight tooth and nail to get there."

"That doesn't mean I don't like it."

The stare he fixed on me was so heated, I was almost sure he would climb across the cockpit and...I wasn't sure what would happen when he got to me, but I was ready to find out.

But he didn't.

The heat slipped away from his expression, his jaw jutting out as he turned to fuss with the rudder. "There were benefits to such a relationship. Trust was imperative for it to work, and we had that through and through. When she said something, she meant it. Every word that came out of her mouth was the truth, unless she was teasing me into play. It was very hard to make her uncomfortable, which was bothersome for me, but she never lied or played me or manipulated me in any way. She never kept crucial information from me for her own benefit."

There it was—his anger from earlier resurfaced. I'd been waiting for it.

"Sounds like a boring marriage," I said. It probably wasn't the best time to sass him. Marion probably never would have. But as he'd not so subtly pointed out, I was not Marion.

He didn't find my teasing amusing, or, if he did, he didn't let on. "She was the one who left me, you know."

I did know, but I'd never heard it from him, and now that I had, it was a wake-up call. His heart had belonged to someone else—might still belong to her, for all I knew. I couldn't tell if that was the point he'd meant to make, but if he'd wanted to hurt me, he had.

"Why?" I asked, taking the bait. "You weren't bossy enough for her?" Hell, if I didn't amuse him, I sure amused myself.

His cheek twitched as he considered his response. "She wanted to be my whole world. She submitted everything, hoping to earn that spot, and she never did."

"You had other women?"

"I never cheated on my wife. On either of my wives."

Just like that, the knife he'd pierced through me only a moment before was gone and his words were a salve in its place. He hadn't been with another woman since he'd married me. That confession tilted my world even more than the rocking of the boat.

"At least not with a woman," he clarified. "Marion took second place to my other ambitions."

His career? It seemed the obvious answer, especially knowing what I knew about what it took to be a successful leader of an international business such as his.

Then the real answer struck me, and maybe it was also about his career, but I was nearly convinced there was something more to it. "Ambitions like destroying my father, you mean."

He didn't answer, and a minute later he stood to adjust the boom, slowing down our speed. Then he walked around the steering wheel to peer off the stern of the boat.

I stood too, gazing over his shoulder, wondering what he saw out there in that great expanse of nothing. Wondering what he was thinking. Wondering his motives for taking me out here and saying these things—these earth-shattering things that were too real and precious and enormous to have put on me and not have to adjust my stance.

"This is where I was going to do it." His voice was low, almost a hum, but in the stillness of our surroundings, he was easily heard. "This was how. I'd push you off out here, in a spot just like this. I imagined it a lot—the ride out here, the time of day, the surrounding circumstances. But in my head, no matter how well I tried to plan it, I could never get to that moment, the moment where we stood here, and I did the thing that was supposed to happen next."

My breath shuddered in my lungs.

He was safe, I told myself. He wouldn't be telling me any of this if he wasn't safe. He was being honest with me now, the same way I'd been honest with him.

At least, I thought so.

There was the possibility that I was wrong.

With shaking limbs, I stepped up beside him so my arm brushed against his. At his side, I looked out at the same emptiness that had stolen his focus. "I've been on yachts plenty, but I've only been sailing a handful of times. Definitely never been sailing without a motor and if anyone had ever invited me to do so, on an ocean no less, that would have been a 'hell, no.' Lakes are okay. Bays are okay. There are borders there. Land corralling the water, and even on the big lakes where you can't see the land, you know it's there. Your head knows that wherever the wind blows, you're still contained.

"Sailing like this, out here on the open water, it's an entirely different thing, isn't it? The breeze could pick up and, next thing you know, you're miles and miles from any shore. Completely a slave to the whims of the wind. That's why I never came out on the ocean like this with anyone before. I've been asked—trust me, I've been asked. The idea was always too terrifying."

I could feel his gaze on my profile, and I turned to meet it. "It's validating to find the real experience is as terrifying as I'd imagined."

Because I was scared. I wanted him to know I was scared.

But I was still here. Not entirely at my will, but I was here. I was in this with him.

His lips turned up into a smirk. "And exciting too?"

"Yes. That too."

The breeze sent my hair blowing, leaving a strand across my face. He reached out to brush it back behind my ear, his fingers igniting my skin as they grazed my cheek. "At the whims of the wind doesn't mean helpless," he said. "The only reason you're frightened is because you don't know how to sail a boat."

Then, he expertly demonstrated how very much in control of the *Vengeance* he was, deftly steering us across the ocean, safely bringing us back into port at Amelie.

TWENTY-TWO

The sun was setting when we got back to the house. I walked in ahead of Edward, my shoes in my hand, having finally succumbed to taking them off. The house was empty, which I'd expected since my husband had informed the staff not to plan on us for dinner, and for Joette to leave plates for us in the fridge.

Despite how little I'd eaten, food wasn't of interest. Nor was the hot shower that I'd told Edward I wanted to take when we got back. The orange and pink streaked across the scene outside the window didn't have my attention either. As I stood behind the couch gazing out at the spectacular display of light, it was the man behind me that held my awareness.

He was complicated and terrible. A devil and a jackass.

And I was falling for him.

Spiraling, actually, in all the good ways and all the bad. He made me dizzy and overwhelmed and alive, even when he terrified me, which was almost all the time. I was pretty certain there was no happy ending with a man like him, not coming from a situation like ours, and it didn't matter.

It couldn't stop my motion. I was still already tumbling down into whatever mess lay at the end, and, if I were honest with myself—something I was being more often than not these days—I wouldn't try to stop even if I could. I wanted this.

I wanted him.

I wanted him to want me with as much intensity, with no regard to reason. I wanted it so badly, I could taste it. I could feel it. The wanting was as real to my senses as the sunset ahead of me.

I didn't look back when he came in, but I heard the door open and then there was the sound of the cooler set down on the ceramic floor. In the glass, I could just make out the hint of his reflection, frozen in place, his eyes seemingly pinned on me.

"Celia?" His voice lilted up slightly like it were a question or possibly an invitation, but all I heard was my name on his lips spoken with the husk of desire.

Turning around, I let my shoes drop to the floor, and within the space of a breath, I was in his arms. I had no idea who'd moved first, who had made the first step, who started the kiss. One minute I'd been wishing and wanting. The next, my body was crashed into his, my mouth desperately trying to keep up with his frantic lips. His tongue felt hot and thick as it tangled with mine, each stroke feeling like a promise, each swipe awakening every nerve ending in my body, making my pussy swell and sob.

His hands mimicked his kiss, furiously running over my body, through my hair, grabbing my ass, as if to leave their prints on all of me. As if to leave no part of me untouched.

I curled my fingers in his shirt, taking what he gave,

hanging on for dear life.

My knees were weak and my lungs empty of air when he drew back, bringing his palms to cradle my face. His expression was unsure as he studied me, searching for something in my eyes.

I held on and let him look, not knowing what he wanted to see there. I only hoped he found it or something close because what *I* wanted to see was in *his* eyes—desire and concern and interest—and I'd do anything for him to keep looking at me like that. Anything for him to keep touching me. For him to kiss me again.

And then he *was* kissing me again, his mouth greedy and demanding as he pushed me backwards until my legs met the sofa. There, he turned me around and pressed my head down until I was bent over the back of the couch.

"Spread your legs," he ordered, though he was already spreading them for me, his shoe nudging my feet until they were wide enough.

His hand traveled from the back of my head and down my spine, a long, possessive caress. Then it disappeared, only to reappear a moment later with his other hand under my dress. He flipped my skirt up then swiftly removed my panties, kneeling in the process. Both of his hands palmed my ass cheeks, his fingernails digging into my skin as his tongue licked along my slit, rimming my wet channel before swiping up to my asshole.

I gasped at the invasion. Shocks of pleasure jolted through my body as he did it again, and again, licking me with fierce, predatory enthusiasm. I was quivering within minutes, and he hadn't even touched my clit.

"Rub yourself, little bird. I want you to come on my tongue."

I shook my head, even though I wasn't sure he could see the movement with me bent over the couch like I was and his head between my thighs. My fingertips were pressed hard into the sofa cushion. They were the only thing holding me up. They couldn't be spared for other activities.

"Do it," he demanded, when I hadn't moved. His tongue speared inside me, prompting me in ways his words hadn't.

"I'm going to come anyway," I moaned. The knot of sensation pulsed low in my belly, each throb bigger than the last. I'd never come so quickly, and I was more than halfway there without clitoral stimulation.

Three sharp smacks fell in rapid succession against my right asscheek, the sting making me cry out. Automatically, my body jerked, trying to pull away from the assault.

Edward pulled his mouth from my body and gripped my hips, anchoring me in place. "I didn't ask, Celia. Put your fingers on your pussy or I'll put mine, and believe me when I say you won't find that as pleasant."

He waited this time, denying me his mouth until I responded.

Having learned how "unpleasant" he could be when he went down on me, I hesitated to obey.

But I didn't want a dozen orgasms this way. I wanted his cock inside me, and it seemed I had a better shot at that if I did what he said.

Lifting my belly from the sofa enough to get access, I slipped my hand down between my legs to the sensitive bud buried in between the folds of skin. I set the tip of my finger to it, scared that any more would set me off, and I wanted to wait to explode on his tongue like he'd asked.

His breath scorched across my aroused cunt, and that

alone nearly devastated me. "Rub it like you mean it, Celia, or I can send you to your room like this, alone."

"Don't you dare," I panted, but I swirled my finger across my clit, drawing the edges of my climax in closer.

Another biting thwack sang against my skin, a punishment for the sass, I assumed because his next words were a soft purr. "Good girl."

Then his mouth returned to my hole, his tongue thrusting into my heat with determined drive.

I lasted all of three seconds before my orgasm had seized me. My legs shook aggressively, my knees knocking against the sofa. "Oh, my Godddddd," I roared, the pleasure blinding me with flashes of white.

I was still shuddering when I was snatched up by the hair and spun around to face my husband.

"When it's my face between your thighs, it's my name out of your lips," he scolded.

"Yes, Edward," I said, only to have the words swallowed by his tongue as it shoved into my mouth. He tasted like me, which made me all kinds of hot, especially when he kissed me like it was a punishment, like I'd been bad. Like I deserved to be suffocated with the wrath of his desire.

When I was completely breathless, he abruptly pushed away, only to swing me into his arms. He carried me to his bedroom, bride style, kissing me the entire way. When he got to his closed door, he set me down so he could open it and usher me in.

It was the first time I'd been to his room when I'd been invited. The significance of the moment wasn't lost on me, despite the distraction of my lust.

We hadn't made it past more than the threshold when he tugged on my clothing. "Take this off," he ordered.

I worked the dress over my head while he kicked off his loafers. I couldn't remember having ever seen his feet bare, and the sight was entirely too sexy for what it was. They were long and pedicured and manly. How was it possible that was such a turn-on? I didn't even like feet.

"And the bra," he said, as he began to undo his pants.

I watched him as I threw off the last piece of my clothing, watched as his greedy eyes skimmed across my naked body. Eagerly, I waited to be able to do the same to him, but he'd only gotten his cock out when he lifted me up, letting my legs wrap around him before he pressed me against the wall across from his door.

"I want to be inside you." He rubbed the length of his cock, hard and hot, against my throbbing pussy.

"Yes. Yes, Edward, yes!" I bucked my hips up, inviting him to slide inside. Begging him.

His crown notched at my hole, and I reached down to help guide him in, but he yanked my arm away and pinned it with the other above my head. He held them there with one hand as his other stroked the underside of my breast.

"You know what I mean when I say that. Tell me you know what I mean."

I paused, wanting to be connected with him like this—with understanding—even more than I wanted to be connected with him with my body. I replayed his words in my head. He wanted to be *inside me*. Inside all the way. Not just physically, but in *every* way. Mentally, emotionally.

Didn't he know that he already was? Hadn't that been his goal all along?

Yes, it had. So he did know. Or he guessed. Maybe what he needed was to know that I knew too.

"I know," I said earnestly. "I know who you are."

He closed his eyes and growled at that, tilting his pelvis to slide his cock through my folds. Still, he didn't enter me, keeping his lids squeezed shut as if trying to hold onto control.

When he opened them again, he brought his hand from my breast up to grip my chin. "You have to choose this. I'm not deciding this for you. You choose if I put you down and let you walk away. Really walk away. Or you choose to keep put. But as soon as I'm inside you, that's where I'm going to stay. You will be mine. Tell me you understand."

I don't know why I hesitated. I understood what he was saying, and I'd already made my choice. Months ago, when I'd first shared anything real with him, the decision had been made. Maybe even before that. When I'd let him put a ring on my finger. When I followed him to Europe.

When I'd taken that goddamned meeting with a stranger, and he'd seen me for who I was. Maybe all the way back then.

Now he was giving me a chance to walk away? To *really* walk away? From this house, from this island, from this marriage. From his threats and his ruin.

A smart woman wouldn't believe him.

Maybe I didn't either.

It was a serious ultimatum, too important to be discussed in the midst of orgasms and the temptation of his beautiful cock. He could very well have said it only to make me uncomfortable. To turn himself on.

Not that the steel rod pressing against my pelvis needed it. The bead of pre-cum at his tip certainly seemed to indicate he was fully aroused.

Still, it could have been just words.

But the possibility that they weren't words, the possibility that he truly meant the rest—that I'd be his, that he'd be inside me permanently? It somehow seemed worth the risk.

"I understand, Edward," I said, sure of the decision if not sure of him. "And I'm not going anywhere. I choose to stay."

I hadn't even finished speaking when his mouth claimed me, simultaneously shoving his cock into me with a vigorous thrust. Over and over he drove into me, his pace rapid and controlled. He released my hands, needing to use his to hold my thighs around him, and I threw them around his neck, winding my fingers through the back of his hair.

He kissed me as he fucked me, his mouth straying occasionally to suck on my neck or pull at my nipple with his teeth until I was squirming from the pain. Then he'd pound into me with even more force, plunging into the deepest parts of me.

It was rough and uncomfortable. My back was going to have bruises from the edge of the closet door frame that slammed into me with each of his thrusts. My breasts were already tender from his bites, my legs ached from how tightly I was wrapped around him, and still it was more pleasurable than any sex I'd ever had. Another orgasm was already gathering, fueled by his frantic tempo, the tilt of his pelvis against my clit, and the skillfully angled stabs of his cock.

And I knew then, if this was as far inside of him that I ever got—him fully dressed, barely in his room, his secrets never to cross the threshold of his lips—it would be enough. I could be the exposed one of us. I could be the one who was opened up and put on display. I could be raw and pulverized and broken down. For him. I could be that for him, and he would never have to give me anything more than he'd given me so far.

Because I was already more loved than I'd ever been, and I could die happy in that.

With this realization, I came, my pussy clenching around Edward's cock so hard I pushed him out of me.

He let go of me so quickly I almost fell. Thank goodness for the wall. I stepped toward him, lifting my mouth for his, but he stepped away, a smirk on his lips.

"I'm going to have to fuck you twice as hard for that," he said, sweat beaded on his brow. "On the bed."

As I walked by, he changed his mind and grabbed my ass with one hand to pull me into him. He assaulted me with a kiss, his chest pressing against the bullet tips of my breasts as he walked me to his bed. As soon as the back of my calves felt the frame behind them, he pushed me to the mattress.

I crawled backward up the bed to make room for us, my eyes never leaving him as he shoved his pants to the floor and worked the buttons of his shirt.

He was always so magnificent to look at. Naked, he was otherworldly. Too perfectly chiseled to be a man. Too manipulative and deviant to be a god. More of a devil in bare flesh than he ever had been in a suit.

Jesus, I thought, dizzy at the sight of him.

But what I said was, "Edward," my tone threadbare, even to my own ears.

278 | LAURELIN PAIGE

"I'm here," he said, stepping up to the mattress, his cock drenched from my juices, jutting out in front of him. He took it in his hand and jerked it up and down, wielding it as confidently as he wielded any other aspects of his power.

He still had a grip on it as he crawled up the mattress beside me, letting it go only to cradle my face when I reached my mouth toward his. He took my lips this time, kissing me even more zealously than he had when he'd had me against the wall. I tried to turn my entire body toward him, wanting my chest against him, but he had other ideas, snaking his hand around my waist and twisting me to my side before pulling my ass up to meet his pelvis. His hand at my face slipped under my head and around so he could hold my chin in place.

While his tongue continued to fuck my mouth, he nudged his cock between my thighs, easily sliding into my soaking pussy.

There was something more romantic about this position, even though he was fucking me from behind. Everywhere we were skin to skin, the contact so intense I felt it on the insides of my entire body. His kiss was deeper. His cock, too, his languid thrusts hitting the most sensitive parts of my pussy.

And even when his hand at my face found its way to my neck, even when his fingers scratched at my throat, pressing against my windpipe, making it hard to get a good breath, even then being in his arms felt good. He was dangerous, yes. He wasn't trustworthy. He was as cruel as he was beautiful.

He was still a devil, but now he was the devil I knew.

And I'd never in my life felt so safe.

TWENTY-THREE

I woke up in the dark, the sheets tangled around me, the bed empty. It took a minute for me to remember where I was, how I'd fallen asleep in Edward's arms after marathon sex. My eyes were still heavy, and it would be easy to curl into the pillow that smelled like him and go back to sleep, but his absence nagged at me. Our relationship, strange and fragile and unformed as it was, captivated me. I wanted it to be as big as it might be, wanted to allow it to swell and grow, and shutting my eyes to it now didn't seem like the best move.

With a groan, I threw my arms overhead and stretched, feeling every delicious way my body had been used before climbing out of the comfortable bed. Snatching his discarded shirt to wrap around me, I went to the bathroom then set out on a search for my husband.

I crept into the dark hall, straining for any sound of movement, finding only thick silence. With no light, I fumbled to the library and found it also dark, but a faint flicker drew my attention out the library window. It was coming from the top of the pool house at the back of the yard. The firewall was lit. I'd found him.

I pushed out the side door and stepped barefoot into the breezy night, circling around the pool to get to the stairs beyond it that led up to the sanctuary I'd built. It gave me a prideful thrill to know Edward was up there. Beyond signing off on the plans, he'd never acknowledged the finished work, which had been fine enough. I'd made the space for me. Still it was nice to know he appreciated it as well.

At the top of the stairs, I paused to take in his profile. He was sitting on the sectional, dressed only in his linen pants, his expression tight as he stared out at the nearly full moon reflecting on the ocean. A bottle of amber liquid sat in his lap, half empty. While I watched, he brought it up to his mouth, taking a swig. From the shape of the container, it looked like Hennessy, which meant it probably hadn't been a full bottle when he'd come out since there had already been one open in his bar, so I couldn't know for sure how much he'd drunk. My guess was enough, since the bed had been cold on his side, and his usually straight posture was slouched.

I'd been quiet, and with the crash of the waves, I wasn't sure he'd heard me approach so I cleared my throat before emerging from the shadows, not wanting to startle him.

He didn't look over until I was standing at the other end of the sectional, and even then it was only a quick glance.

It wasn't like I didn't expect it. Every time we'd fucked, he'd pushed me away after. Why should tonight be any different?

This time, though, when he pushed, I didn't intend to budge.

"May I join you, Edward?" It was a question, but my

tone was clear that I meant to sit whether he said I could or not. That was a trick I'd learned from him. How to command even while maintaining a polite appearance.

"You may," he said, and whatever notion I had that I might be able to dominate this moment fell away because his tone clearly said he was still in charge.

I sighed as I plopped down in the corner spot, three cushions away from him. *Too far* away from him. But I didn't know how to be closer, not with the invisible shield I could feel present around him. Not with the distance he'd already created by sneaking out here in the night. Not with the bottle he held as tightly as I wished he were holding me.

I curled my feet underneath me and waited in case he had something he wanted to say. If he was in charge, he had the first rights of conversation. He had the ability to take this anywhere he wanted.

But he remained silent, wrapped up in his thoughts and his cognac, and maybe it was an obvious message that he wanted to be left alone.

I was tired of being alone, though. Tired of being alone on this island, but also tired of being alone in my whole life, and something about the chemistry that clearly existed between us made me think he might actually be tired of being alone too.

He appreciated honesty, anyway. And honesty for me at the moment was being here with him, telling him my thoughts, even if they disrupted his own.

"I don't know what's going on between us," I said, hesitantly.

If he knew, it would be fanfuckingtastic if he clued me in.

When he said nothing, I gave him more rope. "Or if you even think anything is going on between us." My skin prickled with that nervous excitement that comes from putting something brave out there. He could cut me down now. Dash all the hopes I had for us with only a glare.

Or he could surprise me and tell me something wonderful.

I waited in case it was the latter.

His only response was to take another swig of brandy.

Guess I was talking to myself then. "It sure feels like something to me," I muttered, turning my gaze from him to the lone bird circling the edge of the water, his wings caught in the gleam of moonlight.

"What kind of something does it feel like?"

My head shot back toward Edward who was peering at me with a curious gaze.

Well, shit, that backfired. I'd wanted him to tell me what it was, not the other way around.

But that was the way with us. I kept the truth hidden inside me, and he tugged and pulled until it was outside of me, a living thing, wriggling in his hands. Like I was giving birth out of my mouth, and he was the proud doctor who took all the credit.

And I liked that way about us, for the most part. It had gotten us this far, anyway. So I resumed my role. "It's confusing," I admitted. "You told me you were going to kill me. You alluded to it again today. You keep me trapped as your prisoner on this island, and yet..." And yet I felt things. Enormous things. About him.

Saying that felt too big. Like I wasn't dilated enough for that. I needed some sort of epidural.

I leaned forward and reached my hand out toward the cognac.

"Oh, come on," he said, relinquishing the bottle to me. "How trapped have you been really?"

I practically choked on the swallow I'd just thrown back. I wiped at my mouth, coughing.

"Uh. Pretty trapped."

"How hard did you try to get away?" He stared intensely at me, forcing me to really think about the answer.

I had tried in the beginning. But I certainly hadn't exhausted my avenues. After learning what Edward had told the islanders, I hadn't attempted to talk to anyone besides Joette about the real circumstances of my confinement. I hadn't tried to seduce any of the Spanish-speaking workers who'd helped with my redesigns. I hadn't tried to steal a boat in the middle of the night. I hadn't tried to hack Edward's computer to get to the internet or even searched the staff's quarters for a laptop or a satellite phone, both of which surely existed.

I couldn't begin to say why I hadn't tried harder. It hadn't been because I was scared. It might have been a little because I was lazy. The truth was, though, when I really thought about it now, there hadn't been enough reason to want to leave. What did I have waiting for me beyond Amelie? What did I have waiting for me beyond Edward?

The revelation threatened to knock me off balance.

Then the look in Edward's eyes definitely threw me off balance. It said, *See? Not so easy to define what's going on now, is it?* Because what must he have been thinking leaving me here? Had he expected me to be gone when he came back? Each time he arrived, was my presence a surprise? Had he wanted me to escape?

Had he been glad when I hadn't?

I shook my head, more confused than I'd been before. "If I'm not your prisoner, Edward, then what am I?"

It was his turn to sigh and reach out for the bottle, which I passed without comment. He took a slow draw off the neck then settled it back in the crook of his arm, his brow furrowed as though searching for what he wanted to say.

I brought my knees up to the sectional and hugged my arms around them, letting him take his time, the same way he'd coaxed me with patience in all of his sessions.

Finally, he spoke. "You asked me earlier today what sort of relationship I had with my father."

I blinked, caught off guard by the apparent change of subject. "Sure. Yeah. I did," I said, curious where he was going.

"We weren't close, exactly. Stefan Fasbender wasn't a mean man or cruel in anyway, but, like your father, he worked all the time. He did make quite an appearance of being a family man—everyone said he lived for his company and us—but both Camilla and I knew that what he really loved besides his job was our mother."

"Amelie." I twisted the ring on my finger, the one that had belonged to her. It had felt significant that he'd given it to me. Even more so now that I knew it represented a deep love.

"She really was a lovely woman. It was easy to see why he was so enraptured by her. She was physically beautiful, something you can tell just by looking at photographs— dark hair, pale skin, plump lips. But all that was magnified when you were actually in her presence. She radiated joy, and if you've never seen that on a person, it's incredibly attractive. She made everyone around her feel it with her. It was infectious, and the three people most infected were my father, Camilla, and me. She doted on us. Spoiled us with love and affection. She was better than Father Christmas. She was magic like that."

I smiled at the image. "No wonder you named the island after her. It's magic here too."

"Yes." He gave a respectful nod. "You can imagine how devastating it was for all of us to discover she was terminally ill. I was almost eleven. Old enough to understand that what was happening was not normal, but not quite old enough to understand the intricacies of something as complicated as ovarian cancer.

"The real indicator that it was serious was how my father behaved. He stepped away from his job for weeks at a time, desperate to be at her side through every treatment, through every bout of nausea, through every crying jag. I remember making a huge effort to protect Camilla from it all. She was only six, and I'd ignore homework to keep her entertained so that she wouldn't go searching for my mother's attention. But then, when she was asleep or busy with the nanny, I'd sneak up to my parents' room and watch from the door frame as he tended to her, unnoticed by her because of the fog of medication. Unnoticed by him because of his preoccupation with her."

My throat ached with sympathy, and I wanted to say something, but the cadence of his words indicated he was getting to a point, and my condolences weren't it. So I took my cue from the way he always behaved in his sessions with me, holding back and just listening.

"Understandably, the business suffered from my father's absence. Accelerate, was the name of his company. Not impressive compared to Werner, by any means, but it was substantial. A handful of television stations and some newspapers. He'd inherited a lot of money and bought into media at the right time. He'd built most of it before he'd even met my mother. (He was forty-two when they met, a dozen years her senior. I came along three years later.) He was so blinded by his devastation with what was going on with my mother that he didn't take the time to take proper measures at Accelerate. He should have stepped down as CEO. He should have pulled himself from operations, but he didn't. Which made the company vulnerable, and soon it was ripe for takeover.

"When he realized what was happening, he tried to retaliate. Tried to buy stock in the company that was purchasing, but stock options weren't available. Tried to get his entire team to resign—a tactic known as a poison pill—but the purchasing company didn't care to retain the management team. There's probably more to the back and forth of the negotiations—I was only thirteen by the time this came to a head, so my knowledge has been only pieced together from accounts from other board members years later. The point is, he lost Accelerate.

"And two months later, he lost his wife."

My inhale was sharp and audible, despite having already known the bare bones of the story. The sound brought his eyes to me as I covered my mouth with my hand.

"We weren't completely destitute, mind you. We hadn't lost everything. Money was exchanged in the takeover, though a lot of that went to pay the medical bills. My father had gone all out in search of experimental treatments, each of which were costly and didn't work in the end. There was money in a trust, still, but it wasn't going to last forever. He tried to return to Accelerate as a high-level employee, but the new company had no need for his expertise, since all they planned to do was tear the company apart and sell it piece by piece. Which they did, rather quickly, I might add. He was devastated watching his life's work be demolished, and, after the death of my mother, his two reasons for living were gone."

"He killed himself." The words came out of my mouth before I meant to say them. I'd read this too, but it hadn't been quite so shocking without the details.

"Yes, he did." Edward's eyes were dark and unreadable. "The trust was left to me and my sister, and our care was put in the hands of a cousin we'd only met once before. She and her husband were the trustees and, with no one monitoring them except each other, they sent us to foster care and spent all the money. What money there was after the fall of all the Accelerate stocks, which were worthless after the company was torn apart."

He looked at the bottle in his lap, but instead of taking another swallow, he put the cap on it and set it on the ground. Then he leaned forward, bracing his elbows on his thighs. "The foster system separated us, and Camilla ended up in an abusive family. Burned and beaten for years, until I could get her out of the clutches of that man. The damage had already been done. My situation wasn't nearly as bad. I was moved around a few times, no one wanting an angry, maladjusted teenage boy—and I was certainly both. The homes that took me in along the way were hardly stable. The neglect and lack of supervisory attention did give me time to plan, though, and even before I knew about Camilla, even before I discovered all the money was gone, I knew that one day I'd get my revenge. One day I'd take back what was owed."

He turned his head toward me, his eyes searing into my skin. "I've been living and planning and working for vengeance since I was thirteen, Celia. Before you were even in preschool. It's taken years to find the right path. So many times I've been close, but never as close as now. Do you understand what I'm saying?"

My stomach dropped like there was an anchor in its place and it had been thrown out to sea, taking all of me with it. Because suddenly I did understand what he was saying. "The company that took over—it was Werner Media, wasn't it?"

He didn't have to answer for me to know I was right, and he didn't. He just kept his gaze pinned in place, watching me react. The brandy on an empty stomach suddenly seemed like it had been a very bad idea.

"But...but...but that's just business!" I exclaimed. Though, I knew that there were ethical business practices and less ethical ones, and from his description of the situation, I guessed this had been the latter. "And what about the cousin? The one who took all the money? Or the foster dad who hurt Camilla? Things turned out shitty, but it wasn't all my father's fault. There were other demons in this story, too."

"And those demons have already been taken care of."

A chill shuddered up my spine at the ominous pronouncement.

"For that matter, my father is also to blame, and I acknowledge that. He was a pathetic coward, taking his own life instead of caring for his children, and, believe me, if I could kill him again for it, I wouldn't hesitate."

His tone was as vicious as his words, his demeanor as cruel as his intentions, and, if I'd ever forgotten, here was the reminder—Edward Fasbender was a devil.

And I'd fallen in love with him. Crashed into love with

him. There wasn't a part of me that wasn't mangled and damaged from the impact. The best I could hope was that he'd crashed into love with me, but now that I'd heard his story, I could see why that outcome was unlikely.

I swallowed back the ball at the back of my throat and blinked away tears. "I've only ever been a tool. A means to get to him. To ruin his life the way he ruined yours."

The slight sag in his shoulders said everything.

It was stupid to be so surprised. He'd outright told me he wanted my father's shares. But I hadn't truly under-stood. I'd thought he wanted to move into the U.S. market because he was a ruthless businessman. That felt somehow easier to handle than being the means to execute a plan that was emotionally motivated. Especially after knowing the details of his story. If I'd lived through something so brutal and painful, I'd want revenge too.

Except, the man he wanted revenge against was my father. A man I loved, despite his flaws. "You still want to take him down, don't you? Even now. Even after us."

He didn't bother to deny it. "I won't let you get taken down with him."

I bit my lip, holding in a sob. "Really? You've already taken me down. Broken me. All this time you were doing that—you were only ever interested in finding out things you could use to get to my father, weren't you? Hoping to make me 'yours' so I could manipulate him for you some-how. Was that the reason you kept me alive?"

He scowled. "Don't be ridiculous. I wanted you to be mine because you belong with me. I wanted you to be mine so that I could justify—to myself, at least—not go-ing through with plans I've worked a fucking lifetime to implement."

He was still torn, the evidence in the frayed pitch of his words. Still divided between wanting me and a revenge scheme that consumed him as thoroughly as any of my games had consumed me.

Or maybe he was just angry about the situation. About the cost that came with keeping me alive and giving up access to my shares. Fuck, I'd give them to him if he asked me to. If he'd just say he didn't need his revenge anymore because he had me. If he'd just say he loved me.

But I'd never been anyone's first choice, not even my parents'. My mother preferred her gossip and social hour to time with me. My father preferred his golf and his empire. Hudson preferred The Game and then Alayna. Edward preferred his revenge.

"I guess I understand what it must have felt like for you as a kid, not being the priority of your father's affections. Of anyone's affections." It was childish and passive-aggressive, and now he knew how hurt I was, and even without outright telling him that I was in love with him, he would be stupid not to have figured it out.

"Bird…" he said, his arms starting to reach out before thinking better of it and retreating into his body.

I shook my head, denying the term of affection. "It's not your style to pretend like you're worried about my feelings. You don't need to start now. I know what my value is in this world. I'm practiced at being the one who matters less."

The memory of my father spanking me flashed in my head. He'd put me in second place then too. Believing someone else's word over mine.

Edward started to say something, something I heard nothing of because of where my thoughts had led me.

"Wait. Accelerate was a London company." I did the math in my head to be sure I was right. "That wasn't my father who screwed your dad over. He didn't run that branch of the company back then." It had been Werner Media's brief venture into the European market, a disastrous one from what my mother had told me in later years.

"Don't try to protect him," Edward said.

"I'm not trying to protect him. Lord knows he's failed at trying to protect me."

He put a finger up, as if bookmarking the topic. "We're going to revisit that."

Despite the course the evening's conversation had taken, with the promise of a future session, of Edward wanting to know about a pain I had yet to tell him, a bud of hope sprung inside me.

"But tell me who you think I should be blaming if not Warren. It was a subsidiary of Werner, yes, but your father was the CEO. He oversaw everything that happened under him."

"He did, and he didn't. Not back then. The branch that went into England had autonomy."

"Then who was behind the decision?"

The hope bud inside of me blossomed into something bigger, fed by an odd combination of relief and exhilaration. See, I understood the want for revenge, too. I just had never been ambitious enough to try to go after it. Not when my father had shot down my first attempt.

Now, though, with Edward, perhaps it was time to think bigger.

I almost smiled when I gave him my answer. "A man I'd fully get behind you hurting—my uncle, Ron."

TWENTY-FOUR

Edward

She'd changed everything.

From the moment she walked into that conference room at the St. Regis Hotel, my course had veered. Her eyes. The tilt of her chin. The way her lips formed into a natural pout. I'd been transfixed.

Then, little by little, she altered me. Changing the very nature of who I was. I'd been a vessel, a piece of stemware full with the wine of revenge, and she'd shattered me into a thousand shards of glass, and now I didn't even recognize myself.

Discovering Warren Werner might not be the enemy I thought he was, brought the biggest change of all. A death of sorts. If what she said was true, if there was another villain behind the destruction of my family, then I couldn't be the man I'd been anymore. I'd have to become someone new, someone who didn't live and breathe to bring down Werner Media. I didn't know who that man was. I didn't know how to be him.

She thought I'd ruined her?

She'd ruined me. In every dangerous and noble way.

I needed time to process it. Long hours of examination and research, but I couldn't do that yet because of her. Because she was sitting three cushions away from me, on the verge of shedding another layer of skin, and I needed to devote all my thoughts and energy to her. To whatever pain this was that had her tense and snarling.

I didn't just need to—I *wanted* to.

I wanted to know everything about her, the good and the bad, but especially the bad. I knew what it felt like to carry agony, how it corrupted and controlled. How it turned into poison. Without someone willing to burrow and excavate and scrape out the heartache, it grew into a cancer that compelled actions of evil. It was too late for me, but for her—I wanted to replace those pains in her, wanted to weed them out and take them on myself. She didn't have to be the angry, destructive woman she'd been inhabiting for years. I would be her wrath for her.

Starting with Ronald Werner.

"When did it start?" I asked, making my question too direct for her to sidestep.

Her eyes widened, startled. Then she settled into a frown. "Are you guessing?"

"Am I wrong?" I knew I wasn't. As soon as I'd seen her reaction to the man when he'd shown up at our wedding reception, I'd known he'd hurt her in some contemptible way.

And there was only one usual way that men like that hurt younger women.

Even without her confirmation, I wanted to rip his balls

off and shove them down his throat so he couldn't scream out while I raped his ass with my fist. It still wouldn't make up for however he'd touched her, however he'd harmed her. But it would be a good start.

Her body sagged as she looked out to the ocean, then toward the fire, the light catching the moisture in her eyes. Finally she turned her gaze back to me. "He didn't rape me, if that's what you assume."

My jaw clenched. If it wasn't rape...

"Would rape have been worse?" I asked, my mind already taking me to darker places. Scenes informed by the terrible things I'd witnessed other powerful, depraved men do. Images I could barely stand to imagine let alone discover they were real.

I was prepared when she shook her head, her chin trembling. "No. It wouldn't have."

She curled her legs into her chest and wrapped her arms tightly around them. I ached to pull her into my arms instead, to wrap myself tightly around her, but I resisted the urge. That would only be sealing the cap on the poison. She needed to let it out before I could fill her with something new.

"When did it start?" I asked again, giving her a place to begin.

Her lips pursed. "Is this a session now?"

"Do you need it to be?"

She started to say no. I could feel her dismissal of the subject in the air, firm and resolute.

But before the word made it out of her mouth, she reconsidered, her eyes drooping with the honesty of her realization. "Yes, Edward. I think I do."

"Have you told anyone before? Your parents? A counselor? A friend?"

The shake of her head was barely perceptible. "Just my father."

"The time he spanked you. When he didn't believe you." It wasn't a question because I already knew. It was only said to let her know that I did.

A nod. "After that it seemed like too much work to talk about it. And pointless. So I just…" She took a deep breath, her eyes searching the horizon as if that would give her the answer.

"You pushed it down inside you. Tried to forget it. Hoped it would disintegrate with neglect, but instead it rotted and splintered until it was jabbing into everything else in your life."

"Yeah, that." She almost smiled. "Maybe you should do this for me."

Ah, little bird, I would that I could.

I reached down for the bottle at my side, feeling the need to guzzle the whole thing down. As much as I needed it, I knew she needed it more. I unscrewed the cap and offered it over without bringing it to my own lips.

Her face paled. "No. Thank you. My stomach can't handle it."

I regretted not having more for her out here—a plate of food, crackers. A bottle of water. The temptation to pick her up and carry her inside where I could properly care for her was hard to resist, but I feared the momentum would be lost, and we had so little already.

I recapped the bottle but kept it in my lap, simulating our usual sessions with the routine of a drink in my hand.

"Whenever you're ready."

Her sigh was heavy as she brought her hand up to absentmindedly caress her throat, as though there were an invisible talisman strung around her neck. It was the very spot where my fingers had grazed only hours ago as I'd buried myself inside her. Could she still feel me there? Clinging to every part of her?

I hoped she did. I hoped it helped.

"My grandfather and I were close," she began, and my pulse turned sluggish, realizing she'd tried to tell this story to me before. "I spent a month with him every summer at his country home from the time I was two until he died, which was when I was six. Ron inherited that home, and, I guess because my parents thought I was attached to the routine—or, more likely, because they liked the freedom without me around—they decided to keep up the annual trips when my uncle offered to continue them.

"So I guess it started when I was seven, though it didn't necessarily feel like it started then. It was gradual, so gradual that it was impossible to pinpoint a beginning. I was a frog in a hot pot and, when I first got in, the water wasn't even warm. I have no idea when it started boiling."

Seven years old. Bile formed in the back of my throat. I could remember Genevieve at seven, still a small child. Practically a baby.

"Did he touch you?"

Her brow furrowed in confusion. "Yes, he touched me. There was always touching. But it didn't feel nefarious, not back then. It felt like love is what it felt like. He adored me. He pampered me. He gave me pretty dresses and brought people in to do my hair and nails. I was a princess when I was with him. He made me feel special, and our relationship was special because of that. So, you know, it wasn't really a big deal when he would bring out his camera. It was fun, honestly. I'd pretend I was a model, posing for him in all sorts of goofy ways. Pretending I was older than I was.

"Or he'd take me out to the garden. He'd put up a wooden swing on one of the trees—a great big wooden swing, big enough to seat an adult. Never mind that there was an entire playscape on the other side of the house that my grandfather had installed for me. Ron said the swing was *our* place. He'd let me on it when I was all dressed up—my mother would have made me change into play clothes, but Ron didn't. And he'd push me so high, it felt like I was flying. And I'd laugh and laugh, and he'd laugh too, and it felt really good to make someone that happy. Because that was new to me. I'd never made anyone happy. Not like that.

"After he pushed me for a while, he would say it was his turn, and he'd sit down in my place, and I'd try to push him for all of two seconds, and he wouldn't budge, of course, because he was so much bigger than me, so then he'd laugh and pull me into his lap with him, and he'd hold me while we rocked back and forth, back and forth. And, if he held me a little too tight and a little too long, and if his pants would get rigid underneath me—well, that was just part of it."

I bit down so hard on my tongue that I tasted blood. Castration wouldn't be enough. His punishment would have to be prolonged.

"You didn't tell anyone?" I could barely keep the disgust out of my voice.

"It never occurred to me that I should. Not early on. My parents didn't ask enough about my vacation for it to come up, and I was brought up in one of those *children should be seen, not heard* environments so it wasn't like there was an opportunity for me to spout out the details. And, like I said, it had been fun, and Ron made me feel good, so there was no reason to protest when they sent me again the next summer.

"It escalated from there. The touching grew more intimate. The lap sitting happened more often, and not just on the swing. Squirming, I discovered early on, made it last longer. He liked it too much. So I learned to sit very still. The whole time he'd say lots of nice things in my ear. He'd tell me how pretty I was, how beautiful my body was. How good I was. How *special* I was. He'd tell me he loved me. In detail. Then he'd urge me to tell him I loved him, and after I did, he'd make me promise not to tell anyone about our love because it was so special, it had to be a secret. No one would understand our 'special love.' And it was weird, but it was all right."

"He was grooming you." In general, I tried not to interrupt her monologues with commentary, but I wasn't sure how much she understood of the situation. She'd been a child when it all occurred, and if she hadn't looked back at it very often, she might not have had a chance to apply adult wisdom to the memories.

My suspicion was confirmed when her head jerked toward me, her expression startled. "That's right. He was."

Quietly, she chewed on her lip, her eyes dazed as she likely put pieces together, looked at past memories with this new light. There would be a lot to unpack from this, and I'd do it with her, when she was ready. Right now, though, she had to just get to the end, to the moment that finally pushed her to tell her father. To the place where the water was boiling.

I searched for the right question to ask, the right bait to draw more of the poison from her. Before I could find one I was happy with, she spoke on her own.

"He was very clever about it. About how he trained me. How he *groomed* me." She over enunciated the word, tying it firmly to the situation that had played out with her uncle. "It was subtle and very focused on me. On *my* pleasure."

It was hard to note the color of her cheeks in the weak light of the fire, but I could tell she was embarrassed, and my chest tightened.

"He, uh, he'd put some sort of stimulants in my baths. They made my body feel...relaxed. And fuzzy. Then he'd turn on the jets and show me how to sit so they'd, uh, hit me in the right place. And I'd sit there like that, feeling good while he read me erotic stories. Twisted fairy tales where Red Riding Hood got devoured by the wolf in a carnal way and where Sleeping Beauty was woken up with kisses in obscene places.

"His touch wandered too. Beneath my dresses, into my panties. Never going all the way inside me, but stimulating all the areas around it. He trained my body to his touch. Before I'd even had a period, he taught me how to respond. I thought I was made for him."

"Celia..." *You were made for* me. The words caught in my mouth, not wanting my devotion confused with her repugnant uncle, but feeling the need to say *something*. Anything.

She waved me away with her hand, knowing better than I did that it wasn't the right time. "He didn't make me call him sir until I was ten," she said. "From then on, it was always, 'Yes, sir.' 'No, sir.' 'What should I do for you, sir?' That was when I first remember being really unhappy about our relationship. It took that long. Isn't that stupid?"

"No," I said harshly, even though I knew the question wasn't for me.

She ignored me. "It started to feel like a chore then. The special princess feeling was still there, but it took more and more effort to get his love. And that was *my* fault, or so I believed. He'd done all these nice things for me and spent all this time with me, and I couldn't understand why I was so resentful about it all. Why I didn't appreciate it. I figured I was spoiled and ungrateful, just like my mother liked to say when I was acting out."

I brought a fist up to my mouth, a reminder to keep it shut. There were so many things I wanted to say to her, and none of them were important. She barely even acknowledged my presence anymore. She was in it, regurgitating the memories without any need of prompting.

"Then the parties started when I was eleven. And that's when I began to hate him. The first one was innocent enough—a bunch of men drinking and smoking cigars while my uncle paraded me around in a fancy dress. Several fancy dresses." She let out a disgusted chuckle. "He told me to pretend it was a fashion show, and then afterward, I was to mingle with 'my fans.' Nothing salacious really, but it felt creepy all the same. How they'd reach out and pet me like I was a dog or a doll. Passing me around to sit on their laps. Twirling their fingers through my hair.

"The next year was…" She shook her head slowly, her eyes closed, and I could only imagine the horrors that she relived behind her lids. When she opened them again, she let out a long breath before speaking. "I don't know why I didn't tell my parents that year. I knew it was wrong, and I didn't want to go back, but I felt trapped. I felt like I'd agreed to it all, somehow, sometime, and of all the things he taught me, he'd never taught me how to back out.

"So, when I was thirteen, I returned. And I was nervous about it already, especially after...after the last time."

She'd tell me about that too, eventually. She needed to expel it more than I needed to hear it, but I needed to hear it too. I needed to hear every evil thing that had been done to her so that I could properly make up for it.

Later, though. When she was ready.

"I'd already decided that if he had another party, I was going to find some way out of it. I'd pretend I was sick. I'd make myself sick, if I had to. I'd even brought a bottle of Ipecac syrup I'd stolen from the medicine cabinet back home, planning to use that to prove my illness, but the fucker didn't warn me this time. He'd sent me to bed for the night early, and I'd thought that got me off the hook.

"It must have been after midnight when he came and woke me. He gave me a sheer nightie to put on—it was a rule that I slept naked when I was at his house, then he took me down to the conservatory, the room where he entertained. There were fifteen men there. Maybe a few more. The room had a level change, a couple steps up to a stage-like area, you know, for, like, a band. He led me up there and then he…" She swallowed then cleared her throat. "He untied the straps of the gown and let them fall so I was naked. I tried to put my arms around me, to cover up, but he batted my hands down, and made me stand there like that. Everything on display. I mean, really on display. He showed me off like I was merchandise. 'Look at how pert her nipples are.' Then he'd turn me around and spread my cheeks apart. 'Look at her virgin ass.' 'See how pretty her virgin pussy is.'

"Then he auctioned me off."

She stopped, and I was relieved, unable to take another second of her story, but also desperate to hear every last word. I warred between the choice of telling her it was enough and pushing her on.

Because it was about her, because she was so close to the finish line, I prodded her on. "He *sold* you?" When I'd asked how she'd lost her virginity, she'd wanted to know what I'd meant exactly. She hadn't had her cunt penetrated, but there were a lot of other ways she could have been violated. I could picture the scene in my head and still couldn't wrap my head around it.

"Yeah. Basically. He was decent enough to stipulate that no one could actually fuck me. No dicks could come in contact with any part of me, but that was the only rule. They could touch me anywhere without penetration, and no one was to touch my ass—still a virgin there, thank God. They were allowed to come on me. They could use a vibrator for stimulation. They just had to pay for it."

"*Jesus*," I muttered, under my breath. I gripped the bottle in my lap, wanting to throw it. Wanting to destroy something as badly as this monster had destroyed Celia. It took everything in me just to bring it to my lips instead, letting the burn temper my rage. How dare a man do this to a child? To his own flesh and blood?

"Five of them offered the right price. They took turns, right there, in front of everyone else. Two of them helped Ron lift the chaise up to the stage so they could prop me how they wanted me. They touched me everywhere they were allowed. All five of them came on me. On my back, on my belly. On my tits. Two of them on my face. It was in my hair. I accidentally tasted some that was on my lips. The worst were the vibrators, though. Ron had several for them to choose from and they used them all at least once.

They loved making me come. Over and over. That was the most humiliating and confusing part, because it made me feel like I must be enjoying it, while I was dying inside. *Dying*."

I cringed, thinking of how I'd used her orgasms as a punishment, justifying it at the same time because I hadn't used a vibrator. And then wishing I had so that that memory might replace this terrible one.

"You know, I don't even know what any of them paid because the offers were whispered into Ron's ear. He'd either nod or give a thumbs up to indicate he wanted more. Sometimes I imagine they paid very little because that would serve him right. Other times I imagine they paid a fuck-ton because those fucking bastards deserved to pay up.

"It was after that, I told my father. He didn't believe me, and eventually I shut up about it, and the next summer, I was prepared to convince my best friend to invite me to her churchy camp so that I wouldn't have to go stay with Ron, but I didn't have to. My parents took me to Europe with them instead. And then they never mentioned going to Ron's again, and I don't know if it's because my father secretly believed me or if he just decided that he didn't want to deal with my protests, but it was over, and I was so relieved.

"But I was also only ordinary after that. And maybe that was the most horrible part of all of it. As glad as I was to never go back there, I've spent my life since wondering if anyone will ever give me the time and attention and adoration that Ron did. Sick, huh? No wonder I fell for my captor." Immediately, she brought her hands up to her forehead, shielding her eyes, as if she regretted saying the last part.

What was sick was how my entire being lit up at the admission, even in the midst of her horrible tale. She'd fallen for me, and I didn't deserve it, and I wasn't noble enough to try to convince her of that truth.

I couldn't be away from her a second longer, whether she had more to say or not. I was breaking for her and dying to hold her. I needed her touch as much as I was sure she needed mine.

I moved to kneel in front of her and grasped her wrists, peeling her hands away from her face so I could look her in the eyes. "None of this is your fault, bird. None of your reactions are wrong. Your uncle is a fucked-up psychopath and deserves to face severe repercussions for what he did, and none of this is your fault."

She shook her head vehemently, and so I said it again. Slower. "None of this is your fault, and you don't have to be brave about it anymore."

Her expression faltered, and I thought she was going to go there, was going to release herself to the pain, but the moment passed and her face turned hard.

"What, Edward? You think you understand me now?" She tried to yank away from me, but I held my grip.

"I know I do," I said solemnly, never moving my eyes from hers.

"You don't understand anything."

"I do. I understood you before too. This just gives clarity."

She was quiet for a beat, and I let go of her so I could move up beside her, intending to pull her into my lap.

But as soon as I was sitting on the sectional, she jumped to her feet. "It confirms my worth, doesn't it?" She began rapidly unbuttoning her shirt—*my* shirt. "I told you I knew what I was good for. Now you know too."

When she had the shirt loose, she dropped it to the ground and climbed onto me, straddling my lap.

This was all wrong. She was hiding behind this seduction routine. Building walls, trying to distract herself from the emotions she still hadn't let herself really feel. "Celia... what are you doing, bird?"

She began gyrating against me. "What I've been trained to do. What I'm best at."

"Don't." I sat back, bracing my arms on the back of the sectional so I wouldn't be tempted to touch her. It was harder to convince my cock not to react, but somehow I did.

"Am I too damaged for you now? Too used?"

My chest pinched. "Never."

"Then fuck me. I need to feel good. Make me feel good."

Her plea was desperate and heart wrenching, and I wrestled with the lure of her body, the smell of her arousal, the nearness of her mouth.

"Stop," I said, the word coming out tight and gritted.

Her lips pressed against my jaw. "What's wrong? You have to be the aggressor? Are those the rules between us? Just let me know because I'm good at rules, but only if I know them."

She was intoxicating. Hard to resist.

But the revulsion of her tale still hung in the air around us, and there was no way I could let this moment turn lustful. No matter how much she thought she wanted it now. She'd appreciate my restraint later, when she was thinking straight.

Abruptly, I flipped her to the cushion, pinning her wrists over her head. "I said stop."

"Not good enough for you to fuck now, am I?" Her chest heaved with each breath, her fury wrapped up in the movement of air through her lungs.

There wasn't anything I wouldn't do to take her pain from her, if I could. But since I couldn't, she had to actually *feel* it. It was the only way to get through it, and I'd be there for her every step of the way if she let me.

Just not like this. "I don't want fucking me to be associated with this place you're in right now."

"You're supposed to replace it."

"And I will. But not yet. Not this way."

She wrestled away from me, and I let her go, deciding that her retreat was progress, especially when she snatched the shirt off the ground and secured it around herself with two buttons.

But she was angry at me. Some of it misplaced anger, some of it masking other emotions. "What good are you then? Fuck you."

She started to walk toward the stairs, and I jumped up to block her. "You shouldn't be alone right now. If you want to go someplace else, that's fine, but I'm going with you."

"Confining me to this island isn't enough? Now I'm a prisoner in this house too?"

"We can argue about your prisoner status at a later time. Right now I care that you're my wife, and I'm not leaving you alone in this state."

"Your wife?" She balled her hands into fists and threw

them against my chest. "Fuck you." When I didn't budge, she hit me again. "Fuck you!"

I stood my ground, then, when she veered around me, I stepped in front of her and held her at her upper arms.

She struggled against my hold, the tears finally reaching her eyes with her frustration. "This isn't fair. If you aren't going to make it better then let me go. Just let me go!"

I pulled her closer, and spoke calmly at her ear. "I am going to make it better, but being alone is not what you need right now. And neither is sex."

"It's exactly what I need right now," she said, wrestling against my grip. When she realized I wasn't letting her go, she shoved at me with her palms. "Asshole." Another shove. "Devil." She pushed harder this time. "Fuck you, Edward. Fuck you for making me talk about this." Her voice cracked, the dam about to break.

"Keep going. I can take it." I braced myself for an onslaught.

Her next shove felt more like a punch. "Fuck you for thinking this would be good for me," she said, the tears flowing freely now. Another punch followed. "Fuck you for making me feel special." And another. "Fuck you for making me feel good. Fuck you for using me like that. Fuck you for breaking me down. Fuck you!"

I wasn't sure anymore if her curses were meant for me or for the uncle who had damaged her so reprehensibly. Possibly she meant them for us both, it didn't matter. I deserved her hatred and her pain, whomever the target was. I wanted to carry it all. It would fuel me in the future when I needed it. When my wrath was carried out appropriately.

For now, I tucked it away.

And when her bellows morphed into weeping, when her body convulsed with gut-wrenching sobs, I picked her up and cradled her in my arms, whispering sweet, soothing words while her tears soaked my skin, and she finally found release.

TWENTY-FIVE
Celia

I swept my hair to one side, and held it out of the way so that Edward could fasten the chain at my neck. "Is this for my birthday or our anniversary?" I asked, watching him in the mirror.

With deft fingers, he worked the clasp, then trailed the tips along my nape sending a delicious shiver through my body before moving his hands down to grip my hips. He met my eyes in our reflection. "The necklace is for your birthday." He pressed a kiss at the side of my throat. "The night out is for our anniversary."

I fiddled with the bird charm, a pretentious showcase of colored gemstones and diamonds, normally too gaudy for my taste, but the most perfect gift because of its symbolism. "By wearing this, I feel like I'm giving in to something. I was supposed to be a dragon that night, not a bird."

He chuckled. "It's always the tiniest dogs with the biggest barks."

I turned to face him directly, his man and musk scent smacking me so abruptly my thighs clenched automatically. "What's that supposed to mean?"

"That the smallest creatures always think they're scarier than they are."

He leaned in for a kiss, and I leaned away. "You think you can just kiss me after you belittle me like that?" I teased.

His hand came to hold my chin in place. "I think I can do whatever I want with what belongs to me, so yes."

I didn't fight when his mouth took mine, eager for his lips despite my taunting. It was a thorough kiss, one I felt down to my toes, and I wondered briefly how hard it would be to convince Edward to celebrate at home.

Then I remembered our date was taking me off the island, for the first time in a year, and I wasn't missing that for the world. I put my hands up to his satin lapels and pressed slightly, trying to keep some distance from him before he swallowed me up whole. As if he hadn't already.

He took the hint and, after another deep swipe of his tongue, he pulled away. "Anyway, it wasn't an insult. It was an observation." He rubbed at the spot below my lower lip where my makeup had smeared. "This lipstick isn't going to cut it. I plan on doing that a lot tonight, and you won't be given the opportunity to fix it everytime I do."

"This lipstick will be fine," I said, shooing him away. "You just need to give it time to dry before you do that again."

He twisted his wrist to glance at his watch. "You get five minutes. Then we're off." In a rare show of consideration, he left me so I could touch-up what he'd ruined without interference.

I took a deep breath, an attempt to settle the nerves he'd riled up, and turned back to the mirror. After fixing the lipstick, I studied my appearance. The dress he'd chosen was black with gold touches on the arms and at the waist. Though it was floor-length and long-sleeved, it was definitely one of the most revealing outfits I'd ever worn, the neckline plunging all the way to my waist. A slit up the front of one leg went all the way to my upper thigh, and Edward's refusal to let me wear panties made my pussy dangerously vulnerable to exposure.

"Better access," he'd said, when I'd questioned him about the choice earlier.

"Does that mean you're planning on taking advantage of that access?"

"We'll have to see how the night plays out, won't we?"

My cheeks reddened remembering the conversation, but even without the blush, my pallor was better than it had been in more than a month. Our session of confessions on the rooftop lounge had lanced open deep wounds. I'd been a wreck of myself afterward. Emotions that I'd smothered and ignored grew to vibrant life in the air, emotions that were toxic and corrupt and needed to be felt. Memories I'd buried resurfaced in waves. I spent days at a time crying, releasing the pain of a childhood I'd never been allowed to lament.

Edward had been at my side through the worst of it, holding me. Touching me. Forcing me to eat and move. Refusing to let me stay in bed and sleep away the agony. I'd tried more than once to make it physical, wanting his cock to distract me from my suffering, but he'd remained as chaste as he had in the earlier days of our marriage, insisting that sex would only confuse the things I was working through.

312 | LAURELIN PAIGE

He'd been right, admittedly. Not that I'd wanted to see
that at the time.

After a week of sobbing, I'd woken up with a new energy. Not better—not by a long shot—but determined to
start moving forward. And that required something that
Edward couldn't directly provide. I needed therapy, and I
needed time. He arranged the first without a debate, flying
in a psychiatrist to stay at Amelie and give me one-on-one
counseling.

The second, took more convincing. He'd insisted on
staying with me, and I'd insisted that he leave. When I had
pointed out that ignoring his business in favor of walking
me through my mental health wasn't any different than his
father's choice to abandon his career during his wife's illness, Edward had finally seen reason. He'd been gone for
almost four weeks, and while my therapist had pressed for
it to be longer, my husband refused to stay away for my
thirty-third birthday, which fell on our one-year anniversary.

Though we hadn't talked about it, things had definitely changed between us. It was most evident in the lax
of the rules that had surrounded my captivity before. Besides bringing in a doctor who spoke my language, I was
now allowed on the internet, and Edward and I had spoken
by phone several times a week. The conversations were
always short, mostly perfunctory, but they'd made me
feel cared for all the same. Never once had we discussed
the nature of our relationship. He hadn't given me rules
of what to say or who not to contact. There had been an
agreement of trust when I hadn't taken his offer to walk
away, and maybe I appreciated it too much to defy it or I
was too absorbed in my PTSD, but I hadn't once thought
to use my privileges to "escape." There wasn't anything I
wanted to escape from, except the scars that the past had

inflicted upon me, and I truly felt I had the best shot at that right where I was.

Even so, I was beyond excited for the outing he'd planned.

"You're really not going to tell me where we're going?" I asked after we'd been in the air for an hour. I'd been surprised when he'd taken me to the airstrip instead of the dock, assuming he'd meant to take me to Nassau for a fancy dinner. Apparently, his plans were grander than that.

Though I was fully aware of the bedroom in the back of the plane, we'd spent the flight talking, mostly about my therapy sessions, which had been uncomfortable, at first, then better as we'd talked on. I'd told him a lot of the most terrible things my uncle had done to me that night on the roof, and the initial telling of it should have been the worst part, but in my game-playing I'd learned there was a human tendency to feel the shame after the words were out, and my reaction had been exactly that. It was easier to try to forget I'd said those things, forget that he'd heard them, but he refused to let me, digging in and picking up the burden of those confessions as if they were his own. He wanted to know it all, every detail of the horrors, every memory as I uncovered it, and I found myself wanting to tell him all of it as well. There was still so much to go through, so many parts to remember and process.

But now, the plane had begun its descent, and I wanted to put aside the awful and focus on our anniversary night.

"It was never a secret," he said, linking his fingers through mine. "You just never asked. We're going to Exceso, a private island between Cuba and Haiti. It's owned by a wealthy man I'm acquainted with who knows how to throw a certain kind of party."

I didn't know much Spanish, but I took a guess anyway. "Exceso—*excess*? As in extravagant?"

"Muy bien, pajarita," his Spanish accent doing things to my lower regions. When I frowned, he translated. "Very good, little bird. Esteban touts the island as a place for men with questionable ethics to negotiate business deals. While there is a fair amount of that occurring, it's mostly a hedonistic pleasure resort."

My stomach tightened. "Like The Open Door?"

"Yes. With fewer rules and more dubious consent."

"Oh." I withdrew my hand from Edward's so I could wrench it with the other in my lap. Anxiety bubbled up through my chest and my mouth suddenly tasted sour. It had taken a lot for me to convince myself to go to the party in New York, and that had been knowing the club was well-monitored and safe. And now, after all the focus on the ones Ron had forced me to attend, an unstructured sex party felt especially disarming.

No wonder Edward hadn't volunteered the information sooner.

He reached over to my lap and took both hands in his, putting a halt to my fidgeting. "You'll be with me, Celia, and that means you'll be safe. Do you trust me?"

He'd shown over the past month that he trusted me. It felt ungrateful not to offer him the same.

And I did trust him. Didn't I?

I mostly did, but that didn't mean I didn't question his judgment. "Is there a reason why you chose this event for our date?"

"Several reasons. First, some of the men who go to Exceso own the women they bring with them."

"As in slavery?" My heart felt like it was beating through mud. My captivity had been nothing like the horrific situations so many other women were in. Situations where they were beaten and abused and forced into all sorts of sick, depraved sexual acts. "How can you be friends with a man who allows such a thing? Why don't you do something?"

"I never said we were friends. Going against Esteban Merrado is not something a person does haphazardly. Besides, it's difficult to differentiate those women who are willing to be owned and those who aren't. It's merely my suspicion that some may not be there of their own volition. If I ever witnessed any abuses that I was assured were real, I would most likely involve authorities—if I could safely—but I have not as of yet. The situation does give me an advantage, however. No one at Exceso pays too much attention when a woman cries kidnapped. In other words, it's a place I can take you and not have to worry about you trying to get away."

So much for having gained his trust.

I tried to remove my hands from his grasp, but he kept them pinned in place.

"Secondly," he continued, "I owe you a response to your last session. It's time I gave it."

My eyes shot up to his, my spine tingling. I'd forgotten about the second part of those sessions. His responses, it seemed, were meant to replace the bad experiences from my past. Did he want to take me to a sex party where I had fun instead? So I wouldn't remember the ones with Ron?

I didn't know that it was as simple as that.

But it was a sweet gesture. And a sex party with Edward wasn't entirely off-putting. Not at all, actually.

"Third, I enjoy seeing you uncomfortable, as you are well aware." He gave me a smug smile. "It's my anniversary, too. You shouldn't get all the fun."

I scowled at him, but it was hard to hold it. He was too charming, and though his charm was far from innocent, I liked the way he used it on me.

He was my husband. And I was in love with him, and for good or bad, that meant I would follow willingly where he led.

"Fine. I'll go." As though he'd given me a choice.

"Somehow I knew you'd come around. I brought you something that might make it easier." He released my hands and reached down into the cabinet at the side of the couch where we sat and pulled out a familiar-looking box, which he handed to me.

"Another present?"

"Not quite. It's already yours."

Puzzled, I opened it up to find my red feathered mask, the one I'd worn at The Open Door. "My dragon mask!" I lifted it to my face and slipped it on.

"Pajarita," he corrected, but I was too touched with the gifts and the moment to even pretend to be offended.

We landed soon after, onto an island that was probably twice the size of Amelie, from what I could see on the descent, and was a lot more built up with various structures. Edward had called it a resort, and I could see why. I counted no less than four swimming pools, and dozens of cabanas lined the beaches.

From the airstrip, a planked path flanked with tiki torches led a short way through forest to an outdoor entertainment area. Evening was upon us, and the festivities were already in full swing. Spanish music played through speakers attached on pillars surrounding the space. Two open bars bookended a large wooden floor. Hammocks were hung at the perimeters and various seating arrangements dotted the expanse. Men in tuxes and women in cocktail attire were spread around, conversing and drinking the way people did at parties my parents hosted back home. There was no signs of debauchery. No signs of dubious consent. Innocent, by all appearances.

I relaxed, doubting suddenly the need for my mask.

Before I could reach to remove it, Edward had his hand at my back, guiding me toward a silver-haired man who was approaching us.

"Edward Fasbender!" the man exclaimed with a heavy accent, followed by some Spanish words that I surmised was a question of how my husband was doing based on the answer he provided.

"I've been well, Esteban. Busy, but well."

"And your little project? How is that going?"

I shot questioning eyes at Edward.

"It's, uh...delayed," he said, his eyes darting toward me making me wonder exactly how much of his Werner revenge scheme he had shared with his acquaintance. "I'm preoccupied with other things, at the moment. Allow me to introduce you to my wife, Celia."

He hadn't included my maiden name in my introduction, making me suspect it was on purpose.

"Ah!" Esteban said, his eyes lingering too long on my very exposed cleavage. "Quite exquisite, I must say. Hard to tell with the mask, but it seems you've gone with a younger model."

318 | LAURELIN PAIGE

I already hated the man. He was smarmy and vile, and that could be gleaned just from his leer. If I spent more time with him, I could imagine how much more of his personality I would find I loathed.

"A younger model, yes. A better model, definitely." Edward's charm wasn't enough to counteract the repugnant stranger, but I held my tongue, gritting my teeth.

Since I hadn't been directly spoken to, there was no reason for me to speak.

Esteban moved closer, his eyes leaving foul stains on my skin. "Tell me, does she like to play the way your last one does? Should I have you escorted to the Resistance Room?" He reached out to run his knuckles across my jaw, and I flinched.

I didn't even want to know what the Resistance Room was. The name alone made me shudder. Though the suggestion that Marion had been there with Edward in the past spiked a curious jealousy.

Edward wrapped his arm around my waist, subtly pulling me into his side and out of Esteban's reach. "We're still learning what we like, at the moment. Tonight, we have something specific planned, however. The Base is open, isn't it?"

The man tsked. "Never any time for fun with you, is there? Yes. There are a handful of other workaholics already down there. Just a moment, and I'll summon one of my angels to take you there."

I followed his eyes as they landed on a woman I hadn't noticed before, wearing a white bikini and kneeling on the rough wood floor near the bar. Her head was down, but as Esteban clapped a syncopated rhythm, she looked up, then stood when she saw him gesture her over.

The whole interaction gave me the creeps. I'd studied the submissive thing, of course, seen it played out at The Open Door, and I could admit to seeing an appeal. But after Edward's hint that some of the women here might not just be submissive, but, rather, slaves, I didn't have the stomach for it.

My expression must have given me away because Edward shook his head. "No need. I well know the way. Take care, if we don't see you again on the way out."

Esteban flicked his hand, dismissing his angel with a glower before beaming again at my husband. "That's too bad you don't have time to stay awhile. It would be a delight to watch you break your bride in. The learning phase is definitely the most fun."

His lecherous stare made my hand fly up to fiddle with my necklace, covering myself with my arm.

Edward understood, already steering me away as he gave his parting words. "Yes, indeed. Still, you know I prefer to do the learning in private."

"Forgive me for hoping you'd changed," Esteban called back, followed by more words in Spanish.

Then we were walking out of the arena down another planked path, and I let out an audible sigh of relief. "That man is disgusting."

"He is," Edward agreed. "Which is why I try to come here only when I need to."

"When you 'need' to?" His response had a thousand reactions warring in my head. What kind of business did Edward *need* to do with men that associated with Esteban? And what kind of playing had my husband done here in the past? "I'm sure you *needed* to bring Marion here," I said, the most petty of my thoughts making it to my lips first.

"I didn't need to bring Marion here as much as she needed to be brought here. For very different reasons than you need to be here. The needs that I've had met here have not been sexual, though I have enjoyed those activities here on occasion." The path wound through more forest, breaking off here and there to lead to one structure or another. Signs indicated where the routes led with names that had my head spinning such as Mistreatment Room and Sharing Sector and Recovery Center.

I tried to ignore the distractions of my surroundings and concentrated on what Edward had said. There were questions I should be asking, questions about what he thought I needed here and what needs he had met. I was terrified of what his answers might be, but that wasn't why I didn't ask. My preoccupation with his former wife held too much power over me.

"You said Marion was submissive. Like that woman back there? Esteban's angel?"

"Mm."

"Did she kneel like that for you? Would she come when you summoned her with just a snap of your fingers?"

He studied me as we walked, looking for what, I wished I knew so I could be careful not to show him. Not that he could see much behind the mask, but hiding from Edward was never truly possible.

"She did," he said after several silent steps. "When it fit appropriately into our lives. Which wasn't as often as she would have liked."

"What about you? Did you like it when she obeyed?"

"Very much."

My chest burned, and I blinked away the white spots in front of my eyes. I didn't have to dissect myself too much to understand my anger was with myself, not Marion. As much as I admittedly liked the times that Edward took control and dominated me, I could never be so docile as to kneel in a corner waiting to be summoned. I could never be completely obedient. And because Edward liked it, I wished I could be that. Longed for that nature with a desperation that ached as it rattled against my ribs.

"Is that what you want with me?" My voice was barely over a whisper. We hadn't even discussed what kind of future we might have, if we had one at all, and here I was asking like we'd decided we'd try.

But this answer felt important, like it might decide whether or not a future was something we *should* even discuss.

"Complete submission?" he asked, seeming to consider his response carefully. "I don't believe that's what you want to give me."

His ability to always see me usually made me feel divine. Right now, it made me feel like a bug on a windshield. I'd been flying high in our relationship until this topic smacked me in the face.

I pulled away from his hand at my back and stopped walking. "I'm not asking what you believe I want. I'm asking what *you* want."

He went another couple of steps before he realized I'd halted. When he turned back, his brow was furrowed, his expression impatient. "This wasn't exactly the place I planned to have this conversation, nor the time. But if you need to hear something, I'll make it simple. I want to own you. Does that mean I want you kneeling at my feet like a well-trained dog? No, it absolutely does not. It does mean I want respect and deference, and yes, obedience, in measures that I believe you'd like to give, even if you don't know that you would. I definitely think you're capable. Most primarily, though, I need there to be honesty and trust between us. You didn't answer before—do you trust me?"

It was my turn to wear furrowed brows. His words made me feel warm and hopeful, but also hesitant, because what if he was wrong about what I could give? What if he was wrong about who I really was?

And because I had those doubts, it was hard to say that I exactly trusted him.

Honesty. He wanted honesty.

"I trust you, Edward, as well as I can right now. With as much as I can."

His eyes flashed with disappointment, so fast I almost was unsure I'd seen it. "That's a start. Let me ask you something smaller, then. Do you trust me with you here tonight? Do you trust that I have only your best interests in mind? Do you trust that I know what you can and can't handle, that I will care for you body and soul until we leave this island?"

I bit my lip, considering. It was a fair question. We were at a sex club, a place where trust was important, and I wanted to be here with him, even though he still scared me.

He scared me, but he'd never truly hurt me. And more than once he'd understood what I wanted and needed better than I did myself.

"Yes, I trust you," I finally answered. "But it doesn't mean that I'm not worried too."

He smiled slyly as he crossed the few steps back to me. Tipping my chin up with the knuckle of a crooked finger, he said, "I enjoy your apprehension as much as I enjoy your submission. I think this will work out just fine."

"Okay," I said tentatively. But there were still so many questions about what he wanted from me, what respect and deference and obedience looked like. What he expected out of our marriage. What he expected from me. "What about—?"

He cut me off. "The rest can wait." He nodded to the sign at the path that veered behind him. *The Base*. "We're here."

TWENTY-SIX

My knees were shaking as we approached the unassuming building before us. There were no windows, which made it all the more intimidating. The only kind of buildings I could think of without windows were the scary kind—prisons, dungeons. I shivered at the possibilities.

A security guard stood outside the two large wooden doors, which didn't help my trepidation. Especially when he scanned us both with a wand before we were allowed to enter. So Esteban didn't want weapons in his play spaces. Did he prefer to provide them himself?

As soon as the guard had cleared us for entry, I stopped Edward, grabbing him by the arm. "I know what I said to you about being able to take anything that you could dish, but I gotta tell you—I was all talk. I really don't like pain. Not real pain. I mean, the spankings are nice, but whips and floggers and other torture devices just aren't my thing. If you're really into them, I'll try. I really will, but I already know I'm not going to be very good at it because even the idea has me sweating and scared, and please don't make me do it. Please, Edward, please."

The guard laughed out loud behind me. "Newbie?"

Edward, at least, tried to hide his amusement. "I think it's obvious," he answered, then focused on me. "Why don't you step inside and take a look around before you work yourself into a panic?"

I pursed my lips. It was bad enough that I was terrified. Worse to be laughed at.

But Edward's voice was calm and his hand at my back, soothing. "Fine," I agreed, hoping my heart didn't beat out of my chest.

With a small smile, he wrapped his hand around the large metal handle and pulled the door open, stepping aside so I could go in ahead of him.

I took two steps and then froze, surprised by what I saw. I'd forgotten another type of building that didn't have windows, the kind of building that held objects that could be damaged by the light—a library.

The Base was the largest private library I'd ever been in. Bookcases wrapped around the walls of the massive room. On top of that, a wooden spiral staircase led to a second level housing more shelves. So many books. I felt dizzy from the sight. I'd been ecstatic with the collection Edward had given me the previous Christmas, but that gift was miniscule compared to what lay before me. My fingers itched to circle the perimeter, to drag their tips along the spines, to pick up each precious volume and hug it to my chest. I could live in a room like this without complaints. I could die here, and I'd be happy.

"I didn't realize it was so easy to make you orgasm," Edward said at my ear. "I've been doing it wrong."

I laughed, the sound more boisterous than intended as

my wound-up nerves released into it. "I do like my books. But believe me, you haven't been doing anything wrong."

"I'm relieved." His tone, though, suggested he'd never been too concerned in the first place. "Let's go get a drink, shall we?"

I blinked, taking in the other aspects of the room I'd originally overlooked, too blinded by the array of books. The room wasn't quite a library, but more like a den. Couches and recliners were set up in various tableaus. There were also conference tables and more than one area set up with computers. And there was a full bar tucked neatly next to one of the fireplaces.

"Smoke and alcohol around books? Disgusting." It was the same with most private libraries I'd been in, but it didn't make me any less appalled.

"Francesco hasn't even brought out the cigars yet," Edward said, leading me toward the bar with his hand at the center of my back.

It was then that I truly noticed the people surrounding us. Twenty or so of them divided in groups throughout the space, mostly men in tuxes. The few women in attendance appeared to be accessories. Toys, rather, considering the lady giving a blow job underneath a table while her partner sipped his amber-colored beverage and spoke nonchalantly with his peers.

While Edward ordered our drinks, I scanned the room again, noticing more sexual play that I'd missed at first look. A woman in a white bikini—another of Esteban's angels, likely—knelt at the feet of one of the men in an armchair. Across the room, the man dressed in traditional Middle Eastern garb was fingering the woman on his lap, even though he was engaged in an intense discussion with the balding gentleman sitting across from him.

"He's a sheikh," Edward said as he handed me the tumbler. "Believe it or not. The man next to him is in oil. The man he's arguing with is an arms dealer."

I took a sip of the brandy, suddenly understanding why there'd been a security check. "Legal arms dealer?" I asked optimistically.

"Very little of what happens here is legal, bird."

My insides felt cold. "What is this place?"

Edward brought his tumbler to his lips, taking a swallow before answering. "It's a negotiation room. I told you before that Esteban touts the island as a place for men with few ethics to do business. This is where that business occurs, in this room. It's neutral territory. Many powerful enemies meet here to discuss nefarious deals."

"And this is the part of the island that meets your needs." I couldn't decide if it was thrilling or despicable to realize that. "What am I doing here, Edward?"

"You like the books, don't you?" It was less of an answer and more of a distraction, and I wasn't dumb enough to think anything else. "Why don't you finish your drink while you look around? Esteban will have small plates brought out soon, if you're hungry."

I looked at him with narrowed eyes. "And what will you be doing?"

"Conversing with old friends. Catching up. Nothing you should worry about."

I could feel the corners of my mouth turning down, but I was determined not to pout. I'd already known Edward was a devil. My father had even warned me that he was a man with questionable ethics. This sort of scene was part of that. Part of him. I should be grateful not to know the details, keep my head down, and my mouth shut.

It wasn't in my nature, but it was our anniversary. Behaving could be the gift I gave him. Absentmindedly, I rubbed the bird charm between my fingers. "Fine. I'll be perusing. But don't you dare think I'll be summoned with a clap of your hands."

He smiled. "Never."

I spent the next three hours combing through the stacks, breaking once when the food was brought out to cushion my stomach before refilling my brandy. Despite the pleasure the sight of all the books gave me, there were fewer treasures than I would have hoped for. Most everything was nonfiction, many were books on law and tax codes on various countries in various languages. There was also a large section devoted to business strategy as well as war strategy, and another larger section on the history of almost every nation.

Upstairs, though, I found some items worth savoring. First editions of a few of my favorite classics as well as a very impressive wall of rare books. I took my mask off for these, carefully inspecting fragile bindings, noting the strange typesets and languages inside. It was enough to keep me preoccupied, and I only found myself looking for Edward once or twice. I felt his eyes on me, however, constantly.

Eventually, when my eyes started to grow weary and raw—apparently Francesco had brought out the cigars by this time—I put my mask back on and went back down the stairs in search of my husband. Attendance had grown over the evening, doubling in size. A few more women had arrived, most wearing little or nothing at all. The hair at the nape of my neck stood up as the scene reminded me less of a party at The Open Door and more of the kinds hosted by my uncle.

I was ready to leave.

Hopefully, Edward was as well.

He was easy to find, tucked comfortably into the corner of one of the sofas, a cigar in one hand, a tumbler in the other, his expression carefully guarded. When he caught sight of me, he set down his cigar in a nearby ashtray and stood to meet me.

"Hello, my dragon," he said after thoroughly kissing me. The endearment and the taste of him suggested he might have had more than a couple brandies while I'd been away. Especially when his hand wandered inside my dress to roughly fondle my breast.

"Edward," I admonished with a blush, my eyes darting to the crowd.

"Yes, yes, you're right. I must make introductions." Apparently he hadn't correctly interpreted my reprimand, but he moved away to set down his drink and now his hands were off me, and I missed his touch more than I wanted to admit.

I needn't have worried. A moment later, his arm was around me again, settling at my waist as he turned to face the group closest to us.

"Gentlemen—and ladies, but mostly gentlemen," he said, his voice loud enough to reach those seated farther away as well. He paused to chuckle with those who laughed. "Allow me to introduce you to my wife, Celia. She's new to Exceso, and it's our anniversary. I promised her a good time."

Eyebrows rose and glances exchanged. Some hoots and hollers filled the air. Whispers could be heard but not made out. The weight of several leering gazes hit me at once.

It wasn't that I didn't like to be watched. There were situations where I found the notion quite appealing. Watching Edward with Sasha at The Open Door had been arousing, and I could only imagine how much more arousing I would have found it if I'd been the one being played with.

But this audience was not that audience. These men were not good men. These men were the kind that had my skin crawling and my stomach churning.

I coiled into my husband. "Edward, can we go?" I asked quietly.

"Not yet, bird. Patience." His hand made its way back to my breast, this time pulling on my nipple until it was fully erect.

It was impossible not to react to his touch, uncomfortable as I was with the surroundings. He knew how to manipulate my body, how to make me erupt in birdsong.

"She's remarkable, Edward," said a man nearby.

"Flawless," said another.

"Obscenely beautiful," said a third.

Edward basked in the compliments as though they'd been about him, and, of course, in a way they were, since this was an environment where women were nothing but mere possessions, and I belonged to him. It was to be expected, considering.

What I hadn't expected was Edward's response. "You should see her when she comes."

I could feel the heat spread down my neck. I was mortified.

"Does she come on command?" a thin, pale-skinned man asked, the woman accompanying him turning her head, but not before I caught her frown.

Yeah, lady, I know how you feel.

"She's more work than that." He pulled me tighter to him with one hand, the other reaching down to stroke my pussy through my dress. "Aren't you, my dragon?"

I gasped from the contact as well as the conversation. "Edward," I whispered. "I'm really uncomfortable right now."

"But she's worth it," he went on, not hearing me, perhaps. "The taste of her pussy alone is worth it."

Despite myself, I got wet. My pussy liked being talked about. Liked being talked about by Edward, anyway, even in shady company.

"That's not fair to taunt like that unless you're willing to share." The accent was South African, but I'd missed who said it.

"I could be willing," Edward said, and my stomach dropped. "What's your offer?"

"What are you doing?" I hissed. Was he drunk? Did he think this was fun?

"Ten large to lick her cunt," the South African replied.

A wave of nausea roiled through me. I was going to be sick. This was too much like that night at Ron's. I couldn't do this again.

I tugged at Edward's jacket sleeve. "We need to go."

He pulled my hand from his arm and held it tightly in his grasp, his eyes remaining on the man who'd spoken. "Ten thousand? That's all you have to offer for the taste of the divine?"

"I'd give you twenty to let me come on her tits," said someone else.

"I'm not even going to respond to that. I'm insulted."

This was his response, I realized. This was his way of replacing what Ron had done. But this didn't feel good. It felt just as wrong, just as dirty. It made me feel as much like a whore as my uncle had ever made me feel.

"Edward," I pleaded. "Whatever you think you're doing, this isn't helping. Okay? It's not helping. Please, stop."

"A brick then," the last negotiator countered. "Still insulted?"

Edward glanced at me and for a moment I thought he'd heard me—finally heard me.

But then he turned back to the man. "Look at her, really look at her. A brick for these?" He let go of my wrist so he could once again slip his hand inside my dress. He lifted my breast up and squeezed. "Her tits are perfection."

A tear slid down my cheek behind the mask. "Is this all staged?" I asked, with sudden optimism. He'd been alone down here for so long. Maybe this was all a setup. Maybe these men weren't really bidding for me. "Did you tell them to say these things?"

"Don't be ludicrous," he said.

"You're genuinely worth paying to touch, sweetheart." The oil man winked as he rubbed the crotch of his pants.

I turned my body so I couldn't see him, but Edward, seeming to think I meant to leave, tightened his grasp at my waist, drawing me back into him. My panic escalated with being pinned, and I struggled to get free, only to be overpowered when he brought his other arm into the battle.

"One million to fuck her." This from the arms dealer.

Edward perked up. "One million?"

"I'd want her all night."

"I've seen what you do to women," Edward scoffed. "She's no good to me broken."

The tears started in earnest. This wasn't staged. This was real, and I realized with dread that I didn't really know the man I'd married. How had I been so drawn in to him? I'd let him pull the wool over my eyes. Let myself believe he cared for me, when he was really just as vile as anyone else in the room.

He'd never professed to being a good man. He'd been clear he was a sadist, turned on by the discomfort of others. Just as I'd feared, he'd taken my past and was using it against me. He was really doing this, not for the money, but for fun.

"Two million," someone else offered now. "All night, comes back the way she came. Except happier." Laughter scattered throughout the room, a menacing contrast to the terror happening inside me.

"Fucking let me go, right now." I yanked harder, determined to run.

With an annoyed grunt, Edward twisted his body around mine to get a better hold.

"She doesn't seem to be interested in you, Juri," a man with a French accent laughed.

Juri harrumphed. "She doesn't seem to be interested in being shared at all."

"Half the fun, right?" Edward said with a sneer.

"Please, stop this," I sobbed. "Please. Why are you doing this?" My knees had lost all ability to hold me up. The only reason I wasn't in a pile on the floor was because Edward had me constrained.

And no one would help me! Everyone sat and watched,

amused by the entertainment, not caring that my husband was offering to sell my body against my will. They had to know I was upset, despite my covered face. My entire being shook from the force of my crying.

"Has she been fucked in the ass?" a voice came from the back.

"Virgin," Edward responded, and I gasped in horror.

The bids came out faster and higher after that.

"Four million."

"Five."

"Ten and you can watch. All of you can watch."

The world went dark at the edges, my heartbeat whooshing in my ears. The sounds around me became muffled and I retreated into myself. I'd managed to live through what happened in my past, but I wouldn't live through this. I couldn't survive a night forced in a stranger's bed. Edward's betrayal alone was enough to kill me.

But what if it wasn't betrayal? He'd always seen me as I was, even when I couldn't. Maybe he saw what my uncle had seen in me because that was what I really was—nothing. Useless. Only worth my physical appearance and my body. What could be done with my body.

Only honesty between us, he'd said. Then his honest message was that I had no value, and as hard as it was to accept it, it didn't make it any less the truth.

Then, through the din and darkness, Edward let go of me. My knees buckled, taking me to the floor as he exploded with a roar. "She's not for sale! Do you hear me? No one here can have her."

The room went abruptly quiet, stunned into silence, and I lifted my head, blinking away tears to look at my husband.

His expression was furious and intense, his face red, his teeth bared. He scanned the room, making sure everyone saw his anger. "There's not enough money to let any one of you come near her let alone touch her. A single breath from her body is worth more than any of your entire lives."

I couldn't move. I couldn't get air into my lungs. My jaw hung open. I felt dizzy and cold.

"Fuck, Edward that was a good one. Next time I'll kill you for it, so enjoy this one for a while."

Vaguely, I was aware of similar chattering amongst the crowd before people returned to their former conversations. Then Edward was kneeling in front of me, peeling off my mask so he could dab at my eyes with his handkerchief.

"Do you hear me?" he said, tenderly. "Your value cannot be named. You are priceless."

I didn't realize I was shaking my head until he spoke again.

"Listen to me, Celia. You are worth more than anything. There is no amount that would be enough to let anyone use you. No amount in the world."

Another tear slipped down my face. "But I'm nothing."

He gripped my chin between his fingers and held me tight, but not to the point of pain. "You are not nothing," he rasped, sternly. "If you were nothing, my world would not be completely changed by your existence. If you were nothing, I could give you up, I could walk away. If you were nothing, I would not have been moved from the trajectory that I've been on since my father took his own life. You are a planet of an obstacle, and, as hard as I've tried to fight it, I am in your orbit now. You are not nothing. You are *everything*."

There was no refuting him. His tone was adamant and final, and I believed him, not just because I wanted to, but because his constant insistence on honesty made it impossible to believe he'd tell this lie.

But this truth was so enormous, so overwhelming that I was left speechless. With my lip quivering, I could only respond with a single nod.

Then he stood and lifted me into his arms, and I clung to him as he carried me out of the hedonistic den and into the light of the dark black night.

TWENTY-SEVEN

Outside, Edward put me on my feet and escorted me on a path back to the airstrip that bypassed the welcome arena where we'd met Esteban. We walked in silence, my hand clutched in his, my head too dazed to do anything but follow.

Once we reached the plane, however, I found myself. It was like coming out of a fog how one minute I was content to be led and the next, I wanted the reins for myself. I was in love with this man, so deeply and recklessly in love, and he'd said some pretty noble things to me back at The Base, things that were planted in me like little seeds that I intended to help grow.

But he'd also been one-hundred percent a dick.

I came to a halt at the foot of the stairs, snatching my hand away from his. When Edward turned back in question, I pressed my palms against his chest and pushed, catching him off guard.

"You fucking asshole," I spit. "How could you do that to me?"

He put his hands up in surrender. "Hold on, now. Let's not overreact."

I pushed at him again, putting more of my body into it. "Overreact? Are you kidding me? You fucking tried to *sell me!*"

"I would never have really sold you, and you know that."

"I don't know that! I definitely didn't know it when it was happening. And after my past…! Do you know how traumatic that was for me? Do you? *Do you?*" I pressed forward, twisting to shove him with my shoulder.

This time he caught me at the upper arms, his eyes meeting mine with a stern gaze, but when he opened his mouth to speak, I lunged forward and kissed him.

His grip on me loosened in surprise. Then, when I threw my arms around his neck, he pulled me in closer, meeting the thrust of my tongue with a slide of his own. There was still anger in the way my mouth worked his, but also gratitude. A lot of gratitude.

We were both breathless when we drifted apart. He rested his forehead on mine. "Ah, bird," he sighed into me. "I do know how traumatic it was. That was the point. If it was unremarkable, the new ending wouldn't be remembered. It had to be significant enough to replace the old."

A tear slid down my cheek. All the years of never crying, and lately I'd been doing it a lot.

"Why are you doing this for me?" My voice was a whimper. His motives were beyond my grasp, and the confusion left me as raw as his kindness.

Edward swiped my tear away with the pad of his thumb. "You're a smart girl. Can't you figure it out?"

I wanted to make a guess, but I wasn't brave enough. I wanted him to say it.

This wouldn't be the moment for those words, however. Instead of a declaration, he let his hands fall and took a step back, away from me.

"Celia." His tone was formal, only a hint of the affection he'd shown only a second before. "I need you to listen to me, now."

I frowned, afraid of what he would say next. "I'm listening."

"The plane is fully fueled. Igritte and Marco are prepared for a longer flight, if..." He trailed off, seemingly unsure how to proceed. "They'll go anywhere you want them to. You can board right now and tell them where you want to go, and they'll take you."

Confusion transformed to disbelief. "You mean, go without you?"

"I can easily get back to the island later. Don't concern yourself with that. Your passport is in the cabinet inside, where I'd had your mask. You shouldn't have any problem at customs."

The tears were back. The anger fueled. The hurt, unbearable. "After all that? After what you just did to me, *what you said to me*, you're going to leave me?" I rushed at him again, ready to beat him to a pulp, never mind the fact that he could easily overpower me. "Fuck you, Edward! How can you do this to me? How can you be such a monster? After everything, how can you expect me to live without you?"

I pummeled him with my fists, getting a few good hits in before he seized my wrists. "Shh. Shh." When I met his hushing with a string of curse words, he changed tactics.

"Hold on, now. Listen to me. I am not leaving you, do you hear me?"

I paused my wriggling, waiting for him to expand.

"I'm not leaving you," he said again. "I'm giving you a chance to leave me."

He let that sink in.

He was giving me the option to walk away, unharmed. No longer his captive. It had been weeks since I'd considered myself a prisoner. I'd somehow forgotten that I still technically was.

Edward released one of my hands so he could sweep my hair behind my ear. "I'm giving you a chance to go, even though it is absolutely ruining me to say those words, and every second we continue to stand here, my resolve to let you do so slips away. So, hear me—take this chance. Get on that plane. I won't bear to be able to give you this opportunity again."

My breath shuddered through my lungs. "You've given me this option before. I already made this choice that night in your bedroom on Amelie."

"It wasn't fair to force that decision from you in the midst of sex. Right here, right now. This is the real choice."

I didn't hesitate. "I don't want to get on that plane alone. The only place I want to be is with you."

A spark of light flashed in his eyes. "If we board together, you understand what that means? You understand that you're accepting that you're mine?"

Mine.

He'd said it so many times and in such cruel ways that I hadn't ever really heard it for what it was. Possessiveness, yes. A claiming. But with the whole heart.

A kind of euphoria winded its way through my body, twining around my limbs, coiling in my chest, pressing against the steady beat of my heart. Our wedding had been a sham, our vows spoken under false pretenses.

Here, in this moment, this was where our marriage really began, and as the script is for all brides, I gave him an earnest answer. "I do."

The kiss that followed was rushed, both of us eager to get on the plane and off the island. Edward insisted that we buckle up for take-off, and somehow we managed to sit in our seats until we reached cruising altitude, our hands clasped together, a lightning storm of energy between us.

As soon as the pilot gave the indication that we'd reached altitude, Edward was on the ground, kneeling in front of me. I hadn't even undone my belt before he'd pushed my dress up my thighs, pulling me to the edge of the seat. He threw a leg over his shoulder, spread me wide and then his mouth found my pussy, greedy and weeping for him.

He easily drew two wicked orgasms from me before abruptly standing and yanking me to my feet. With our lips wrapped around one another, we stumbled to the bedroom where I eagerly worked his jacket off. Then his tie. Then began on his shirt buttons, my mouth never leaving his. He tasted like me and cognac and secrets and desire, and I wanted to lick every flavor out of him, until it was mine as well. Until our taste was the same.

His hands were busy as well, one wrapped around me to keep me steady while the other thrust two wicked fingers inside me, rubbing at my G-spot and coaxing another climax to take me over. When I was gasping his name, lost in another reeling whirlwind of pleasure, he pushed me backward to the bed. He found the top of the slit in my dress, now pushed up around my waist, and with an impressive show of determination, he split the material up the seam, all the way to where it dipped at my cleavage.

I wrestled out of the sleeves, leaving the tattered gown beneath me. He stared down at me with heated intensity, his gaze taking in every inch of my bare skin. I flushed from the warmth, and I distinctly thought that I would never get used to the way he looked at me. The way he opened me up and really saw me.

"Spread your legs," he said as he furiously stripped his shirt.

I did, bending my knees and resting the heel of my shoes on the edge of the bed so he could really see me. His eyes grew dark and hooded, and even next to a man with such fierce command, I felt powerful.

"Pinch those pretty nipples," he ordered next. "Pretend they're my fingers, and make them hurt."

I pinched hard, digging my nails in until I winced, and by the time he was naked and crawling over me, I was ready for his mouth to take over the work. He licked one steepled nipple, soothing the sensitive skin before his teeth nipped sharply.

My cry was lost to the jagged moan that erupted from my mouth as his cock plunged into me. His thrusts were deep and savage, each stab winding me tighter and tighter. He bent me in half, draping my heels over his shoulders and moving his knees to the outside of my hips, hitting me at an angle that found places inside me I'd never known. We were an orchestra of sound, my gasps and whimpers harmonizing with his primal grunts, the slap of his thighs against the back of my legs, a driving percussive beat.

And when we came, it was nearly together, his climax

only a half-step behind mine, and I spiraled somewhere higher than I'd ever been, higher than the number displayed on the altimeter in the cockpit, and for the first time in my life, I found I wasn't afraid of flying.

Afterward, he collapsed at my side, only the edge of his body touching mine, but when his breathing returned to normal, he turned to his side and gathered me close to him, his legs twining with mine.

And then my heel dug into his calf, and he untangled himself only long enough to remove the dangerous items before wrapping back around me.

We lay quiet and content, me stroking the length of his torso while he caressed the side of my face. There was nothing awkward about the silence, but words bubbled inside me, loosened by the events of the night, and for once, I wasn't too intimidated to let them be said.

"Once upon a time," I said, trying to remember the way I phrased it the first time I'd begun this story. "I met with a businessman because I thought he wanted to hire me. I gave up my career, moved to London, and married him." I brought my hand up to his cheek. "Then he took me captive and threatened to kill me. Which he did. Slowly, but surely, he killed the worst parts of me, and I'll never be the same, and I wouldn't have it any other way."

He kissed me, tenderly, and I felt it then, how I truly did belong to him. Why else would he care so much about healing me? Why else would he sit patiently through sessions, responding to them thoughtfully?

"You didn't reveal anything about yourself this time," I said, missing that traditional component of his response.

His knuckles brushed along my cheek. "Didn't I?"

I thought about it. Thought about the things he said

at The Base, then the words he'd said outside the plane. *"You're a smart girl. Can't you figure it out?"*

"You told me how you feel," I said, my chest blooming with the revelation.

"Go on."

I hesitated, nervousness creeping in like an old friend. "It's…" I hesitated. "It's the same way I feel about you."

"Which is?" A smile played on his lips.

I could feel his cock thickening at my thigh, and even now it was astonishing to see how my discomfort made him react. "You're turned on by this."

"Quite." His expression grew serious and stern. "Tell me."

Only honesty between us.

I took a deep breath. "I love you."

"Yes," he rasped, the evident weight of the syllable on his tongue, as raw as if he'd said the words instead.

He kissed me then, and as other kisses we'd shared had shown me what he wanted to do to my body, this one showed me what he wanted to do to my heart. Protect it, cherish it. Heal it. Love it.

I was bubbling and bouncing and overwhelmed and the unknown future that loomed over us was daunting but thrilling, and I couldn't wait for it. Couldn't wait to be with Edward in it, whoever I was anymore.

"You won," I sighed, realizing suddenly that I'd lost, and that it was wonderful. "You won, I'm yours. You've ruined me. You've broken me down. Now what?"

His gaze touched every part of my face—my swollen lips, my tilted chin, my flushed cheeks, my questioning eyes.

And when he answered, I knew it was the beginning of the next chapter, the beginning of something so much bigger than I could imagine.

"Now, I build you back up again."

Edward and Celia's story continues in Slay Three: Revenge.

Edward and Celia's relationship changes once again when his focus for the future includes a past she wants to leave behind.

Also by Laurelin Paige

Visit www.laurelinpaige.com for a more detailed reading order.

The Dirty Universe

Dirty Filthy Rich Boys - READ FREE
Dirty Duet: Dirty Filthy Rich Men | Dirty Filthy Rich Love
Dirty Sexy Bastard - READ FREE
Dirty Games Duet: Dirty Sexy Player | Dirty Sexy Games
Dirty Sweet Duet: Sweet Liar | Sweet Fate
Dirty Filthy Fix
Dirty Wild Trilogy: Coming 2020

The Fixed Universe

Fixed Series: Fixed on You | Found in You | Forever with You
Hudson | Fixed Forever
Found Duet: Free Me | Find Me
Chandler
Falling Under You
Dirty Filthy Fix
Slay Saga Slay One: Rivalry | Slay Two: Ruin
Slay Three: Revenge | Slay Four: Rising
The Open Door

First and Last Duet: First Touch | Last Kiss

Hollywood Standalones

One More Time
Close
Sex Symbol
Star Struck

Written with Sierra Simone

Porn Star | Hot Cop

Written with Kayti McGee under the name Laurelin McGee

Miss Match | Love Struck | MisTaken | Holiday for Hire

Let's Stay in Touch!

I'm on **Facebook, Bookbub, Amazon,** and **Instagram**. Come find me. I totally support stalking.

Be sure to **join** my **reader** group, **The Sky Launch**, facebook.com/groups/HudsonPierce

Check out my website www.laurelinpaige.com to find out more about my books. While there, sign up for **my newsletter** where you'll receive a **free book every month** from bestselling authors, only available to my subscribers, as well as up-to-date information on my latest releases.

Only want to be notified when I have a new release? Text **Paige** to 21000, and I'll shoot you a text when I have a book come out.

ABOUT THE AUTHOR

With millions of books sold worldwide, Laurelin Paige is a New York Times, Wall Street Journal and USA Today Bestselling Author. Her international success started with her very first series, the Fixed Trilogy, which, alone, has sold over 1 million copies, and earned her the coveted #1 spot on Amazon's bestseller list in the U.S., U.K., Canada, and Australia, simultaneously. This title also was named in People magazine as one of the top 10 most downloaded books of 2014. She's also been #1 over all books at the Apple Book Store with more than one title in more than one country. She's published both independently and with MacMillan's St. Martin's Press and Griffin imprints as well as many other publishers around the world including Harper Collins in Germany and Hachette/Little Brown in the U.K. With her edgy, trope-flipped stories of smart women and strong men, she's managed to secure herself among today's romance royalty.

Paige has a Bachelor's degree in Musical Theater and a Masters of Business Administration with a Marketing emphasis, and she credits her writing success to what she learned from both programs, though she's also an avid learner, constantly trying to challenge her mind with new and exciting ideas and concepts. While she loves psychological thrillers and witty philosophical books and entertainment, she is a sucker for a good romance and gets giddy anytime there's kissing, much to the embarrassment of her three daughters. Her husband doesn't seem to complain, however. When she isn't reading or writing sexy stories, she's probably singing, watching shows like Game of Thrones, Letterkenny and Discovery of Witches, or dreaming of Michael Fassbender. She's also a proud member of

Mensa International though she doesn't do anything with the organization except use it as material for her bio. She currently lives outside Austin, Texas and is represented by Rebecca Friedman.